ON MESSAGE

~A Jillian Hillcrest Mystery ~

JOYCE T. STRAND

McCloughan and Schmeltz Publishing

ISBN: 978-0-9839262-0-7

Printed in the United States of America

McCloughan and Schmeltz Publishing LLC
2360 Corporate Circle Suite 400
Henderson, NV 89074-7722
www.mccloughanandschmeltz.com

Cover and Interior Design by: Gwyn Kennedy Snider, www.gkscreative.com
Cover Photograph: Elizabeth Strand
Author Photograph: Erin Kate Photography, www.erinkatephoto.com

For information about the author: joycestrand.com

On Message is the first of the Jillian Hillcrest mysteries.

To my husband—my favorite chef

Author's Note

Inspiration for the Jillian Hillcrest mysteries came from two key sources: my experiences as a Corporate Communications manager and relevant cases from current events. I freely admit that I never encountered any murders in my career and had to look elsewhere for insight into the world of crime fiction.

Fortunately, being the news junkie that I am, I turned to current events for inspiration. Each of the Jillian Hillcrest mysteries is inspired by actual events in the news—murders or crimes that could possibly touch Jillian's life as the Senior Director of Investor Relations and Corporate Communications at a small biotech company in Silicon Valley.

On Message grew out of a case in San Diego, Calif. of the murder of an angel investor who was a former biotech executive. The circumstances surrounding the motive for the murder and the unique capture of the suspect helped fuel my imagination. To assure that I anchored the events in reality surrounding Jillian's interactions with the police, I researched and spoke with several law enforcement officers about police procedure.

You can read about the San Diego case on joycestrand.com where I have placed several articles describing it. In the meantime, enjoy exploring Jillian's world and helping her solve her first murder mystery as a Corporate Communications executive.

Joyce T. Strand, Author
Jillian Hillcrest Mysteries

Acknowledgements

First, thanks to my husband Bob for the suggestion and encouragement to write a book.

I also wish to express gratitude to Noel Lanctot, retired after 30 years of service from the San Jose Police Department; Lieutenant Patrick McGuire, Retired, San Jose Police Department; and Lieutenant Randy Sutton, Retired, Las Vegas Police Department, for their guidance on police procedure.

For early consultation on credibility and consistency, thanks to Pat Becker, Bob Strand, David Strand, Laura Strand, Liz Strand, and Gail Troutman. For more detailed editing to transition to a smoothly flowing book, thanks to Brooke Habecker. Special thanks to Laurie Gibson, editor extraordinaire, for helping my words tell a story.

Finally, I want to express my appreciation to Jared Kuritz for making me believe I could actually become a published author.

Despite all the incredible assistance from so many people, I take the blame for any errors, typos, or inconsistencies. Sometimes I just don't listen!

O h, damn, damn, damn.

"So sorry." Jillian did not believe what she was seeing—her boss, Brynn Bancroft, and the CEO in bed together—naked, of course and, well, breathing heavily. Of all the hotel rooms in Geneva, the reception desk had to give her the wrong key to THIS ONE! The appropriate end to a cantankerous day of travel, and definitely career-limiting.

Damn. She backed out as unobtrusively as possible, dragging her one roller bag with her, half-running to the elevator as fast as her slender, 5-foot 7-inch frame would carry her after being cramped on an airplane and shuffling between connecting flights for at least 15 hours between San Francisco and Geneva.

At that very moment—of course—her mobile phone was playing its "answer me" tune, and the display indicated that it was a key reporter she had been trying to reach for days. She had to talk to him. She continued to make her getaway from the violated hotel room and walked as quickly as possible toward the elevator as she answered her phone.

"Hello, this is Jillian Hillcrest."

"Jake Durham from *The Wall Street Journal*, here. Got your call. What can you tell me about the trial results?"

Jillian reached the elevator and pushed the button, deciding to risk losing the connection in order to get off this floor as soon as possible. Hopefully cells were strong enough in Geneva that she wouldn't lose him. However, just in case, "Hi, Jake. Thanks for calling back. I'm in an elevator so can I call you back if we get disconnected?"

"Sure, no problem. Use my cell number, which you have. In the meantime, what can you tell me about the timing of your new drug, and will it actually cure lupus? And will you be able to use this drug for other indications besides lupus?"

Jillian reviewed her prepared pitches in her mind—how to keep on message and entice Jake to write a story on the preliminary data that her 200-person biotech company was preparing to announce. "The data look promising, but, of course, the drug candidate has only completed the first part of Phase Two trials. And, as you probably know, we are conducting Phase Two trials to assess whether the drug is effective, and early results suggest that it is. However, the FDA is the only one who can say upon approval whether the drug is safe and effective. Given all this background, we would like to offer you an advance on the data. If you are interested, I'll send you a copy of the press release within the next half hour, assuming, of course, that you'll embargo it until we release it."

"Sure. Do you have any idea yet when you'll start Phase Three trials and when you might file for approval with the FDA?"

"We think it's too soon to know when we might file. However, as you'll see in the press release, we are going on record to say that— assuming the Phase Two trial results of the two hundred patients continue to be as positive as they have been to date—we would start the more comprehensive Phase Three trials in the middle of next year."

"Cool. Good job. Two things. Assuming that you announced the Phase One results to assess human tolerance to the drug, can you send me that press release as background—unless you included information about the Phase One results in the current press release you're sending me? Then that will suffice. Second, can I get an interview with Tim today?" Tim Wharton was the CEO of Jillian's company, who she'd just seen in bed with her boss.

At that moment, the elevator door opened in the lobby and Jillian was face-to-face with Tim's wife.

Jillian quickly greeted her and motioned for her to wait a moment hoping to stall her long enough for the elevator doors to close, preventing the wife getting anywhere near her boss's room. Given that her boss and the CEO were in what was definitely a compromising position, Jillian doubted that even the most understanding wife would appreciate the situation. She told the reporter on her phone that she would send him the press release shortly, promising that the *Journal* would be the only business publication to get the advanced information and trusting he would embargo it until time of release. She also would arrange an interview with the CEO.

She turned her full attention to the CEO's wife.

"Hi, Stephanie. How are you? I didn't know you were coming to Geneva." Jillian hugged the attractive 50-something brunette. Although Jillian herself was in great shape, with a layered V-line cut displaying her thick dark hair, probably 15 to 20 years younger, and professionally and stylishly dressed as her position of the head of corporate communications required, Stephanie Wharton always made her feel dumpy, fat, frumpy, and like she was dressed in hand-me-downs. Why Stephanie's husband was not faithful was a mystery to Jillian.

"I decided to surprise Tim. We haven't had much time together what with the latest financing road trips for the company and the clinical trials—which are so exciting, by the way! I can hardly believe that we might actually have a product that works for lupus. You may not be aware that both Tim and I had family members with lupus. You don't happen to know where he is, do you? He wasn't in his room so I was just heading up to Brynn's room to see if she had seen him."

Of course. Brynn was Jillian's boss. Jillian didn't want Stephanie anywhere near that room, as she pondered what Stephanie might see if she knocked on Brynn's door and encountered her husband and the very attractive Brynn together in bed. Somehow she suspected that Stephanie would not exactly understand, no matter what excuse they might muster. And that did not bode well for a successful announcement; the CEO and the CFO both were needed to provide interviews and Jillian did not want them any more preoccupied than they already were.

So she hoped she sounded normal. "Actually, I just got here myself and I still need to check in. Believe it or not, they gave me the wrong room key," that in response to Stephanie's inquisitive nod at the room key in Jillian's hand. "We are all scheduled to meet in about an hour to prep for tomorrow's announcement. Let me call Brynn to see if she has seen him." Jillian quickly pushed the pre-programmed button to call Brynn, before Stephanie could object. Thankfully Brynn answered quickly and Jillian professionally asked her if she had seen Tim, as his wife was in the lobby. Visions of Tim's bare white derriere popped into Jillian's head. After a moment's hesitation, Brynn responded with equal professionalism that Tim was probably in the bar, as that was where they were to meet shortly.

"Oh, look, there's Archie," said Stephanie as she headed toward the company's VP of Business Development and Strategic Planning, in response to his wave. She called to him as she approached, "How are you? It's great to see you. Have you seen Tim, by any chance?"

There seemed to be multiple bars in the lobby, but Jillian followed Stephanie to let her know that the most likely place to find Tim was in the bar. Stephanie and Archie decided to go there—Jillian was still not sure where "there" was—but she had done as much as she could.

Now, to the front desk to get her room sorted out.

The conference in Geneva was being held for biotechnology companies to showcase their latest drug research results. It was an annual affair and well attended by reporters and investors eager to keep current or get a scoop on the latest "next best thing." Deals were often struck here between companies, while analysts and investors gathered information for investment decisions. Everyone benefitted by companies having a platform on which to present their latest data.

Jillian's company, Harmonia Therapeutics, was there to present some encouraging results from Phase 2 clinical trials on its newest product candidate as a therapy for lupus, one of the more difficult diseases to diagnose and treat. Lupus is an autoimmune disease of unknown cause in which an over-active immune system results in detrimental symptoms, such as kidney disorders, arthritis and other joint swelling, seizures and/or psychosis, skin disorders, and cardio-pulmonary involvement, frequently mimicking rheumatoid arthritis and occasionally resulting in death. At least 1.4 million Americans have been diagnosed with lupus, 90 percent of whom are women, and a disproportionate number are women of color.

After completing Phase 1, in which they established that their drug candidate was tolerated in 35 healthy subjects, they proceeded to Phase 2 trials in approximately 200 lupus patients to determine if the drug was effective. They were in the process of presenting preliminary results from 180 of the 200 patients from this Phase 2 trial at the Geneva conference.

Once they completed the Phase 2 trials and assuming that the data from the trials indicate that the product candidate is effective, they planned to proceed to the larger and more comprehensive Phase 3 trials, which they had determined would be 2,000 patients, most of whom would be women, divided into proportionate numbers of Caucasian, African American, Hispanic and Asian. By the conclusion of the Phase 3 trials the company's investment would be six years and millions of dollars into the product candidate. However, they still would have at least a year to go before approval, as they would need to prepare the data in accordance with Food and Drug Administration (FDA) requirements, and then submit an application to the FDA which, once they accepted the application, has an approval process lasting at least ten months that includes a review by an independent Advisory Panel as well as by the FDA itself.

What this long approval cycle meant to the company, in addition to the expense and resource investment was that every step of the process would be analyzed, reviewed, and judged by investors, patients, and physicians. So how the company communicated the success and/or issues associated with a drug's progress would influence investment, employee recruitment, partnering, and potential customers.

Therefore, Harmonia was pleased to be announcing these preliminary results from the Phase 2 trial of its new lupus product candidate because it appeared to slow the advancement of the disease; this news would be perceived as a positive indication of its potential. With the exception of a recently released product, most of the current standard therapies for lupus were inadequate, and, until recently, no new therapy for lupus had been approved since 1955, when corticosteroids and an anti-malarial drug (Hydroxychloroquine) were approved by the FDA for lupus.

Harmonia researchers hoped that their therapy would combine with the recently launched new medication from a major pharmaceutical company to help suppress a lupus patient's over-active immune system without the typical side affects of immunosuppressants endangering patients to various infections. Many companies had tried and failed to develop such a therapy, and Harmonia was potentially risking its very existence—and investors' funds—in its attempt to make it happen. Investors, the media, and patients all had high hopes heightened by the previous success of the founder, a patent holder of a marketed AIDS therapy from a former company. AIDS is also considered an autoimmune disease although it is somewhat the opposite of lupus, given that the AIDS problem is an under-active immune system.

When Jillian got to her room—which she entered gingerly, to assure that it was empty—she immediately pulled out her computer so that she could send the press release to the reporter. Of course, it was highly likely that in the next 24 hours the press release would be altered—it was Jillian's experience that CEOs had a habit of tweaking the words until the very last minute. Hopefully, she had incorporated as much information as possible into the current, already-reviewed draft to enable any re-writes without the need for additional scientific scrutiny. She again briefly wondered how to minimize the last-minute tinkering beyond the multiple steps she had implemented since starting at the company a year ago.

Yes, yes, she was willing to hock her most valuable whatever to pay for the link to the Internet service offered by the Geneva hotel. Just make it work—PLEASE! She again marveled that the more expensive the hotel, the higher the cost of Internet access. At the local Best Western, it was free. Here, the price was outrageous. Fortunately, the computer gods were generous today—the connection came up immediately, and she e-mailed the draft press release to the reporter with a message offering an interview with the CEO that evening.

Now on to the preparatory documents for the meeting with her boss and the CEO. A knock on her door alerted her that the printer she had requested was being delivered. The front desk was being especially solicitous to offset the mistake they had made putting her in the wrong room, and so had offered her access to an in-room printer free of charge. Given how incredibly uncooperative this day had been, she was surprised at how easily she connected the printer and how quickly it spit out enough copies for the meeting.

She took one last look at the presentation, grabbed her laptop and the printed copies, and headed for the conference room she had reserved for the meeting. A bit apprehensive about greeting the compromised CEO and her boss—she could only hope they had been preoccupied and not seen her when she opened their hotel room door—she approached the conference room with quiet and efficient professionalism.

Only Archie was in the rather ornate conference room with its walls of tapestries, and deep red velvet tied-back drapes at the floor-to-ceiling windows. The presentation screen at one end of the table intruded into the ornate room, as did the projection equipment. However, the trays of food laid out on the buffet looked incredibly inviting, and Jillian realized how hungry she was as she helped herself to a plate of prosciutto-wrapped white asparagus, a variety of cheeses, shrimp, vegetables, and freshly baked baguettes that called out to her. She mentally patted herself on the back for having the forethought to order food.

Archie Linstrom was working patiently at his computer expecting that the other participants would be late. Punctuality was not a key attribute of Harmonia's senior executives. "Hi, Archie. The food looks great. How was your day? Did you line up any meetings for tomorrow?"

He nodded. As head of the company's business development efforts, he was constantly on the lookout for new deals. He was also in the process of considering whether to sell off or partner the new lupus product to a large pharmaceutical company for commercialization or build the company's infrastructure so they could do it themselves.

"Not as many as I would have liked. One big one, though." He finished typing. "How much time have you allowed for briefing Tim on specific meetings?"

Jillian checked her agenda. "Actually, as much time as you need. Unless Tim has some concerns, we're well prepared with no last-minute issues so we shouldn't need too much time to review the press release or to prepare responses to questions."

Archie returned his attention to his laptop. Jillian often wondered why he gave up his VP of Corporate Development position at a large pharmaceutical company to work at a small biotechnology startup. But he seemed to really enjoy his work, so perhaps he just preferred the entrepreneurial aspect of always being on the edge of the next financing to the bureaucracy of fighting for financial and human resources.

Jillian connected her laptop and projected the agenda for the meeting on the screen just as Brynn, her boss, entered the room. Brynn Bancroft, a Harvard MBA, had started at the company as the comptroller and was promoted within two years to Chief Financial Officer. Brynn's measurements were only overshadowed by her intelligence. A well-endowed, perfectly proportioned woman, she was blond and blue-eyed. What was atypical was her IQ—she was extremely bright, a MENSA member, knew her numbers, was a clear-thinker, able and willing to make decisions when needed. Jillian just couldn't figure out why Brynn felt the need to sleep with the CEO. Brynn's husband was equally bright and good-looking and seemed to be an attentive partner.

"How are we coming along? Were you able to get *The Wall Street Journal* lined up?"

Jillian held up her phone. "I'm waiting to hear. I connected with him and sent the press release. Can you and Tim do an interview this evening?"

Just then Tim walked in with Stephanie. "Hi, everyone. Look who showed up to surprise me!" Tim Wharton did indeed look the role of a CEO. His lean 6-foot, 3-inch frame and graying hair gave him a distinguished air of competence and reliability, and his self-assured approach inserted him into the room. He was in great shape since he worked out regularly. Although definitely an entrepreneur interested in reaping the profits of building a business, Tim was also dedicated to finding a cure for lupus; his sister had died unexpectedly in her teens of the disease. A Stanford MBA with a BS in biochemistry, he chose biotechnology as his career specifically to make a contribution. "How long do you think this will last, Jillian? I'm kinda tired."

Jillian pointed to the agenda being projected and handed out copies of the press release and the list of anticipated questions with some proposed answers. "The press release is final, right? No more changes? Then let's get to the Q's and A's."

During the next hour they reviewed potential questions and discussed how best to respond to them to assure they were not divulging any proprietary information prematurely, particularly material or contractual information. During the process, they made five or six changes to the press release, which Jillian noted. She figured it would only take an hour to finalize the release with no need for additional review, and the changes were easy to explain to the reporter, who was reviewing the earlier version. It allowed a full day of advance notice to the *Journal*, which she wished could have been longer—but the presentation was late tomorrow afternoon and the data was too material to hold.

Just as they were finishing with the questions, the reporter called and asked for an interview. Maybe Jillian's luck was changing. She arranged for the CEO and her boss to talk with him right then and called him back using the hotel's telephone to assure a clear connection and to use the speaker capability to enable the group to participate, if needed.

The reporter began with some background questions about the

company. "Before we get started, can you tell me how your company got its name? What does 'Harmonia' have to do with lupus?"

Tim laughed. "Actually we develop and manufacture drug products to curtail the harmful attack by the immune system against its own cells, know as autoimmunity. Phil Montgomery, our founder, sings tenor for a nationally competitive barbershop quartet, and he named the company. He compared balancing the human immune system with singing in harmony. In Greek mythology, Harmonia is the goddess of harmony and concord."

"Interesting. I guess that's as good a name as any. Thanks for explaining. I often wonder how companies get their names, particularly in biotech. I'll add that story to my list."

Jake continued to ask questions, which Tim and Brynn answered thoroughly and without hesitation. The interview was going swimmingly when all of a sudden the reporter asked a zinger. "I hear that several patients in the trials became very ill and had to be removed."

Jillian jumped in—as any protective PR professional would—and asked, "Where did you hear that, Jake? You saw in the press release that we reported the adverse events that we've seen to date. Are you looking for something beyond that?"

"Yes. I heard that some patients reported kidney failure." The reporter was sure he had a scoop. However, kidney failure was a common problem with lupus patients and the trial patients could have had kidney failure with or without the drug. Jillian looked to the others in the room, who all shrugged. "Well, kidney failure is a common problem with lupus patients. We'll have to get back to you whether there were any in the trial. The adverse events that we've seen so far are clearly stated in the press release, which you have. Did you have any additional questions?"

"No, that's it for now. Get back to me on the kidney failure."

Jillian looked at the others and shrugged. "I'll do my best. Thanks for the opportunity."

After the reporter hung up, Jillian looked at everyone and again asked if anyone was aware of any renal failure among the patients. "O.K., I'll get in touch with Reboto to see if there were any, and we can decide how to handle it." Dr. Leonardo Reboto, an independent clinician, was the lead trial investigator. He was in Geneva to present the results at an event scheduled by the biotech organization responsible for the conference as part of their annual meeting. "If it was someone on placebo, it is a no-brainer. If it was someone on the drug, we'll have to think about our response, especially since it will be way too early to determine if it was drug- or disease-related."

This was more how Jillian expected her long and convoluted day to end.

Jillian weaved her way slowly through customs at SFO returning to San Francisco following four days at the conference in Geneva. She was exhausted. *The Wall Street Journal* article had turned out primarily positive. Jillian had discovered from Dr. Reboto that there was only one incidence of a patient with renal problems, and it was a patient taking the placebo, or non-drug—a member of the group participating in the trial for the sake of comparison. The reporter wrote a brief but basically positive story.

The other activities surrounding the conference also were productive. Dr. Reboto did a comprehensive job presenting the preliminary data from the Phase 2 clinical trial at the conference to a room full of scientists, investors, and reporters. Jillian was still gathering the results of any audience activities, such as articles or analyst reports, although the net-net was that the company's stock value had risen. Archie lined up several pharmaceutical companies interested in considering a deal to join in the commercialization of the new drug. The CEO and CFO presented the company story to a dozen or so investors while in Geneva and then Zurich. Jillian herself talked to a half-dozen reporters, and the data was well reported in articles in daily and biotech journals throughout Europe and the United States.

Jillian was also pleased with the number of new contacts she made. In addition to meeting several new investors and analysts, she spent some time with a particularly savvy financial advisor, Mr. John Bowersox, a CPA from San Diego, who seemed very astute about investing in biotech companies. He was very knowledgeable about the most recent genomic research, and also up to date on the latest deal making. He sat at Jillian's table at a lunch gathering along with several other investors and reporters, and the conversation was quite lively. Jillian was pleased when he agreed to consider speaking on her panel at an upcoming symposium, if he was available and visiting Silicon Valley at that time. If nothing else, Jillian was convinced that he was now familiar with Harmonia and would follow the company, possibly even recommending it as a stock purchase to his clients.

However, despite these successes, Jillian was somewhat disappointed that Harmonia had not secured more coverage in the business media, particularly on television outlets. The company's PR agency had warned her that the data was not far enough along, and that lupus itself was not perceived as a "newsworthy" disease, so it was not likely to get broad coverage. However, both she and the agency had tried to alert potentially interested science and medical reporters. At least they had familiarized an increased number of reporters and bloggers with the name of the company and the lupus drug candidate in anticipation of future announcements.

Regardless, Jillian returned from the conference somewhat exhilarated; she truly enjoyed the rush afforded by the discipline of effective communications. She wasn't about seeing her own name "in lights." However, she appreciated the intellectual exercise of putting together the pieces of a news item to position a key message that a company wanted to share. For her, it was all about "C²", i.e., Comprehensive Communications, or telling the total story like painting the whole picture with the individual news items filling in the picture, much like an Impressionist paining where the brush strokes combine to form the whole picture.

Perhaps she had first come to realize the importance of the relationship between the individual bits of news to the whole story when she studied political science, her major at Cal. Trends were an important component of reaching conclusions. Without understanding the influences of the world or the country, policies were less likely to be effective and citizens less likely to be engaged. At any rate, she loved to practice the science and art of communications in its broadest context addressing all of the relevant audiences.

Of course, there were caveats. Jillian thought of herself as extremely ethical and she practiced her art strictly within the rules of the regulatory bodies, such as the SEC and FDA, which she studied regularly to assure her strict compliance. As an employee and as an executive, she also required that her company be ethical and respectful of its employees, patients, investors, and partners, or else she would seek employment elsewhere.

It had taken Jillian years to gain this perspective, and she was wise enough to understand that it would continue to evolve. Reared in a small town by a single mom, she had arrived at Cal in Berkeley relatively unsophisticated socially. She quickly learned about great food by dining at the many fine restaurants in the Bay Area when she could afford it; fine wine by visiting Napa and tasting wine at the many wineries there; classical music by attending concerts by the San Francisco Symphony conducted by Michael Tilson Thomas, known by symphony aficionados as MTT; drama (and comedies) by seeing plays performed at the Berkeley and San Jose Rep, the ACT, and Broadway touring groups. She even learned to appreciate the unique San Francisco Victorian architecture.

So it was not a big surprise that she decided she wanted to stay and work in the Bay Area, especially given the many high-tech and biotech companies in Silicon Valley. After a year of job-hunting following graduation from Cal, she had secured an entry-level position at a high-tech company writing its marketing newsletter. There she met a fellow communications enthusiast who was head of that company's corporate communications function who recruited her to become part of the public relations department. This was where Jillian first experienced the rush of seeing an article in print and on blogs that incorporated a press release she had written. She quickly embraced the discipline and spent time attending conferences and seminars to learn more about the science of communications.

One day after eight years of progressive promotions to senior director at the high-tech company, she received a call from a recruiter. Would she be interested in interviewing for a position as Senior Director of Communications at a new biotechnology company, which was listed on NASDAQ but was basically a startup? At first she was not interested, but the more she investigated the company, the more she was intrigued. She was startled to learn that although listed on stock exchanges, the majority of biotechnology companies are not profitable. Given that biotech products have such a long development and approval cycle, these companies need to raise capital to fund the research. Therefore, the typical indicators of earnings per share, or profit margins, were not as relevant for the majority of these companies. So, in order to invest early in biotechnology companies, both institutional and retail investors required knowledge of the field. The result was that there were institutions and banks that specialized in biotechnology finance. They followed companies by marking their progress with clinical trials and other announcements that corroborated their potential.

Jillian was also enticed to biotechnology by the relatively recent use of DNA to develop drug products that would make a difference in people's lives by giving them much needed therapies, such as cures for cancer, diabetes or lung disorders.

Jillian was hooked. To her it seemed that communications of the steps of progress was very important to the success of a biotech company. So she enthusiastically interviewed for the position brought to her by the recruiter after doing significant research to enable her to speak intelligently about biotechnology in general and the company specifically. Following the first round of interviews, she prepared a mock communications plan for the company to illustrate her skill set, painting the broadest picture possible. She was rewarded with an offer of Senior Director of Corporate Communications and a large number of stock options pending the fulfillment of certain performance requirements. That was just over a year ago.

The Geneva conference was her first real test since starting at Harmonia, and she was basically pleased, despite her desire for even broader results. Now it was time to consolidate the company story and prepare for the investor conference coming up in two weeks in New York. In addition, Jillian was to speak at a local symposium of her peers where she was to lead a discussion about the merits of public relations and the ethics of being "on message."

First, however, after the long flight from Geneva to San Francisco, Jillian was looking forward to a shower and at least 100 hours of sleep—well, at least six hours. She decided that she deserved a cab from the airport and headed for her newly refurbished flat in the recently redeveloped Mission Bay Area near AT&T Park, the home of the San Francisco Giants. After paying the cabbie, she grabbed her purse and one overnight bag that included her computer—she prided herself on being a frugal packer and it was one of her rules never to travel with more than she could lift—and entered the building, picking up her mail from the concierge on the way to her large, modern one-bedroom-plus-loft abode that she called home.

Jillian had moved here following her divorce last year from Chad Bradbury, a marketing VP at a local biotech company. They had met while at Cal and married shortly after graduation. However, after ten years of trying hard to remain excited about being together, they called it quits. They divorced with no animosity or offspring and remained friends, often consulting one another professionally. He lived across the

Bay in Alameda in a Victorian house that he took great joy in renovating. The last Jillian had heard he was regularly dating an executive at an Alameda biotech company.

Jillian, on the other hand, was content to live a simple life in an apartment or, in San Franciscan nomenclature, a flat. Her four-story, redbrick building was designed to mimic San Francisco Victorian architecture with protruding bay windows and balconies, and wood trim painted blue and white. The lobby's double doors were also painted blue, with stained glass above. There was someone at the front desk to take care of her mail and deliveries, park her car, call for cabs, and even take messages if she wanted. And it was great to be able to walk to many parts of the city for dinner like in South Beach or Potrero Hill, or to take the Muni to a play or concert without having to drive in the congested city traffic.

Although she was incredibly tired, her curiosity was piqued by one unexpected package in her mail. Other than Amazon.com, the only source of her packages was her mother who lived in southern California near San Diego. However, this package was not from either Amazon or her mother. There was no return address. She smiled. If she were in a Robert Ludlum or Stieg Larsson novel—Jillian was an avid reader of spy and mystery novels given her great appreciation for solving puzzles— she might have been nervous about opening an unmarked package. But this was real life, so she cut open the box and peered inside to discover a packet of papers and a flash drive.

She couldn't easily discover the origin of the papers, but in her tired frame of mind quickly determined that they weren't anything that would be interesting to explore, like a gift certificate to a new restaurant from her ex-husband. So she decided that maybe it was some kind of ill-conceived marketing campaign, aka junk mail that she would check out later just in case it was more than that. Plus she could always use another flash drive. She threw the package onto her dining room table and headed for the shower.

04

Brynn Bancroft nursed her wine as she sat on the plane 40,000 feet over the Atlantic Ocean mulling her options. She was relatively comfortable, as she had used her frequent flyer miles to upgrade to first class given the long flight from London—the location of the last investor meetings following the conference—to San Francisco. Nonetheless she was hardly content. She had never intended for the relationship with Tim to go so far. How could two intelligent, well-meaning people have allowed it? She enjoyed her husband and loved him, she supposed. They had been together for 14 years. And Tim and Stephanie had been married for almost 25.

The flight attendant interrupted her thoughts to ask if she needed anything. Brynn smiled wishing it were that easy. "Yes, could you bring me one more red wine? I'm hoping it will help me sleep."

Brynn reflected on the past week and how many near-misses the secret couple had had. She wondered why Stephanie had decided to fly to Geneva to surprise Tim. Did she suspect something? Did she suspect Brynn? Or did she just miss her husband, because he had been traveling a lot lately for the company? Stephanie had not left his side since the conference. The two of them together along with Brynn had visited at least a dozen investors to entice them to buy stock in Harmonia.

European institutional investors were among Brynn's favorites; in her experience they were thorough and took their time to get to know a company. Although that meant that they were slow to purchase stock, it also meant they held it for a long time, which was helpful in stabilizing the stock price. They also kept in touch with the company's progress and would frequently add to their portfolio, which was helpful in increasing the value of a company's stock. Harmonia was a good long-term story of growth, so this kind of investment favored the company. Professionally she had enjoyed the past week. It had been very successful.

Personally, however, it had been incredibly demoralizing. She was certainly no saint, and both she and her husband had strayed in the past. Nonetheless, they had re-committed to each other and this most recent affair was a serious betrayal because Brynn really wanted to spend more intimate time with Tim. She found him very compelling and wanted to laugh with him, work with him, attend concerts with him, enjoy dinner and wine with him. And, although Tim was willing to share her bed, it was highly unlikely he would leave Stephanie. He was very committed to her and his family. Nor, for that matter, did Brynn want to leave her husband. She truly enjoyed being with him, although over the years the two had discovered each other's shortcomings and sometimes she just wished he would go away for a while so she could re-remember his positive qualities.

What made this situation even more abhorrent was that she genuinely liked Stephanie. The two of them had become friends—or as close to being friends as Brynn ever managed. They had worked together to raise funds for a nonprofit; they had spent time discussing life in general and relationships specifically; the two couples had gone to numerous functions together. Brynn knew that Stephanie was afraid of losing Tim. She had built her life around him, and, although she was independent, Stephanie was not someone who would function joyfully outside of the relationship. Brynn understood this, which only made matters worse.

If it became known at the company that she and Tim were "together," it could cause serious business problems, as well. As the CFO, Brynn felt this responsibility keenly. She wondered who had intruded on them in Geneva. Although they had hardly noticed the intrusion, assuming it was the housekeeper, something nagged at Brynn about the person's voice. If it was someone they knew, it could be a problem.

Brynn poured the third mini-bottle of wine that the flight attendant brought. Hopefully it would help her sleep so she could ponder the solution to this problem with a clear head. She prided herself on her problem-solving skills and believed she needed to approach this personal issue much the same as she would any business issue. But she already knew the answer—and maybe that was why she was so morose.

05

Jillian was late. She had known it was risky to schedule a meeting early on the morning of her return from a sleep-deprived, four-day trip to Europe packed with interviews and late-night calls to U.S. reporters unable to attend the conference. In fact, it violated one of her rules of scheduling meetings to maximize attendance. However, this morning was the only time she could get the relevant people all in one room (or on the phone) at the same time. She had returned home early in order to participate, missing out on an opportunity to spend a little free time in Europe.

She looked longingly at the stack of mail on her table. However, she knew she barely had time for some yogurt and her coffee. She always ground and brewed it herself and filled a ceramic travel mug—another one of her rules she had evolved over the years as a result of her mother's insistence that she create a list of rules to live by (after she neglected to fulfill some obligations as a teenager): If it was worth putting into your mouth, it was worth preparing properly. She had already called to give the ten-minute warning for her car to be brought from the garage—a service she had decided was well worth the extra charge per month. San Francisco was not a car-friendly city, partially due to its compactness caused by the configuration of water on three sides of it. However, she needed a car to get to her office down the peninsula in Redwood City, south of the airport. Yes, she remembered arguing with Chad that it would be far cheaper and easier finding a place in Redwood City, but she really liked the feel of San Francisco and enjoyed living there. So she paid the premium without too much resentment knowing that it enabled her to live comfortably where she wanted to be.

She grabbed her laptop and purse and headed for her car, which was waiting just outside. She gave Pete, the valet parker, the usual tip to assure his continued good service and headed for the entrance to Highway 101 hoping today was not one of the days that a big rig had overturned to snarl traffic and prevent her from getting to the office in time for her meeting. Fortunately, the traffic gods were on her side this morning and she made it with five minutes to spare.

The meeting was in a conference room of her two-story office building near the Bay in Redwood City. It concerned the marketing plan for a partnered product developed using their combined technologies for the systemic treatment of severe cases of psoriasis, an autoimmune disease where the immune system falsely increases the growth of skin cells. The Advisory Committee called by the FDA had recommended that the product be approved, and although the FDA is not required to follow the advice of the Advisory Committee, they usually do. So, the two companies were finalizing their joint marketing activities that included a sales plan for the partner, since Harmonia did not have its own sales force.

Jillian was more involved than usual in the marketing efforts because her Marketing Communications Manager was on vacation, and Jillian was covering for her. As Senior Director of Communications, Jillian had a staff of two that included the manager and a shared assistant, a position that was currently open, which meant she was using Brynn's assistant at the moment.

When they had finished dealing with the agenda, which laid out key messages, schedule of events, due dates, and assigned responsibilities, Jillian was in the process of disconnecting the conference call phone. Bill Vulkjevich, one of the temporary contract financial analysts, who had called into the meeting through the conference call facility, asked if he could call her back on her mobile phone and speak with her for a minute after everyone had left the room. He preferred not to be on the conference speakerphone to ask her something.

When he reached her, he asked, "Did you get my package?" He seemed a little nervous and tenuous.

"What package—oh, was that from you?" Jillian recalled the package she had reviewed the previous night. "The one with the flash drive? I haven't had a chance to really look at it yet. I'll do so tonight probably. Is it urgent?"

Again, Bill seemed tentative—which was not at all like him. Normally he was brashly barking about the latest San Francisco 49er football or Giants baseball game and was very outspoken about umpire or referee grievances or the latest use of steroids or the latest NFL player jailed for domestic violence. Today, however, he had been uncharacteristically quiet during the meeting, and now he was being cautious with Jillian, who did not consider herself a particularly threatening person.

"Oh, can't you look at it now?"

"No, I left it at home. I didn't realize it was work-related. Will tonight be soon enough?"

"I guess it's not urgent-urgent—but could you call me tonight after you look at it? I'll wait for your call. You have my number."

Jillian was now intrigued, but also a little annoyed. She had plans to go out with a friend who was in town for just tonight—another reason for returning home early from Geneva. They were headed to a new wine and tapas bar on Valencia Street. Jillian loved good food and was in search of the perfect cooked duck and unique pastas with interesting sauces (although she tended to prefer the rich Bolognese meat sauces). Of course, she also enjoyed potatoes in almost any form and desserts with sauces (but not whipped cream or meringue, which she didn't like). She had heard that this new wine and tapas bar had some outstanding duck tapas, and she had been anticipating exploring it with her friend. She would have to do a quick look at the flash drive, call Bill, and then meet her friend. "Sure—I'll go straight home and give you a call—say between 6:30 and 7:00. Will that work?"

"Ah, yeah, I guess that will be fine. I wanted to be sure that you—" Bill interrupted his own discourse with "Oh, hi—I was just finishing—" and he hung up in mid-sentence. A bit rude, but not out of character.

The rest of the day turned out to be productive for Jillian despite her jet-lagged brain and heavy legs. She received input on a variety of projects she had circulated for review while traveling, enabling her to continue to the next step. She had a quick lunch with her Human Resources recruiter who was looking for a new assistant for her—someone with judgment who could write and arrange a meeting with an investor without selectively disclosing material information. She responded to several calls from investors to clarify the recent announcement about the lupus drug data.

Most noteworthy was a meeting in the afternoon with the head of a local growing biotechnology hedge fund. Despite her misgivings about the role that hedge funds could play in manipulating a company's stock value, Jillian was eager to meet with this particular fund manager due to the founder's outstanding pedigree. Dr. Dan Harrington had a stellar background. With an M.D. and Ph.D. from Harvard, he had served as an executive for more than ten years at a leading biotech company and for the decade before that in various management positions at two leading pharmaceutical companies.

He retired in his 50s, heeding a call from the investment community to help fund promising new drug therapies. Without investor dollars, fewer new therapies would be developed, because the approval process is long and expensive. In a very short time, Dr. Harrington's investment concept and its results had attracted others and he had gathered funds, while continuing to grow his company's position. He had also grown his own personal wealth and was successful enough to buy 20 acres in the Napa Valley, where he built a relatively modest 8,000 square foot house on a hill overlooking his acres of Cabernet Sauvignon grape vines. In fact, that day he brought a bottle of his personal vintage, which greatly pleased Jillian, who fancied herself a Cabernet aficionado.

This was the company's third or fourth meeting with Dan, so Jillian was eager to see how he would react to the presentation of the new Phase 2 data by the Founder and Chief Scientific Officer, Phil Montgomery. Dan was interested in Harmonia for a couple of reasons. He knew Tim, the CEO, from his past career at a pharmaceutical company, and, second, Dan really liked following and discovering new small-cap biotech companies with unique, promising products that would make a difference.

Dan Harrington arrived limping and wearing a neck brace. When Jillian asked him what had happened he responded that he'd had a recent bicycle accident in the City. He was peddling uphill when an oncoming car crossed into his lane. Jillian was not a big exercise fan and wondered that someone of Harrington's wealth would be cycling on the streets of San Francisco, but he certainly did appear to be in good physical shape, his recent injuries notwithstanding.

More important, Jillian was not disappointed with his reaction to the data from the recent trial. He seemed genuinely excited and asked lots of questions—always an indication of engagement. She was pleased with the meeting and gave Dan copies of the presentation and promises of follow-up data when it became publicly available. She was a little surprised, however, when he handed her a folder and asked if she would have Brynn review it. She responded of course, although she was not sure when or if Brynn was planning to come in that day. Dan seemed satisfied with that response, although preoccupied with a phone call. Jillian winced in empathy as he limped out of the building while juggling his cell phone.

Jillian did look briefly for Brynn. It was unlikely her boss would have come to the office and not checked in with Jillian. And Jillian was eager to leave for her evening date with her friend. She was also concerned about reviewing the package Bill Vulkjevich had sent. Since Dan had not specified that the folder was urgent, she left it and the bottle of wine on her desk to tend to in the morning. She knew that Brynn appreciated Cabernet, too, and was thinking about sharing it with her.

Jillian was truly looking forward to seeing her old friend from college and resented the need to check into her apartment to review the package of data sent by Vulkjevich rather than going directly to the restaurant. She assumed he had run some numbers regarding the partnered project and wanted to review them with her privately. But why it couldn't wait until the following day or even next week, she didn't understand. Oh, well, she would go home, let Pete park her car for the night, do a cursory review of the package, call Vulkjevich as promised, then grab a cab to the wine and tapas bar.

Although she had allowed plenty of time to reach her destination—another one of Jillian's rules—traffic was backed up for miles on Highway 101 and she could not get anywhere near the off-ramp to her apartment. So, rather than be too awfully late to meet her old friend, she took the next exit from the freeway, which was now a parking lot, and jogged over to 280 via 380 and then went along surface streets using her dash-mounted GPS to locate the restaurant. She amazingly encountered a parking space within a block of the place and arrived just ten minutes late. Lisa was already seated at a table when Jillian walked in, having used the valet parking for her rental car.

How great it was to see her! The two of them had met more than a dozen years earlier while studying in a program abroad in Bologna, Italy. They had stayed in touch, and Jillian almost always stopped by to see Lisa in Philadelphia when she was on the East Coast. They had last visited when Jillian spent a few days with Lisa following her surgery almost a year ago.

Jillian was relieved to see that Lisa looked much less gaunt than when she had last seen her. Lisa had been going through a run of misfortunes—which was a bit of an understatement given the amount and scope of her troubles. First, her life partner decided that she was not committed for life and left Lisa after five years together. Shortly after the separation, Lisa discovered a lump in her breast and had a mastectomy. Her insurance company then refused to cover the surgery costs. Lisa had to take out a second mortgage to pay her medical expenses, and after almost a year she still had not been reimbursed by her insurance company for the cost of the surgery, her hospitalization, or any of the required drugs. In the meantime, her employer had sold the company where she worked and, as is typical, the new owner laid her off. After a year of searching for a full-time job in a down economy and exhausting her savings, Lisa had been unable to find a new marketing position and was therefore in the process of selling her house. She had just barely kept up-to-date with her house payments by doing some consulting work.

You'd think she'd be a little depressed! But, no, she updated Jillian with humor and energy—like she was having great fun beating the challenges thrown at her. She was really happy to be in San Francisco if only for a brief time, especially since the company she was consulting for had paid for the trip.

Accompanied by several glasses of Cabernet supplemented with an occasional Merlot or Zinfandel, and superb goat cheese, duck strudel with a sweet and sour sauce, beets and puff pastry, the two old friends spent several hours working out the world's problems.

Jillian was most emphatic. "We could stop the wars in the Middle East by making oil irrelevant. I favor alternative energy myself."

Lisa agreed. "You know what else? We need to do something about education. It is the key to solving problems in many African nations, along with basic items like food and medicine, of course. Just think how an improved education system would help to solve many of America's problems."

Jillian jumped on this one. "You bet. Do you know that in the biotech industry we can't find enough qualified scientists here in the U.S.? We have to recruit worldwide."

"And what about the lack of funding for the arts? Not only does art, music and literature help in the "pursuit of happiness," but study after study show that students can learn math and science better if they take music lessons. Also, those who take music lessons or paint pictures are inclined to be more creative employees at solving business problems."

Jillian nodded. "How do we create more jobs here in the U.S. if our companies keep employing labor abroad? I think, however, that labor in India, China, Brazil and other countries will soon cost more—if recent demonstrations are any indication—and could push some jobs back to the U.S."

"Or to other poorer nations. Well, now that we've solved the world's problems, what do you think would make the most absolute perfect movie?"

Jillian thought for a moment. "It would have to be action, but with sensitive people who speak great dialogue. Good movies are based on good scripts."

"Well, that's true, but I'm thinking that a movie with Angelina Jolie, Julia Roberts, and Vanessa Williams would definitely be worth seeing, no matter the subject."

"If you add Hugh Jackman, Brad Pitt, and George Clooney, I concur."

The two women were very pleased with themselves but the discussion had to end. Lisa had an early morning meeting and then a flight back to Philadelphia, and Jillian had to be at work the next morning as well. Jillian decided that given her state of sobriety—or lack thereof—it was probably safer to pick up her car in the morning. It was parked near a well-lighted corner, and she knew it was better for her to leave it than to drive it. She would just have to pick it up in the morning before the parking meter kicked in. Given current medication, Lisa was more careful with her wine intake and felt comfortable driving so she happily offered to drive Jillian home.

Lisa dropped Jillian off in front of her apartment building at about 10:00. The two friends gave each other a hug, and parted with promises of seeing each other again soon. Jillian would be in New York within two weeks, and they had discussed the possibility of meeting in The Big Apple for appletinis (which seemed amusing to Jillian at the time). Jillian promised to send her itinerary and Lisa said she'd check her schedule and arrange to travel there from Philadelphia.

As Jillian was entering her building, her cell phone played the ring she programmed for business colleagues, and she was very surprised to see Dan Harrington's name displayed. It was very unusual that he would call her at all, much less this late at night. She answered professionally, she hoped. "This is Jillian Hillcrest."

"Hi, Jillian. This is Dan Harrington. I am so sorry to bother you this late, but I was wondering if you had given that folder to Brynn yet? I apologize for answering my phone just as I was leaving our meeting today, and I couldn't remember what you said about Brynn."

"Oh, no, I'm sorry. I looked for her, but I left the office shortly after you, and I didn't see her. In fact, I wasn't even sure she was in the office today. But I will be sure to give it to her first thing in the morning, as I'm pretty sure she's due back. I hope that's O.K.? Was it urgent?" Jillian waved to Charlie at the desk and then pushed the button for the elevator.

"Somewhat urgent, but tomorrow morning will be soon enough. Could you just be sure to give it to her as soon as you get in?" He seemed anxious, and Jillian felt a little guilty she hadn't searched harder for Brynn before leaving the office.

"No problem. Will do. Is Brynn expecting it?"

"No, actually, she isn't, but there's a note in the folder asking her to call me and I'll explain. Thanks." And he disconnected.

This was turning out to be a really strange day between the package from Bill Vulkjevich and now Dan Harrington's unusual call. The elevator doors opened at her floor, and Jillian headed for her flat. As usual, the neighbor across the hall had decorated her door with a new wreath celebrating the beginning of spring (it was March, after all!) with fresh flowers interwoven with some kind of twigs. The fragrance was actually quite pleasant and Jillian walked close by the door to get a good whiff only to be startled by the door opening by her retired neighbor, Mrs. Anderson, in her bathrobe. Cynthia Anderson was a stocky, not-unattractive woman probably in her late 50s or early 60s, with short brownish hair, muscular arms, the stance of an athlete, and an enticing smile that reached to her eyes. "Oh, hi, Jillian. I was getting a little worried, because I didn't think you had come in yet. How was your trip?"

Jillian sighed. One of the reasons she liked living in a city was the anonymity it offered, as opposed to the busybody atmosphere of many small towns such as the one where Jillian had grown up. Mrs. Anderson robbed her of that, although she was more well intentioned than interfering. The older woman volunteered for a lot of different community programs, and it seemed to Jillian had an overdeveloped sense of community responsibility. She felt it her duty to assure that a single female within her domain was protected.

"It was a great trip, although very busy. I didn't get to do any sightseeing—just work. Sorry that I'm so late tonight." What the hell? Jillian realized she was apologizing for being late to her neighbor, whom she barely knew. "I had some wine with a very good old friend who was here just for tonight. Your wreath is really pretty—and it smells great. Good night."

"Oh, thanks, Jillian. I'm glad you like the wreath. Good night. Get a good night's sleep!"

Jillian entered her flat surprised her lights were on. She didn't remember leaving them on. She must have been more tired than she remembered.

Jillian now regrettably faced the task of reviewing the flash drive and other materials from Bill Vulkjevich before giving in to the wine stupor and her pillow. She had left him a quick message earlier to let him know she would be contacting him later than originally anticipated, but promised to get back to him with some kind of response that night—even if only preliminary. She was a little annoyed he hadn't answered his phone, since he'd led her to believe he would be waiting for her call.

She picked up the package, took out the flash drive, and plugged it into her laptop. While it was loading, she poured some water from her filtered water jug to combat the dehydration from the wine and then turned her full attention to the information displayed on her laptop. Basically what she saw appeared to be a bunch of columns with numbers. Each column was labeled with a capital letter between A and X, which, assuming every letter of the alphabet was used except the last two, would mean there were 24 different columns.

However, Jillian could not understand the significance of the numbers and so looked to the printed pages included in the package. The first one said Patient A, which is when Jillian began to feel uneasy. Was this some kind of data from the lupus trial? If so, how had Vulkjevich gotten hold of it and why had he sent it to her? She was hardly a statistician and not someone who could interpret this kind of data. She continued through the pages and found that each was labeled as a patient with a different letter, i.e., Patient A, Patient B, Patient C, etc.

Then she came to some pages that appeared to contain a legend for the columns. She recognized some of them as the adverse events to the lupus drug that the company had reported as part of its presentation of the data in Geneva and as part of the public announcement. Her heart sank when she saw the category "Renal Failure" with several numbers beside it. The independent clinician, Dr. Reboto, had assured her that the one patient with serious kidney problems in the lupus trial had been on placebo only and not on the company's drug. If the data she was reviewing now was accurate, that statement was wrong and the company had incorrectly represented the results.

Jillian quickly called Bill Vulkjevich again hoping he would enlighten her. Again, no answer. Jillian left another message and asked him to call her as soon as possible. Until she clarified with him the significance of the figures in front of her, Jillian was uneasy about talking with anyone else—except maybe her boss, Brynn, who as CFO would be clear about what procedures to follow (or who to ask for guidance), if the company needed to disclose this information. It was just 11:00 p.m. and most likely not too late to disturb her boss so Jillian pushed Brynn's name on her mobile phone and waited somewhat impatiently to hear Brynn's voice. Instead she got her not-available message, so Jillian recorded her message: she needed to speak with her as soon as possible, and was she coming into the office tomorrow?

Anxious to solve the puzzle, Jillian then turned back to the columns of numbers to see what she could do to decipher them. After another half hour of working on them with little success, she grabbed her mobile phone and set the alarm for earlier than usual since she had to pick up her car. She placed the phone in its charger on her night stand to assure that she didn't miss any calls and also so that she would hear her alarm, and then placed her head on the pillow and succumbed to jet lag and wine.

06 ⋈⫴⋈⫴⋈

Brynn looked at the phone display and saw it was Jillian calling. It was after 11:00 p.m. so she was not inclined to answer the phone. This decision was reinforced by the fact that she had continued to ply herself with wine and did not particularly want her employee to know she was hardly sober. Given that she would see Jillian at the office in less than ten hours, she doubted there was anything urgent enough to need her response tonight. Also, sometimes Jillian over-reacted. So Brynn ignored the call.

Brynn's husband was not home yet. She had been gone for almost a week, and was surprised that he was not there when she returned. She had let him know when to expect her. She anticipated he would at least greet her upon her arrival at their modern 4,000 square-foot, red-tiled roof home in Los Altos Hills, a very wealthy enclave about 15 miles south of the Harmonia office. He liked to cook in the well-equipped kitchen and often would prepare her a light supper when she returned from business trips. However, he was not here nor had he left her a message about where he would be or when he would return. She was actually surprised that his absence made her sad.

Tim had just called to let her know he would not be in the office tomorrow. He and Stephanie were planning to spend the weekend in Paris as part of a delayed anniversary celebration. He asked Brynn to handle a couple of scheduled meetings and said he would see her Monday. Given his professional tone, Brynn assumed he made the call with Stephanie in the room, or else he was trying to tell her that their relationship was finished.

Brynn continued to sip her wine as she reviewed her virtual decision-making chart on the pros and cons of having an affair with the CEO of her company.

07

Jillian had slept fitfully and awakened before the alarm, again annoyed that Bill Vulkjevich especially had not called her. She figured she would see Brynn this morning, but Bill had asked her for an immediate response and yet was not around to receive it. To Jillian, who practiced Professionalism (with a capital P), this was irresponsible at best.

Jillian asked the concierge to get a cab for her at 7:45 so she could pick up her car by 8:00 to minimize the possibility of a parking ticket. She then started the coffee, took a quick shower, grabbed her morning toast and travel mug, laptop, and purse and headed out, taking care to be sure the lights in her flat were turned off. The cab was waiting; she retrieved her car with no problems, and proceeded on some surface streets in the city to enter Highway 101 as far down the peninsula as possible to avoid freeway traffic. She got to work by 9:00—record speed for this time of day.

Neither Brynn nor Tim was in the office yet. Jillian checked with their shared assistant who said she had not heard from either of them. They were not officially scheduled to be back until Monday, although both Jillian and Brynn's assistant expected them that day—Friday was usually Tim's staff meeting, and it was still scheduled for 11:00 a.m.

Jillian headed back to her office and decided to place another call to Vulkjevich to see whether he could enlighten her as to the significance of the columns of figures in the documents he had sent to her. Still no answer. She left another message, annoyed with him for dumping this on her with no explanation. Given her slight hangover and rush to pick up her car, she had neglected to bring the package with her to work, which was unfortunate; she would have liked to show the information to Brynn and others for their input. She wondered if Brynn had additional contact information for Vulkjevich, because Jillian was reasonably sure that Brynn had hired him to help run numbers to support financial reporting and analysis. She would add this question to the list of things she needed to discuss with Brynn.

Her phone buzzed and the display said Dan Harrington. Unbelievable. She briefly toyed with the idea of not answering, but put that idea aside almost immediately as she responded "Jillian Hillcrest" in her professional "I'm very busy" tone.

"Hi, Jillian. Dan here. Just checking to see if you'd had a chance to get that folder to Brynn. She hasn't responded to my phone messages."

"Hi, Dan. I haven't seen her yet this morning. We are definitely expecting her today. She is scheduled to make a presentation at a meeting later this morning. As soon as she comes in, I'll talk with her. In the meantime, is there anything I can do to help?"

"Er, no. I don't think so. Just get the folder to her and ask her to get back to me."

Jillian's phone was indicating another call, so she promised Dan she would relay the message. She was surprised to see that the caller ID indicated Lisa. Jillian thought Lisa had a tight schedule since she was flying home this morning. She answered, "Hi, Lisa—what's up?"

The background noise on the other end was a mixture of sirens, voices, cars, and screeches suggesting that the caller was outdoors. Jillian was startled when a male voice said, "Who is this?"

"Who is this? Where is Lisa?"

"Yes. Do you know a Lisa Baumgartner?"

"Who is this? And why are you asking about Lisa? What's happened?" As Jillian tried to comprehend what was happening, her stomach tightened.

The voice at the other end was calm, but insistent. "Please, ma'am. This is the San Francisco Police Department, and I need to know your relationship to Miss Lisa Baumgartner. You were apparently the last person she called, and since this is a local number I thought that you might be able to help us."

Jillian had to focus on breathing in order to talk. "Her phone, what? What's happened? Lisa was supposed to be on a plane back to Philadelphia this morning. Did the plane crash? What happ—"

The calm but firm voice interrupted. "Please, ma'am, can you identify yourself and can you tell me, is she a friend or relative of yours?"

Jillian was at the end of her patience. She eked out as best as she could and as loudly and emphatically as possible, "Lisa is a very good friend. My name is Jillian Hillcrest. Tell me what's happened!"

"I'm sorry to have to tell you that Miss Baumgartner has had an accident."

Jillian was now even more concerned especially since it seemed that this voice on the phone would not tell her anything.

"What kind of an accident? Is she all right?"

"Is it possible for you to come to the hospital? It's in San Francisco. We could discuss it here."

Jillian was sure something was wrong and believed the call was legitimate. After all, she recognized Lisa's caller ID. Also, the man on the other end of the phone sounded professional and real. So she concluded that Lisa really was seriously injured and needed her. "Of course, I can be there within an hour. I'm in Redwood City."

"That would be great. Ask for Loren Sherwood. I'll meet you in the lobby of the hospital right inside the door." He gave her the name and address of the hospital.

As Jillian disconnected, despite physically shaking she was thinking about what she needed to do to leave the office for possibly the rest of the day—in case she needed to stay with Lisa at the hospital. She checked in with Brynn's assistant and the receptionist letting them both know that she would be out of the office most likely for the rest of the day. She would try to reach Brynn later as soon as she understood better the status of her friend. She had enough presence of mind to grab Dan Harrington's folder and ask the assistant to be sure to give it to Brynn as soon as she got in. She would have to deal with Bill Vulkjevich and his issue later.

Traffic on 101 was mercifully moving at the speed limit; she drove to the hospital while trying to stay focused and calm. She kept trying to reassure herself that everything would be all right, that Lisa had overcome enormous obstacles, and that whatever had happened, she was fine. However, the policeman's voice echoed in her mind and something about his tone and hesitancy led Jillian to expect the worst. Her friend had suffered so much already. Why did the gods keep piling on more? It just wasn't fair.

Her buzzing cell phone interrupted her contemplation. Unfortunately Jillian had left home without her headset, so she opted not to answer, given that it was against the law to drive in California using a mobile phone unless it was hands free. It was dangerous, and Jillian knew that in her current state of mind she was in no condition to add any more distractions. However, she took a quick look at the display and did not recognize the number so figured she could return the call after she reached the hospital.

Her mind wandered back to Bill Vulkjevich and his package. Where had he gotten the data listed in the columns? Was it real or was it a template or what was it? Why had he given it to her? And what was with Dan Harrington and his folder for Brynn?

Oh, please be all right, Lisa.

08 ⋈⋈⋈

The hospital was located on the side of a hill, which always made it seem unapproachable to Jillian. She took the parking stub and headed for the hospital entrance dreading every step closer to learning what had happened to her long-time friend. There was an SFPD police car parked in front of the entrance, and Jillian assumed it belonged to the officer whose name Jillian had already forgotten.

She entered through the automatic doors, and charged the young yet apparently composed receptionist who already had a line of about a half dozen people in front of her. Jillian resented those who cut in line as if they were superior to everyone else who queued up to wait their turn—particularly in a hospital where each person in line could have a need as urgent as hers. Just as she was getting ready to ask the young lady if she knew where a police officer might be, someone gently tapped her shoulder. "Are you Jillian Hillcrest?"

"Oh, yes. Are you the officer who called me?"

"I am Inspector Loren Sherwood and, yes, I called you." He showed her what appeared to be a legitimate badge—not that Jillian would know the difference. "Can you come with me, please?"

Before they could move in the direction indicated by the inspector, a short, middle-aged, balding man approached the inspector and nodded emphatically. Inspector Sherwood motioned to Jillian. "This is the hit and run officer who first investigated your friend's accident. He just gave me some news that confirms my need to talk with you here, and maybe later at the police station. He'll come with me right now to hear what you have to say, and then he'll need to go back to the site at the garage where the event occurred, as will I, actually. Anyway, can you follow me, please? Let's get out of the lobby."

Jillian followed him, now even more concerned. With every step, her trepidation grew. "What do you mean 'hit and run'? Please tell me what's happened to Lisa! I want to see her. Is she all right? We had dinner last night, and she was fine. I know that she has had a lot of health problems, but she seemed so well last night."

The look on the inspector's face was enough to raise Jillian's apprehension. But she was not prepared for what he said next. "Miss Hillcrest, I'm sorry to have to tell you but we suspect that your friend was murdered this morning—struck deliberately, we think, by a hit and run driver. I didn't want to tell you on the phone, because, well, that's just not the right thing to do and it's also contrary to our policy. Please, let's sit here for a moment."

Jillian was sure that her entire body had hit a brick wall. Every movement seemed to take forever and it seemed to be happening at someone else's will. She allowed Inspector Sherwood to steer her into what appeared to be someone's office, and he led her to a chair. It was a soft chair and its print featured red flowers with green leaves. Jillian wasn't sure why she noticed, but the flowers seemed so big. Then she started to cough and gasp for air. Inspector Sherwood talked to her calmly and advised her to breathe slowly, first in, then out.

After what seemed like a lifetime but was probably only a minute or two, she felt her body return to some tired, fatigued place. Inspector Sherwood gave her a glass and encouraged her to drink some water— and that was helpful. "Please—Lisa and I have been friends for many years. Why would anyone want to kill her?" In her current state of mind, Jillian rushed to a possible conclusion and blurted out, "It wasn't a hate crime, was it?"

"Why do you ask that?"

"Well, Lisa was gay."

"Oh, were you . . .

"No, we are just very good friends."

"We don't know what the motive was, and originally the officer at the scene assumed that it was an accidental hit and run. What we know is that this morning in a parking garage a witness heard a scream, and as he was running to see what had happened he saw a white four-door car drive very fast out of the parking structure. He couldn't identify the model of the car. When he got to your friend, he called 911 immediately, but unfortunately she passed away in the ambulance on the way to the hospital."

Inspector Sherwood continued. "The doctor here at the hospital just confirmed that the car must have driven over her more than once given the amount and type of injuries, so we are proceeding as if this is a deliberate vehicular murder. It is unlikely that someone who accidentally ran over her would do it multiple times. We'll have confirmation of that following an autopsy, which will be performed as soon as possible."

He tried to be as gentle as possible in delivering this news, but Jillian felt as if he had punched her in the stomach. "We were hoping that you might be able to help us, and the sooner we can get after this guy, the better the chances are that we'll catch him. Do you feel up to it?"

Jillian definitely did not feel up to it, but her disbelief and fatigue were turning to anger. Her friend did NOT deserve this. "What can I do to help?"

"Well, first, just to get it out of the way, what kind of car do you drive?"

Jillian was too numb to care that he had asked a question implying that she might have had anything to do with Lisa's death. She was aware enough to understand that from Inspector Sherwood's perspective she was probably as much a suspect as she was a witness with information. "A dark red Scion XB—you know the boxy car that looks like it's from a cartoon." She and Lisa had often laughed about it. But she felt like she had to apologize for it. "I like its funky look."

"Thanks. I'm sorry. I had to ask. The car that ran over her was probably white. In addition to the witness who saw the white car, we found some white paint on a nearby car that appears to have been dented by the one that ran over your friend. We understand from her phone and some materials in her car that she was working for a company called Infrastructure Services, or something like that. One of my colleagues is headed to their office to ask them about what she was doing here in San Francisco, since it appears she lives in Philadelphia. You said you met with her last night?"

"Yes, we had wine and tapas here in the City." Somewhere in the back of her mind it seemed silly to provide such detail, like it really mattered that they had wine and tapas. "We make it a point to visit each other whenever either of us is in the other's area. Yes, she lives in Philadelphia. She does contract or temporary work as a consultant and was here, I believe, meeting with a client. We sort of made it a point not to talk about work."

Inspector Sherwood pulled out a small pocket notebook and a pen. "Do you mind if I take some notes?" Jillian thought it was incredibly polite of him to ask if he could take notes, especially since the other inspector had been recording since they entered the room. But Inspector Sherwood seemed to be trying to put her at ease. "No, of course not."

"You said that Lisa was supposed to be on a plane today. Do you know what time her flight was to depart and from where—San Francisco or San Jose or Oakland?"

"She said she had an early morning meeting in San Francisco, I think, and then had to catch her flight—I believe from SFO. Where did this happen?"

"It was at a parking garage near the Moscone Center. You came from Redwood City, I believe. Was there a particular reason that you met your friend in San Francisco?"

"Yes, first I live here, so it was convenient for me, but Lisa also had a meeting here all day yesterday so it worked out for her too. And, well, she really liked the City." Jillian felt a pang inside her when she realized she'd just used the past tense when talking about her friend.

"Did she give you any indication about who she was meeting this morning?"

"No. She hardly mentioned it. I got the feeling it wasn't a client, however. More like it was someone who could help her—you know, like a networking meeting, or maybe even someone with a job lead. What was the name again of the contracting company she worked for? I feel like I should know it."

He looked through his notes. "All I have written down is 'Infrastructure something.' I guess I don't have it. I'll have to get their full name." His cell phone suddenly played the theme from the old Dragnet show. He looked sheepish. "My nephew programmed it. I haven't had a chance to change it back." He answered quickly with a curt "Inspector Loren Sherwood." It was then that it registered on Jillian that she was staring at a tall, well-built mid-30ish man, with a shaved head, dressed semi-casually in slacks and blue sweater, which accentuated his blue eyes.

"What about the meeting this morning?" As she studied him, Jillian was listening closely to his side of the call. "Did you ask her employer why they don't know?" He sounded a little exasperated. "Yeh, I know, they're only her contractor and not her employer. Anything else?" Jillian shared his disappointment. "What about friends or acquaintances?" Short response. "O.K., I'll finish up here and meet you back at the garage. I want to take one more look around." Sherwood turned back to Jillian.

"She spent all yesterday at a client company in South San Francisco where she basically completed her work. The guy she was helping was actually pretty upset when we talked with him. He said that she did good work and was a really neat person and he liked her and planned to hire her again when they needed someone. He said that she was scheduled to return to Philadelphia today. She didn't mention anything to him about an early morning meeting. As far as the contractor company that placed her with the customer, they seem to know even less."

"Yes, she mentioned they were not too people-oriented but they had placed her at various positions throughout the country and sent her paychecks promptly and without any hassle. She was earning far less than she was worth, and they were taking their cut, but she needed the money to make house payments."

He tried to look empathetic, and then glanced at his notes, again. "Can you think of anyone who might have wanted to harm her? Or can you think of any reason—like, would she leave a big inheritance? Or did her work involve her knowing something that someone might not have wanted her to know? Or, anything?"

Jillian searched her memory. "I don't know what to say, so let me tell you what I know. I met Lisa almost 15 years ago in a college program in Italy. We became fast friends and confidants. We hit it off immediately, and enjoyed touring Europe together. She was an excellent market analyst, astute at comprehending market trends that would support the introduction of new products. She worked her way up to a director level position at a Philadelphia pharmaceutical company. At the same time, she actively supported her favorite charities, like a children's museum and a children's arts program."

"You mentioned earlier that she was gay. I need to explore that for a moment. Is it possible that could have anything to do with her death? Did people know she was gay?"

"Oh, yes. She didn't try to hide it. It was while we were in Italy that she figured out she was gay, and I wasn't. It was not easy for her—her family is very, quote," Jillian made the quote sign with the two fingers on both hands, 'religious.' She has not spoken to most of her family for a long time, although her mother and she communicated occasionally, over her father's objections. Hooray for religious tolerance." Jillian couldn't help herself—she had so resented the hateful behavior of Lisa's family.

"She met the woman of her dreams six/seven years ago—I can give you her contact information in Philadelphia, if that would be helpful. They were both very much in love, and lived together in Philadelphia in the home they bought until over a year ago. Although the breakup was traumatic—and definitely not Lisa's idea—it was not acrimonious. They are still friends, and keep in touch."

Jillian paused a moment to consider what else might be helpful. "Since the breakup, Lisa has had one thing after another go wrong—she had a mastectomy, lost her job, insurance didn't pay for the surgery, etc. Given the current job situation, she felt very fortunate to have landed the opportunity with the contractor. I don't know how helpful that is, but that's pretty much Lisa's life. Please—I have to ask—are you absolutely sure that the victim is really Lisa Baumgartner?"

Inspector Sherwood looked a little unsure, but not for the reason that Jillian thought. "We're pretty sure, given her driver's license photo. However, we do need someone to identify the body, and I suppose we could ask her family to do so, but since they are back East, perhaps, er, would you be willing . . .?"

Jillian looked at him as if he were asking her to jump into a pit full of snakes. "You want me to look at the body and confirm that it is Lisa?" There was no way that she could face this.

"Well, we prefer not to release the body until it has been officially identified—and after we've done an autopsy, of course—which means that someone from her family will have to travel here, and I thought maybe you might be willing to spare them. That way they can make arrangements to transport the body without traveling here. The other thing, we'll need to reach her parents, who I assume are her next of kin, and given what you've just told me, perhaps you might want to call them—after the Philadelphia police have informed them of their daughter's death—to help with the arrangements?"

Jillian knew that he was trying to be helpful, but she still remembered laughing about the best all-time movie with Lisa just last night, and how great the wine and tapas were, and how the two friends were solving the world's problems. How could she look at her now-dead friend and talk to a family who had caused her mostly pain?

"I don't know if I can. When would you need it done? I couldn't possibly do it today."

Inspector Sherwood nodded. "Of course. Tomorrow will be soon enough—given that we have her driver's license photo. The Medical Examiner's office is transporting the body right about now, and it would be helpful if you could go there tomorrow. I'll send you directions later when we know exactly where in the building to go."

"I live in Mission Bay, so it's just a short drive. It's not a problem to come tomorrow. What time?"

Inspector Sherwood checked his mobile phone calendar. "It looks like noon would be the best time, but let me confirm that after I talk with the Medical Examiner's office. Will that work for you?"

Jillian just wanted to get out of the hospital and back to some place normal, like home, so she readily agreed to noon. Inspector Sherwood handed her his card, and asked for hers. She dug one out of her pocket—she always had one available—and handed it to him. He promised he would follow up if he learned anything and also asked if he could call her if he had additional questions. "Oh, one more thing. Do you have a photo of Lisa that you could send or bring to me? We can use her driver's license photo but it's not very sharp and seems old. We'll want to show a photo to people in the area to see if we can identify who she met this morning."

"Sure. I can e-mail one to you that's fairly recent—like a year ago. I'll do it as soon as I get home."

As she headed toward the exit, she could hardly believe it was only 2:00 p.m.–less than 24 hours since Lisa and she had laughed and pounded their table with the authority of two people expecting to live much longer.

09

nspector Loren Sherwood watched Jillian leave the hospital as he
checked in with his partner, who was still at the garage where the
suspected homicide had occurred. The hit and run officer had left
the hospital about halfway through Sherwood's interview with Jillian
Hillcrest. The police had initially closed only the one floor of the
garage where the incident had occurred in order to gather forensic
evidence and take photographs. However, upon learning of the doctor's
supposition that it was probably a deliberate vehicular murder, the
police had subsequently closed the floors above and below that one,
which was causing parking problems at the Moscone Center (located in
a very congested part of San Francisco). There was some urgency about
releasing the area for parking.

Inspector Sherwood gave his partner a quick download of his
conversation with Jillian Hillcrest. His partner, Inspector Joe Sodini,
was an experienced homicide investigator who was close to retiring,
but after a full career solving crimes he somehow managed to still care
about the victims and their families. He would work methodically and
carefully to reveal the killer. Sherwood often thought that if criminals
knew about Joe Sodini, they would be less likely to commit crimes.

"Do you think she had anything to do with this?" Sodini trusted Sherwood's judgment. It had proven multiple times to lead them in the right direction.

Sherwood considered his response very briefly. "No, I definitely do not think that she had anything to do with this. In fact, just the opposite. My concern is that she might be a potential victim, although I'm not sure why. There is something nagging at me about something she said. She really seemed to care for her friend. However, I would still stay open to checking her out more—I have certainly been fooled in the past."

"So do you want to come down here and take one last look at the garage? Or should we open it up?"

Inspector Sherwood decided he wanted to explore the area again especially now that he knew more about the victim after speaking with Jillian Hillcrest. "Oh, and the hit and run officer is on his way. It might be useful to have him look over everything again now that we know for sure that this is most likely a murder. I'll get there as soon as I can." Inspector Sherwood picked up the recorder that the hit and run officer left and headed outside to his car to drive to the garage.

It took him longer than anticipated, even though he parked his police vehicle in a close-by "no parking" area (where he was careful not to block traffic). He hurried to the taped-off area and motioned to his partner, who was in a heated discussion with a man in a parking attendant's uniform. Inspector Joe Sodini noticed Sherwood with relief and cut off his discussion, pointing to his partner, who hurried over to the pair. "Sorry it took me so long. I just need a few minutes, and then we can open this back up. It's a mess out there, as you know."

The uniformed attendant looked relieved but not much happier. He was probably being pressured by his bosses who were most likely receiving lots of angry phone calls from officials of the trade show currently being held at the convention center.

Inspector Sherwood stared at the tape indicating where the body was found. Unfortunately for the investigation, the victim was still alive when the paramedics arrived, so they moved her, first to administer whatever aid would help save her, and then, to take her to the hospital. She died en-route without regaining consciousness. What that meant was that the original position of the victim was not preserved, although one of the paramedics had provided a description and the hit and run officer had used chalk to replicate it as best as he could. The forensics team had noted the blood spatters and speculated the original direction of the car, although it looked as if the body had been dragged in two directions. That had led the hit and run officer to deduce that the car had run over her going both forward and backward more than once, corroborated by the doctor's conclusion that she had been run over multiple times. At that point, the hit and run officer had called in the homicide detectives, which is why Inspectors Sherwood and Sodini were now involved.

Sodini joined Sherwood and pointed out the white paint scrape on one of the nearby cars, whose owner they had subsequently identified in their search for Lisa's vehicle. "They took a sample of that white paint assuming that it was from the murderer's car. The witness is positive that it was white, and he seems fairly reliable. The hit and run guys are following up with both him and with the owners of the other cars in the vicinity."

Sherwood tried to imagine exactly how it would have happened and how fast the car would have been going. They had located the victim's car about 20 feet from her body. It was the only one nearby that was a rental, as the sticker on its windshield indicated. A quick call to the rental agency confirmed it was the car rented by Lisa Baumgartner.

Assuming that she had entered the floor from the closest elevator, she would have been walking toward it. The paramedics had found a small backpack-type purse on the victim, and had removed it and given it to the police. It contained her cell phone, driver's license, a packet of business cards, keys, a bottle of ibuprofen, credit cards, and

$40. However, they had not found anything else, so both Sherwood and Sodini now spent their last moments at the roped-off crime scene carefully searching one last time for anything that might provide a clue. They were only two of a team of many who had done so, and it was unlikely that anything had been missed. In addition, they would have the photos that were taken earlier. But both of them always did one last search to be sure.

"I assume that the reason there are so few cars parked here was that it was so early when it happened before too many people had arrived," Sherwood asked the parking lot attendant, who nodded. Then he turned to Sodini. "Was the car towed to the impound lot?" He wanted the crime lab to go through it and was eager for the results.

Sodini said the rental car had been towed about ten minutes ago, and that he had already started the paperwork for a search warrant to investigate it. He also noted that the victim's luggage and some other items were in the car. Once they got the search warrant they could check them out.

The two homicide inspectors took one last look, and then gave the garage attendant permission to open the area to traffic. They reassured themselves that everything that could be done to preserve the evidence had been done. Now they needed to start putting together the pieces of the puzzle.

10

Before Jillian reached her car after leaving the hospital, she remembered the phone call she had received while on her way there. She pulled out her cell phone and listened to the voicemail. It was from an online broker asking her to verify that she knew Dan Harrington; he had used her name as a reference. That seemed very bizarre. Why would Dan need to use Jillian as a reference? Despite her tendency to like to solve such mysteries, that could certainly wait for a call back as she was sure it was a mistake.

She was surprised she had still not heard back from Bill Vulkjevich. His sense of urgency had apparently dissipated. She checked with the receptionist at her office to see if there were any emergencies. She had already decided to go home, rather than back to work. She reached Brynn's voicemail and left her a fairly lengthy message about Lisa's death and Bill Vulkjevich's mysterious package. She let Brynn know that unless she really needed her for some unforeseen emergency that Jillian would be spending the rest of the afternoon at home, but that Brynn should feel free to call.

Mostly—surprisingly—Jillian wanted to talk to her ex-husband. He had known Lisa fairly well. When the four of them were still two couples, they had enjoyed sharing a number of events together—like going to Broadway plays, movies, and dinners when in New York and most recently attending the Sacramento Traditional Jazz Jubilee over Memorial Day, since Lisa's ex-partner loved any kind of jazz. Chad would understand how Jillian felt. As soon as she got home, she would give him a call. Maybe he could go with her to the hospital tomorrow.

Jillian tried one more time to reach Bill Vulkjevich—just in case—but again all she got was his voicemail. She left another message asking him to call her. Then she phoned the receptionist at work and told her she would not be in for the rest of the day. Having done what she could to assure that things would continue without her at the office, she got in her car and headed for home.

When she arrived at her building, she was relieved to see Pete's familiar face and handed the car over to him explaining that she was home early due to the death of a friend. He expressed his condolences, and seemed sincere. Pete was a student at San Francisco State, and was the first member of his family to go to college. He seemed determined to graduate and was officially a sophomore after three years of part-time attendance—part-time because he had to earn the tuition as well as the money to help support his mother and three younger siblings. He said he wanted to become the world's first honest lawyer, because his family had suffered frequently at the hands of shysters, which was part of the reason he had to support the family.

So, Jillian was always happy to tip him and she really enjoyed talking with him. He had a great sense of humor and appreciated hers. Today, however, neither of them felt like joking, and Jillian was just relieved to be greeted by a familiar and friendly face. She handed him the usual tip and headed for her flat. She waved to Charlie, the concierge, explaining to him, too, that she was home early due to the death of a friend, and picked up her mail.

As she approached the elevator, the doors opened and Mrs. Anderson and a young man wearing a Giants baseball cap, whom Jillian didn't recognize, got out. Jillian really didn't want to get into a conversation with Mrs. Anderson, but when the older woman looked surprised to see her, Jillian felt compelled to tell her she was home early due to the death of a friend. Of course, the motherly woman was immediately worried and started to fuss over Jillian. "Thanks. For right now, I just need to sleep. I still haven't recovered from my trip yet and, well, I need to not think."

The young man kept his head down and walked straight to the door. Mrs. Anderson looked at him as if she were a teacher disciplining a poorly behaving pupil. She raised her voice so that Charlie and the teenager—who was hurrying out the door—could hear. "I found that young man skulking around our hall, and he doesn't seem to live here. He said he was visiting someone, but I don't believe him. You need to be more careful about allowing people into this building, Charlie."

Charlie looked truly concerned and would have gone after the young man if he weren't already out the door and running down the street. It would take Charlie a few minutes just to get out from behind the desk, and they could see it was too late for him to do anything. "I'm sorry, Mrs. Anderson. I don't know how he got by me. I'm going to have to keep the front door locked again. I hate to do it because it makes it so inconvenient for everyone—but I don't know how else to keep an eye on the desk and the door. It would help if we had a security guard."

"It's fine with me if you keep the door locked." Mrs. Anderson appeared to be somewhat shaken by the incident. Apparently riding in the elevator with the teenager had unnerved her. "I'd rather be safe."

Jillian just wanted to escape, and the elevator doors closed as Mrs. Anderson continued to express her concern over the lack of security in the building. Jillian looked at herself in the elevator's mirrored wall and was surprised that she looked almost the same as she had yesterday. How could she still look the same? With all that had happened in the past 24 hours she was sure she must be a different person.

Entering her flat, she was shocked to find her lights on again. This was too much. Jillian knew she had turned them off this morning. Perhaps Mrs. Anderson was right. Perhaps the teenager in the Giants hat was somehow entering and robbing the flats. Jillian looked around carefully but everything seemed to still be there. Nonetheless, Jillian knew she had turned off her lights. She decided to report it this time to Charlie, whom she called on the intercom phone. "Charlie, I'm sure I turned off my lights this morning, and yet they were on when I got home just now. Is there any reason for that? Could that guy have somehow gotten into my apartment? . . . No, nothing seems to be disturbed or missing. . . . No there's no need to come up. I just thought you should be aware. Thanks."

Jillian didn't know what to do. Frankly, she didn't want to do anything. So she sat down in one of her dark blue leather chairs and began thinking about Lisa's death, Vulkjevich's package, Dan's folder, and Brynn and Tim's affair. She had still not heard from any of them. Maybe it was time to check in with Brynn so she pushed her boss's number and was only mildly relieved when she answered. "Hi, Jillian. How are you doing? What happened to your friend?"

"Hi, Brynn. Apparently she was deliberately run down—hit and run—and killed. The police say there's no doubt it was deliberate. They want me to identify the body tomorrow to save the family a trip from the East Coast."

"Oh, so she wasn't from around here?"

"No, she was visiting from Philadelphia. She was a contractor, out here finishing up work for a client."

"Why do the police think it was deliberate?"

What had the inspector told her? "You know, he told me but—I think it was that she was run over multiple times. Right, the doctor at the hospital said he thought so, given the amount of injuries. Oh, and they also have a witness who saw a car speed away afterward. Anyway, they are sure. She had a meeting with someone this morning and they are trying to track down who it was. I'm sorry to focus on this."

Jillian changed the subject. "Did you get the folder I left you from

Dan Harrington? He said to tell you to call him if you had any questions. He was at the office yesterday, and Phil gave him an overview of the data. He seemed impressed, even though he was in pain from a bicycle wreck. Apparently he rides his bike a lot in the City. Hard to believe that someone with his wealth would ride the streets of San Francisco."

"Well maybe he just appreciates the views. It is beautiful, you know. And yes, I got his folder. I haven't had a chance to look at it yet, but I'll get to it. You left me a message about Bill Vulkjevich. What was that about?"

It felt good to Jillian to be having a semi-normal employee-to-boss conversation. "He dumped a package on me a couple days ago that seems to be a bunch of data from the lupus trial. He said it was urgent, and I have tried to get back to him repeatedly, but he hasn't been answering his phone. It could be nothing, but I was concerned when it appeared that the data indicated more renal failure than Reboto told us. However, I really can't tell."

"Is it on your desk? I'll go get it and take it to Phil. He should be able to interpret it."

Jillian sighed. "Unfortunately it's here at home. He mailed it to me here. I'll bring it on Monday. By the way, where did you meet Bill?"

"Actually the agency sent him to us and his credentials were very solid. He really knows his numbers and has a keen analytical sense."

Silently, Jillian disagreed, which was unusual as she typically concurred with Brynn's assessments. Jillian found Vulkjevich slow to respond, and he typically was unable to interpret the significance of the numbers beyond the mathematical output. She had assumed that his value came from his attention to detail, not his analytical prowess. However, perhaps she had missed something. After all, she was not a financial wizard herself. "Anyway, if you hear from him, ask him to call me. Otherwise I'll turn the package over to Phil on Monday. I assume your trip back was at least uneventful, if not pleasant?"

Brynn laughed a little. "Yes, it was as fine as a 15-hour flight can be.

I can't complain. Everything was on time, and the wine was drinkable."

"How was the staff meeting this morning? Did Tim get back?"

"Actually, no. We had a brief meeting without him just to review what happened in Geneva. It looks like we won't see Tim until Monday."

Jillian was beginning to lose interest in the conversation, but she was trying hard to focus. "Well if anything comes up over the weekend that you need me for, please don't hesitate to call. I'll be a little shaken tomorrow, I suspect, given the identification at the hospital, but . . ."

Brynn interrupted. "Don't worry about it, Jillian. I can't think of anything that could happen that would require your attention that urgently. We can plan our contribution to the investor relations symposium on Monday or even Tuesday. The moderator of the panel called today and asked to have a conference call to review what the CFO panel should be discussing. Also—they asked about your panel. Is there anything we can do to help?"

"Sorry—I totally forgot. Do you need any help with your topic? Can I do some research for you?" Brynn again said they could discuss it the upcoming week. Jillian continued, with relief, in "work mode." "I also need to contact my panelists, but Monday should be soon enough to remind everyone. I arranged everything before we left for Geneva."

Jillian was in charge of a panel at a symposium of her peers in San Jose just a week from that day. Given increasing criticism that both public relations and investor relations were receiving—especially from "fake news" shows like Jon Stewart's Daily News that Jillian typically enjoyed—she had proposed a discussion on the ethics of being "On Message." The topic of her panel was "Public Relations: Propaganda or Communications?" She planned to kick off the discussion with a brief history of the discipline of public relations reviewing its origins in the United States by a nephew of Sigmund Freud, to the change of its name from the Fascist-used term "propaganda" to "public relations" by early practitioners to improve its image. Then she would follow with a recent clip from some of the coverage that poked fun at multiple presidential spokespeople who all reiterated the same message across multiple venues at different times, i.e., staying "on message."

The panel included the head of a well-respected local PR agency; a financial consultant who described himself as an advisor for the entrepreneur and investor community; Dan Harrington, representing institutional investors; a Silicon Valley *Wall Street Journal* reporter; a retail broker; and one of her company's larger individual investors. She had provided the questions for discussion, some articles on pundit opinions, and only needed to remind her participants about the conference and the schedule and logistics to assure the session's success.

Brynn was appearing on another panel as a Chief Financial Officer representing small-cap biotech companies. Her topics would be moderated by another investor relations executive who would focus on financial reporting and the changing rules of fair disclosure among others. Brynn was well-versed on the topic and Jillian doubted that she needed much support to be a major contributor. She was also a clear and careful speaker, and Jillian was pleased that her boss would be participating. Jillian felt a tiny bit better, and when she disconnected from Brynn, she decided it was time to call Chad to see if her ex-husband would be willing to accompany her tomorrow. He was probably still at work, but she decided to try his mobile phone rather than his office number since it was a personal call. When he didn't answer, she left him a message asking him to call her, and that it was urgent. The letdown she felt when he did not answer added to her current frame of mind and made her wonder if a good cry would make her feel better.

She decided to see if she could sleep, and lay down on her bed. But her mind kept racing from Lisa to Bill Vulkjevich and his package to Dan Harrington and his folder. Who would want to kill Lisa? Why didn't anyone know who she was meeting this morning? Jillian tried and tried to remember if Lisa had said anything specific about the meeting, but all she could remember is that she had an appointment that came up suddenly—something about meeting someone who might be able to help with a job or something about doing some research that would lead to a job? Had she been run over before or after she met with this mysterious person? If only Jillian hadn't had so much wine, perhaps she could recall something helpful.

B rynn disconnected from Jillian, concerned about Vulkjevich. She had hired him against her better judgment because he had been recommended by the agency as one of the few experts in the lupus field—but also because he had intimated he knew something about her and Tim, telling her he had seen them leaving a room at a San Jose hotel together. What was he up to? Where had he gotten the data he had sent to Jillian? And why had he sent it to Jillian rather than her? Brynn was the one who had actually hired him as a contractor.

At any rate, Brynn was not so much concerned about the supposed data as she was about the fact that Vulkjevich sent it to Jillian, which irked Brynn. She felt very confident the trial had been conducted in the best interests of patients and that Harmonia had followed FDA protocol guidelines. Ethics started at the top and she knew that Tim was painfully ethical in business, as was Phil Montgomery. They would never allow falsified information to be created or published.

In the meantime, Brynn needed to prepare a report for the board of directors on the company's progress with European investors. She tried to put her uneasiness to rest. She also tried to eliminate the feeling of remorse. When Tim had told her he would not be returning until

Monday because he was spending the weekend with Stephanie, it seemed to Brynn he was telling her they had to stop—that Brynn and he needed to return to being employer/employee again. And Brynn knew that was the best for everyone.

She was also sure her husband suspected something. He had not returned home until Friday morning and had behaved as if his absence was normal. It turned out he, too, had been traveling. However, he had made her work for this information while he was grabbing his golf clubs and heading for a day on the links. He did not let her know when or if he would be home for dinner.

Her assistant entered to let her know that one of the company's larger investors was on the phone, so she gratefully turned her attention to that call.

12

Chad Bradbury noticed he had a message from his ex-wife. Jillian seldom called him any more, and when she did it was usually something work-related: Did he know so-and-so, the reporter, and what did he think of him? Chad didn't mind, but sometimes he yearned to return to their early days together, when they were just learning about each other. They had joked a lot then, and they each showed the other new experiences. The relationship was active. They both grew. Perhaps that was why they had felt like they made each other whole.

Mostly he missed the laughter. He had recently been dating a really attractive and intelligent woman he liked a lot. He and Mary had learned about each other and had done some interesting things together. They had gone to several plays and concerts, as well as movies and dinners. They discussed a lot of issues, and were politically like-minded. The sex was not terrific, but it was more than adequate. However, she didn't like to laugh that much. His jokes fell flat; she would look at him quizzically asking him to explain.

Jillian, on the other hand, not only understood his sense of humor, she amplified it. The two of them had often spent many a dinner exploring a new restaurant where they laughed continuously. He remembered one time when the waiter started to join in with them and every time he appeared at their table he wore a different hat—first, the obvious chef hat, then a floppy rain hat, then a bowler—which prompted Chad to go out and get a bowler for himself which he wore every day for months, to Jillian's delight.

At any rate, he was a bit anxious about returning Jillian's call. He and Mary had decided to call off their relationship for a while, because Mary wanted to focus on her career, which had become particularly demanding and time-consuming. Through it all, Chad had come to realize he really missed Jillian. He couldn't remember exactly what had instigated their divorce, but he was sure that part of the problem was that he had become too complacent. While he missed her laughter when he was with Mary, he couldn't recall the last time Jillian and he had laughed at more than an occasional joke. Over the last few years of their marriage, they had laughed less and less.

Assuming she was calling for professional reasons, Chad wanted to plan in advance to push for more than just a discussion about a reporter. He decided he would invite her to dinner, and see where that took them. However, he also needed to probe to be sure she wasn't serious about someone else. That would be embarrassing, at best. He was actually very excited when he returned Jillian's call.

Jillian awakened to the phone playing "Once Upon a Time" in her ear. She checked the display to confirm that it was Chad (she had assigned "Once Upon a Time" as his ring) and answered gratefully if somewhat sleepily. "Hi, Chad. What time is it?" It was dark and her clock said it was almost 6:00. That didn't make sense.

Chad was concerned. She didn't sound well. "Jillian? Are you sick? What's up?"

"No, I was just sleeping. Something really awful has happened. Lisa was murdered this morning—here in San Francisco. I just saw her . . ."

"What?! Lisa was murdered? How? What happened? When? Are you sure? Are you all right?"

Jillian was tired, but she understood Chad's reaction, which was not much different than hers had been. "Yes. The police called me at work this morning. I went to the hospital and talked to an inspector. Chad, they want me to go to the hospital tomorrow and identify her body. It's all so awful. Can you go with me? I know it's asking a lot, but it would be so helpful."

"Of course. What time do you need to be there?"

"The inspector said noon, so maybe you could swing by here and pick me up at, say 11:30?"

"No problem. Jillian, are you all right? Do you want me to come over tonight? I could keep you company, and then we could have breakfast and go to the hospital together in the morning."

That did it. Jillian started to cry. "That would be so wonderful. I don't have any food. I just got back from Geneva. I'm so tired." It had been a long time since she had cried and she really preferred to keep it private so she was trying very hard to suppress it.

"I'll be there as soon as I can. It's about 6:00 now—I'll stop for some Chinese. Do you have any wine?"

"Yes—I have some. Thank you so much, Chad."

"What are ex-husbands for? I'll see you soon."

And then she really did cry.

By the time Chad knocked on her door, which Jillian verified by looking through the peephole, she had showered, changed, and reapplied her makeup—what little she wore—and dressed in a comfortable over-sized shirt and jeans. As she opened the door, she caught a whiff of the Chinese food and realized she was indeed quite hungry. All she had eaten that day was toast in the morning. Chad quickly put everything down and gave her a long hug. "Oh, I think I've missed these hugs—I guess you're right—this is what ex-husbands are for. I didn't even ask: How are you doing, Chad? How's the house coming? And Mary? Are the two of you doing well together? I really like her, by the way." She had met Mary one night at a mutual marketing function sponsored by the local Biotech Industry Organization, or BIO.

"First, tell me about Lisa." Jillian proceeded to fill him in beginning with her last evening together with Lisa, and ending with her conversation with the inspector at the hospital.

"I still can't believe it."

Chad gave her another hug. "Hugs are always on the house from this ex-husband. I'm so sorry, Jillian." He decided that a change of subject would be helpful. "Regarding the house, the front porch is almost done—I've been working on cleaning the carvings and fixing and painting the banisters and the roof of the overhang. And Mary and I are no longer together."

"Oh, I'm sorry. I'm not sure what to say. I really liked her."

"Me too. But she doesn't want a committed relationship right now. She is more interested in her career. So we decided to just be friends. Sort of like you and me!"

"Well, all I can say is that Chinese food smells unbelievably good. Here is the wine. I even opened it. And here are spoons and plates and chopsticks. Let's eat." Jillian found it hard to believe she was actually hungry. Just seeing Chad had helped her a lot. And she was greatly relieved he would be accompanying her tomorrow. Just about that time, her phone played the ring she had programmed for "unknown" callers.

Jillian saw it was Inspector Sherwood. Sigh. "This is Jillian Hillcrest."

"Hi, Miss Hillcrest. This is Inspector Sherwood. I am sorry to bother you, but I have a quick question. Do you know if Lisa had any other meetings while she was in San Francisco?"

"Not that I know of. She was here basically to work with her client to finish their project, which was probably some kind of analysis to assess the potential market for a product. Why?"

"Well, we found a folder in her luggage that maybe you can look at tomorrow. It seems to have some information about some stocks in it. It may be nothing, but we want to check out any possible leads."

"I'd be happy to look at it. Also, I hope it's all right—I've asked a friend to come with me tomorrow. Actually, he's my ex-husband." Why did she feel compelled to add that? "He also knew Lisa pretty well, so . . ."

"That's probably a good idea to bring someone with you. It's not the easiest thing to do. I'll see you tomorrow at the Medical Examiner's about noon. I e-mailed you the directions. Oh, and I hate to bother you again, but could you send us that photo of Miss Baumgartner? It would be extremely helpful in identifying her whereabouts this morning."

"Oh, I'm so sorry. I forgot. I'll do it right away. It will just take a second. Thank you, Inspector. Good-bye. See you tomorrow."

Jillian disconnected and went to her laptop. "I need to send the inspector a photo of Lisa to help him find out if anyone saw her this morning. God—it's hard to believe that this all just happened this morning! I wonder why Lisa would have a folder with her about various stocks?"

Chad looked thoughtful. "Maybe she was investing or maybe she owned some stocks and was tracking them?"

"I had the feeling she had already liquidated everything. Anyway, the inspector wants me to review the folder to see if it's a lead."

Jillian searched her photos file and found a year-old picture of Lisa— before her world turned upside down. She looked happy and Jillian felt the overwhelming desire to have her friend with them right now. She also felt angry that someone had taken her life. Jillian hesitated and then sent the photo to the e-mail address on the inspector's card.

She turned her attention to Chad as he handed her a plate with the amazing aromas of lemon chicken, walnut shrimp, and pork-fried rice. Oh, please let there be pot stickers—yes, of course there were. All her favorites. Chad remembered what she liked. Never had food tasted so good, and Jillian suddenly felt guilty that she could be enjoying anything considering what had happened to her friend a short 12 hours before.

Chad sensed the mood change and asked Jillian if she wanted to talk about Lisa. "Did her parents ever come to terms with her and Beverly?"

"No, I don't think so. I really wish that had happened before she died. She overcame so much with so little help from her family. Oh, damn, I should have asked the inspector if he wanted me to call them. He mentioned it earlier today, but I totally forgot."

Suddenly the intercom buzzed. Jillian pushed the button and heard Charlie's voice say, "Hi, Jillian. Sorry to bother you, but it turns out that one of the apartments was burglarized today so the police are here. Mrs. Anderson told them about your lights being on, and they were wondering if they could talk with you."

"Sure, Charlie. Should I come down?"

"No, they would prefer to come up to see where your flat is compared to the one that was robbed. I'm checking with everyone to see if anything was taken. Obviously I'll be locking the front door now, even when I'm here. They're on their way to your place now."

Jillian explained to Chad about the young man in the baseball cap, Mrs. Anderson's concerns, and her lights being turned on two evenings in a row when she was sure she had turned them off. Just as she finished, there was a knock on her door.

Checking the peephole, she saw two police officers in full uniform. She opened the door and greeted them. "Please come in." Policemen in uniform always intimidated Jillian, particularly those who carried guns. To her, their guns seemed particularly big, although she had to admit she wouldn't know, as they were very much not a part of her life. She had never even held a gun, and other than reading about them and seeing them in movies and TV, she had nothing to do with them.

The two policemen introduced themselves and explained they were checking to see if her flat was also involved in the burglary since the one they were investigating was directly above Jillian. Apparently, the things that were taken included a briefcase, a laptop computer, and a couple of folders with some papers in them along with some jewelry and cash. Was Jillian missing anything? And was she absolutely certain her lights were turned off when she left the apartment the past two mornings?

The upstairs tenant admitted she had left her door unlocked when she went downstairs to do her laundry and then out for coffee—leaving her flat open for at least an hour.

One of the officers was looking at the sliding doors to Jillian's balcony, which he found unlocked. "Do you usually leave this unlocked?"

"Actually, yes." She heard Chad sigh and could feel his disapproving eyes on her. "It's three stories up so I figured it doesn't matter."

"Well, maybe. But it's not absolutely impossible that the thief descended from the balcony above yours to get into your apartment. We've had reports of a burglar with gymnastic-like ability who has been active in the City over the past few months. In the future, I'd keep it locked. Again, can you check to be sure nothing is missing? Do you have a computer? A briefcase?"

Jillian knew her laptop was there—she had just used it to send Lisa's picture to Inspector Sherwood. She looked for the package Vulkjevich had sent, and it was right where she had put it in a closed bookcase where she stored important mail and other items. She also checked what little jewelry she had—not that it was valuable, but just in case; and she checked appliances, DVD player, and anything else she could think of. As far as she could tell, nothing was missing.

"I am certain I turned off the lights, but when I came home last night they were on, so I took extra special care this morning to be sure they were turned off." Jillian was more perplexed than disturbed at this point.

So were the police. None of this made much sense to them since nothing had been stolen. "Just be sure that all of your doors and windows are locked, and if you see anything else that's suspicious— like if your lights are on the next time you come home—contact us before you enter. In the meantime, your guy in the lobby is going to lock the front door even when he's behind the desk. I think that's all we can do now other than check to see if anyone else has experienced anything strange."

Once the police were gone, Jillian returned to what was left of her dinner. Since it was cold she microwaved both her plate and Chad's. The aroma of the re-heating food rekindled her appetite, and she again attacked the food. She also thoroughly enjoyed the feel of the Sterling cabernet as she drank it—no, she would not say "guzzled." It was another of Jillian's rules never to guzzle good red wine.

The combination of the food, the cry, talking with Chad, and the wine was making her feel almost human again. When she looked up from her plate, she discovered Chad studying her with focused concentration. At that moment, she was again surprised: she wanted more than just a hug from him. The sex they had shared as husband and wife had been fulfilling and steady. And at that moment, Jillian wanted to be fulfilled. However, her ex-husband simply took her in his arms, and guided her to the bedroom.

"Not tonight, Jillian. You need to rest."

nspector Sherwood printed a copy of the photo of Lisa Baumgartner sent by Jillian and then forwarded the e-mail for processing so that the police could canvass the area around the murder scene. They had not yet found out where Lisa had had her meeting but until now they only had her driver's license photo to show to possible witnesses. This one was much better and would help the identification process, although Sherwood was not hopeful. It was a very busy area, with a trade show in town bringing lots of non-residents. But at least with this photo, they had a better chance.

He studied the photo for a minute or so trying to see into the character of Lisa Baumgartner, willing her to tell him what had happened. He knew this was hopeless and silly, but it helped him to focus. He could see in her eyes and stance that she was someone who met problems head-on. Or was that his opinion after learning about her from Jillian Hillcrest? Well, the photo of her definitely fit the description of her character.

He looked again at the list of companies in the folder that had been in her luggage. Sherwood had never heard of any of them. Lisa had traveled light. She had only a carry-on bag. It was one of those bags with a slot for a computer and room for some clothes. She was wearing a professional-looking pantsuit, but most of the other clothes in the carry-on bag were more casual. However, there was no computer in the bag, so either she didn't bring one or it had been stolen. Given her profession of market analyst, the inspector was thinking the latter. So he added that to the list of items to investigate. What kind of computer did she use? Maybe her employer would know.

The Philadelphia police had informed Lisa's parents of her death; it was customary for such notifications to be made in person. Apparently only the father had been at home at the time, and the officer who made the visit said that his conversation with the victim's father was somewhat unexpected. He reported that the parents lived in a very nice and spacious Pennsylvania stone house in the suburbs. The officer anticipated that the parents would be heartbroken, and had brought along one of his colleagues accustomed to offering early grief counseling. However, the father's response to the news of her death was, "Well, I suppose that's what she gets. It's God's punishment for the choices she made."

As instructed by Sherwood, the Philadelphia officer informed Lisa's father that Jillian Hillcrest would be doing the identification so that the family did not need to fly to California. He then asked who would be making the arrangements for her body.

The father responded that no one from his family cared about her burial, and that she could rot in the morgue for all he cared. Then he closed the door without ever inviting the officers into his house. They never saw the mother.

Inspector Sherwood was heterosexual, but could not comprehend the bigotry against homosexuals. He figured he was somewhat unusual as a cop—even in San Francisco—but he believed people were born as one or the other; choice was not a factor. Plus, as far as he was concerned, and given all the horrific things people were capable of doing to one another, he encouraged love over hate regardless of sexuality.

So he had little time for a father who would say what Lisa

Baumgartner's father had said. However, he felt that much harm had been done in the name of Christianity and other religions. He was an Episcopalian and despite all he had seen, he believed that some sort of superior being existed. Otherwise, how could humanity have been started? He had seen a lot of disgusting and inhumane and unimaginable behavior throughout his career. So he knew the dark side of human behavior. However, he found it hard to believe that any superior being would want Lisa Baumgartner to be killed this way. He studied the photo and promised he would find her killer.

14 ⣿⣿⣿⣿

Jillian and Chad awakened in the morning to the usual city noises of sirens and traffic—sounds that Jillian preferred over chirping birds and rushing streams consistent with her preference of cities over countryside. She glanced at the half-naked body of her muscular, 6-foot-plus ex-husband. They really needed to have a talk so she could remember exactly why they got divorced. Neither of them had really gone on to find another long-term partner, and they both seemed to still enjoy being together. Or maybe it was just the easy way to live their lives. This way, they could be constantly in dating mode, did not need to participate in the give-and-take of a permanent relationship, and did not need to perform the daily chores or errands associated with everyday living. Regardless, her appreciation of and fondness for her ex-husband filled her as she remembered last night and what a huge difference he was making at a very bleak time. Although she was disappointed they had not had sex, she was at the same time curiously relieved.

Unfortunately, not even his presence today could make her feel anything but dread about having to identify her friend's body. Even thinking about it was repugnant.

Jillian grabbed a robe and headed for the kitchen to grind her favorite coffee beans. On normal days, she loved starting the day with a cup or two of Garuda blend, an English muffin smeared with peanut butter and her Kindle to read the morning papers—she tried to read at least the front pages of the *San Francisco Chronicle*, *The New York Times*, *The Washington Post* and *The Wall Street Journal* along with the weekly *The Economist*. She considered it important to be well informed both for professional and citizenry responsibilities. Professionally, she was better able to position her key messages in a knowledgeable context. As a citizen, knowledge enabled her to support causes in trouble, and vote appropriately.

The grinding noise awakened Chad, who mumbled something unintelligible and then headed for the bathroom—sans robe. Jillian was not a fan of the scruffy, unshaven look, but she had to admit on Chad it looked appealing and accentuated his tussled hair, which currently partially covered his hazel eyes. He was saying something about going out for breakfast—why had she started coffee?

"Oh, I just thought I'd have a cup before we head out. It's only 7:00. We have time. Where did you want to go?"

Chad reflected for only a moment. He typically arose very alert and ready to go, as opposed to Jillian who needed a bit more time to become fully functional. As he spoke he moved toward Jillian, and gave her a hug. "There's a great little Mediterranean place a few blocks from here. We could walk there. They have an interesting breakfast buffet on weekends with Greek and Italian specialties. They cook omelets to order and they have fruit and all kinds of stuff. I checked, and they start serving at 7:30 on Saturdays. We can have your first cup of coffee, shower, get dressed and be there in time for a leisurely breakfast. I know it's your favorite meal."

Jillian smiled. "You are the best ex-husband ever."

Although Chad did not drink coffee, the two of them had always been food-compatible; however, he had less of a weight problem than she did. He jogged regularly; Jillian abhorred exercise. She was sure the restaurant would be excellent. He had seldom failed at finding the best places for her to enjoy.

15

The morning had been as good as possible, given what was to follow. The walk to the restaurant improved her disposition, although it always annoyed her when exercise made her feel better, given her dislike of it. The restaurant was perfect. She had eaten more than she should have and enjoyed the lamb, potato, and eggplant omelet.

Chad had decided he would drive them to the Medical Examiner's office rather than take a cab, and for a change Jillian was happy to let him lead. They parked the car in a nearby garage and followed the directions that Inspector Sherwood had provided. As they entered the building, Jillian saw Inspector Sherwood standing near the front desk, talking on his mobile phone, and looking a little angry. As he spoke, his tone grew heated and his movements more animated. He saw her and motioned for them to wait a moment, then disconnected with an annoyed expression.

"The people at Miss Baumgartner's contracting company—not the one in San Francisco but the one that actually placed her with that client—are really dragging their feet about getting us a list of employees and company clients. We want to crosscheck them just in case any connection between her and someone associated with them might turn up. They claim that they hire thousands of people, and they don't have the right to violate their privacy. They won't give us the list unless we have a warrant, which seems kind of suspicious to me, especially since her client company provided us with whatever we asked. But I guess they feel obliged to protect the privacy of their workers—not that they even know who they are."

Inspector Sherwood put away his phone and turned his full attention on the couple. "Anyway, I want to thank you again for coming here. The Philadelphia police talked with Mr. Baumgartner, Lisa's father, last night and told him that you were doing the identification. Apparently he didn't really care. They did not speak with the mother. So I'll leave it to you about who else you might want to contact as a friend of the deceased." Sherwood had decided not to let Jillian know exactly how "cold" her friend's father had been. At the appropriate time, he would bring up the issue about claiming the body, but it wasn't necessary yet. Also he was hoping that the father would realize that this was his daughter, whom he must have loved at some point.

Jillian noticed she was holding Chad's hand very tightly. "Thanks. I probably will try to talk to her mother directly and maybe I should call her partner—what do you think, Chad? Oh, I'm sorry, Inspector Sherwood, this is my . . . well, this is Chad Bradbury. He also knew Lisa."

The two acknowledged each other as Chad nodded. "Definitely. You should definitely call Beverly. We'll take care of that later today, Inspector, and we'll also get in touch with her mother, as Lisa's father might not have shared the news with her in a, shall I say, 'loving' manner?"

Sherwood nodded. "Here is a copy of the printed material that we found in a folder in her carry-on luggage. If you could look at it and get back to me if there is anything that strikes you as familiar about it, or that might give us some sort of lead, I would appreciate it."

Jillian opened the folder. The contents appeared to be a list of stocks with accompanying information about them—mostly printed from Internet postings. On closer inspection, Jillian realized that the companies—which included her own—were all small biotechnology companies, most of them public. She was just about to mention that when the inspector suggested they proceed with the identification and asked them to follow him to the morgue.

The next 15 minutes were a blur in Jillian's mind. Chad had a firm grip on her hand as she approached the viewing window, behind which was a raised table with a body-sized, sheet-covered lump. Inspector Sherwood motioned to the attendant after asking Jillian if she was ready. When she nodded yes, the attendant pulled back the sheet and Jillian felt like she had run into an invisible, immovable wall. She froze, staring. Lisa's face was badly bruised, her skull appeared dented at one spot, and there were all kinds of cuts. But there was no question it was Lisa. Jillian gasped, "Yes, that is Lisa Baumgartner," and the inspector nodded to the attendant, who re-covered Lisa's body. Chad and Inspector Sherwood led her back upstairs to the lobby.

Again Inspector Sherwood brought Jillian some water and again she found it soothing. Chad guided her to a chair and told her to stay there while he spoke with Sherwood. She really didn't want Chad to leave her at that moment, and the look on her face must have expressed that need, because Chad quickly said he would be gone for just a second and would be right back. She watched Inspector Sherwood and Chad as they talked. Finally, the inspector nodded and Chad looked relieved and returned to her.

"Are you ready to get out of here? Inspector Sherwood said he doesn't need to see you any more today and you don't need to do anything else officially regarding Lisa's body. He will want you to come to his office to sign your statement, but that can wait, although he would appreciate it if you could do it tomorrow or Monday at the latest. It's up to you how much you want to get involved with her family. As I said, I really think we should call Lisa's mom and Beverly, as well, but I can do that if you want. He wants your input regarding the contents of that folder—if you recognize anything."

Jillian remembered she had recognized the names on the list were all of small biotech companies, including her own. She handed the folder to Chad, who after a quick review, agreed. She relayed their conclusion to Inspector Sherwood, and promised she would study them some more to try to determine if there were any other connections. Also, she would ask Brynn, who was very knowledgeable about biotech stocks, if she noticed any common denominator. It did seem significant that they were all small biotech companies.

Inspector Sherwood thanked her and, in parting, offered some new information. "We're reasonably sure now that she would have already had her meeting yesterday morning because she would not have had time to make her plane if she were on her way to a meeting. We tracked down her airline reservation and given when the crime took place, she would have had just enough time to get to SFO to board the plane. She was registered at a hotel near the airport—we found her checkout receipt—so there was really no reason for her to be in San Francisco at that parking garage unless she was meeting someone. We're therefore assuming that she was in the garage following her meeting and on her way to her rental car to go to the airport. So we really want to find this person she met Friday morning. We're checking with hotel personnel and people who might have parked in the parking garage. So far, no one can remember seeing her. The photo you sent, by the way, has been a big help. Thanks for that. And, again, please try to remember if she said anything that might help us identify who she was meeting yesterday morning."

"I'll help in any way I can, Inspector. I am very glad to have the identification over—maybe that will help me to think more clearly."

"Have you been able to remember anything else she might have said about this meeting?"

"I tried. The only thing I thought of was that maybe the meeting was about something that could lead to a job and that it came up suddenly—like it wasn't planned before she left Philadelphia. I'm wondering now if

Lisa maybe reviewed these stocks for someone to showcase her ability as a market analyst in order to see if she could qualify for a new job. I'll try to really focus on this list and let you know."

"Thanks. If it's all right with you, I'll keep in touch. Your familiarity with Miss Baumgartner might spark something. I really appreciate your help."

Chad was quick to point out that Jillian needed to rest for a while, and perhaps Inspector Sherwood could hold off bothering her too much, if possible. Jillian would let him know when she would come to the office to sign her statement. It would most likely be the next day. They would definitely call Lisa's mother and her former partner. Jillian typically resented Chad's protectionist approach as she felt perfectly capable of running her own life, but this time she actually appreciated his interference and was willing to go with it.

She had a thought. "If Beverly—that's Lisa's ex-partner—or Mrs. Baumgartner want additional information, should they contact you?"

"No problem. You have my card. And again thanks for doing the identification."

16

The rest of the weekend was reasonably uneventful for Jillian. Chad insisted on staying with her the rest of Saturday and would have stayed Sunday as well except he was scheduled for a business trip that morning. He suggested postponing it, but Jillian said she was fine and that there was no need to put it off. They stopped for food at the supermarket on the way back to her flat—not one of Jillian's favorite chores. The City was alive with Saturday traffic, and seemed not to care one bit that Jillian's friend had just been murdered.

Pete was more than pleased to park Chad's Porsche 911 Carrera. The sporty silver two-seater was truly an awe-inspiring car, sort of at the opposite end of the spectrum from Jillian's Scion-XB. Chad believed that he had earned the car, which had been financed by his proceeds from the IPO of a now-successful Silicon Valley biotech company. He had worked for two years for not a lot of pay—most often seven days a week and certainly 10 to 12 hours a day with little vacation or holiday time off—to make the company successful. He believed the car was a reward. Jillian, on the other hand, believed that the high-cost car was basically a waste of money, as she considered a car just a way to get from Point A to Point B.

So Chad handed the car over to Pete with a little apprehension, and a knowing smile from Jillian, and helped carry the grocery bags to the now-locked front door of her building. To Jillian's relief, when she entered her flat the lights were still turned off. It seemed like a small thing to worry about at this point, but she had felt a little violated at the thought of someone entering her home without her knowledge.

They put away the food, then sat down to consider how best to talk with Lisa's mother and ex-partner. Jillian believed it would be better for her to make the calls, rather than Chad, so she steeled herself for the task and pushed the buttons to reach Beverly, Lisa's former partner. Lisa and Beverly had been so close for so many years—it still seemed hard to believe they had split. Jillian remembered the many good times the four of them had shared and wished she could move back the clock to enjoy their time together again.

"Hi, this is Beverly. Is this Jillian Hillcrest, friend of Lisa and my cohort in so many adventures?" Beverly obviously recognized the caller ID and was not aware of what had happened, as she answered joyously and with laughter. "To what do I owe this call? I must say I have missed talking with you and Chad. How are you?"

"Hi, Beverly. I'm afraid I have some really bad news. I don't know how else to say it – Lisa was, is, was murd—, killed—is dead. Oh, Beverly! It's so awful. The police think . . ."

"Jillian, what are you saying? What happened? Where are you? Where is Lisa?"

"I'm in San Francisco. Lisa was here to visit a client. The police say someone deliberately ran her down and killed her. They don't know who or why yet. I'm doing everything I can to help."

"I can't believe this! Who would want to kill Lisa? She was the kindest, most gentle person I know. This is incredible. I assume you told her parents."

"Actually the police talked to her dad, who was his usual un-warm and non-caring self. The inspector said he seemed cold about it. I haven't talked to Madeline yet. I'll call her on her mobile phone—she might be showing houses and be able to talk." Lisa's mother was a successful real-estate agent in the Philadelphia area. She frequently showed houses to prospective buyers on the weekend, and Jillian had learned that was the best time to reach her so that Harry, Lisa's father, would not hear. Actually, Jillian was a little surprised that Madeline hadn't called her.

Jillian refocused on what Beverly was saying. "This just isn't possible, Jillian. I can't absorb it. Listen, can I call you back? Let me get used to it."

"Of course. No problem. Chad has been with me today. He's traveling tomorrow. And if you want to talk to the inspector in charge of her investigation, I have his contact information."

"Thanks, Jillian. I just need some time."

They disconnected, and Jillian took a deep breath.

"It's time for some wine. Did we finish yesterday's bottle?"

"Yes, we'll have to open another one. Then we'll call Madeline, and after that we are going out for dinner. I know just the place." He turned his attention to opening and pouring the wine and making a dinner reservation. Jillian searched her contact list for the number of Lisa's mother's mobile phone and pushed it, dreading the actual discussion but wanting to get it over with. So she had mixed feelings when Madeline answered in a firm voice, with almost no emotion and strangely toneless. "Hello, Jillian. Thank you so much for calling."

"Madeline, I am so sorry. Can you talk now?"

"Sure. I'm home and Harry isn't here." She continued to speak in an emotionless tone. "I canceled everything for the rest of the weekend. I can't believe it. I just talked with Lisa Thursday night—she said she was getting ready to see you. She was so happy about that. You were such a good friend, Jillian."

"Thanks, Madeline. It's been an incredibly difficult 24 hours." Jillian was speaking quickly to try to pump some energy into Madeline. "By the way, I talked with Beverly just a little while ago, so she knows. And I wanted to be sure to let you know that if you want to talk directly to the inspector who's working on this I have his contact information. I'll e-mail it to you. Is there anything I can tell you?"

"What happened? Harry wouldn't tell me anything other than that she was killed. He acted like she deserved it." Her tone became bitter, but still without inflection. "That's why he's not here right now. I told him to get out, and I'm not sure I'll ever let him back. I should have done it a long time ago." There was silence on her end of the phone, and then she exclaimed more loudly and with some emotion. "Oh, Jillian, I am so ashamed. How could we have turned our backs on her? And all she went through."

"She truly appreciated talking with you, so you can take some comfort in that. Basically, the police are sure she was murdered—a deliberate hit and run. They don't know why and they do not have any real leads yet. We think she had an early-morning meeting, but we don't know if she kept it or who it was with. She didn't happen to mention anything to you about a meeting, did she?"

"I don't think so. Mostly she talked about how excited she was to be seeing you. She said she just had finished a project in San Francisco and that she drove through Stanford—you know, I graduated from there, so she just wanted me to know. But she did say something about a meeting she was having, because she bumped into somebody earlier who asked her for some research. She said there was a possibility it could lead to a project. I thought it was someone from work, but I don't know why. Should I tell the police?"

"I think you should call the inspector and tell him about the conversation you had with Lisa that night. It's hard to say what information will be helpful. His name is Inspector Loren Sherwood. How are you holding up?"

"I really don't know, Jillian. My sister is coming to stay with me. I don't know if you ever met her. She lives in Carlisle, near Harrisburg. She is a college professor at a small liberal arts college there. She should be here soon."

"That's good, Madeline. I can tell you that Lisa and I had a great time Thursday night. She was very happy, and we enjoyed our time together very much. I just wish . . . well, I just wish it was all a bad dream."

"Thanks, Jillian. It looks like my sister has just arrived. Send me the inspector's number and I'll give him a call. You take care."

As soon as she disconnected, Jillian pulled out Inspector Sherwood's card and e-mailed his contact information to Lisa's mother. Then she gratefully took the glass of wine Chad offered, munched on the cheese, apples, and crackers he had prepared, and sat there with little to say. It felt good just to sit and share the silence with him. They still had a few hours before it was time for dinner. While Chad was checking his e-mail, Jillian turned on her Kindle and checked the *Chronicle* to see if there was a story about Lisa. She found a small article in the local section about a hit-and-run victim found in a parking garage. The article clearly stated that the police were searching for someone who might have had a meeting with the victim and provided a phone number to call. Otherwise, there was no additional information.

Jillian started to think about what Lisa's mother said about the person Lisa had bumped into, resulting in a scheduled meeting. It was possible that the inspector would learn something useful when he talked to her—like whether Lisa said where she bumped into this person; or even why she thought there was a potential job opportunity. The *Chronicle* article might also draw the person out.

17 ⋈⋈⋈

Madeline Baumgartner put down the phone after speaking with Jillian. She had lied to Jillian. Her sister wasn't due to arrive until the next day. She just couldn't bear to talk anymore about it. She knew Jillian blamed her and her husband for abandoning Lisa. How could she explain? She had always supported her husband and assumed he would get over his issue with Lisa's sexual orientation. But he never had. And he had said some very hateful things to Lisa. Worse still, he had passed his hatred onto their son, who also ostracized Lisa—all in the name of God.

Madeline didn't know how to move on. She didn't know what to do in the next five minutes, much less for the rest of her life. She deeply regretted she had not taken a more active position to support her daughter. She also clung to Jillian's statement that Lisa had appreciated speaking with her—even though she knew it had hardly been enough to make up for denying her.

Her laptop pinged and she saw that Jillian had sent her the contact information for the inspector in San Francisco who was handling Lisa's case. Somehow it seemed like the right thing to do to check in with him. Also, Madeline realized she would need to make arrangements for bringing Lisa's body home. Perhaps the inspector could help her.

She called the inspector's phone and waited apprehensively for his answer. "Inspector Loren Sherwood here."

"Inspector Sherwood? Hello, my name is Madeline Baumgartner. I am Lisa Baumgartner's mother. Jillian Hillcrest gave me your contact information."

The Inspector seemed wary. "Hello, Mrs. Baumgartner. How can I help you?"

Madeline was gaining courage the more she talked. "Inspector, can you tell me what happened? I know the police here spoke with my husband, but he didn't tell me very much. Also, do you know who I should contact about bringing Lisa home?"

Inspector Sherwood seemed more forthcoming as he gently told Madeline about her daughter's death. He seemed very kind, telling her he was sure Lisa hadn't suffered; she died shortly after the accident without regaining consciousness. He asked Madeline for her contact information and said he would send her the name of the person to talk to about shipping Lisa's body. He suggested that a mortuary in Philadelphia would know how to take care of it for her.

"By the way, forgive me for asking, but when was the last time that you spoke with your daughter?"

"Actually, I am so grateful I spoke with her Thursday—it must have been about 5:00 in California, because it was about 8:00 here. She was very excited to be going to see Jillian. They are such good friends, you know. Anyway, she said she regretted she had an early-morning meeting—she said it was at 7:00 with someone she had met earlier that day or the day before at her work, I believe. She thought it was a good lead for another job. She was working to earn money to pay her hospital bills—she had breast cancer, you know. And that awful insurance company refused to pay her bills—something about it being pre-existing, which is absurd. Anyway, she said she didn't care that the meeting was early the next morning—she was going to stay out as late as she could because she really enjoyed Jillian."

"Did she happen to say where she was meeting this person?"

"Now that you mention it, she said she had tried to get him to meet her at the airport but he—and she did say 'he'—had to be in San Francisco, which is why they were meeting so early."

"Can you remember anything else? Did she happen to mention what the job was about?"

"No, I'm sorry, Inspector. We had to hang up about that time because my husband came home. He didn't like me to be talking to her. He is very religious, you know."

"Really? I didn't know that . . ." Sherwood stopped himself. This woman didn't deserve his retort. "You have been very helpful, Mrs. Baumgartner. Please feel free to call me with any questions, or if you have any difficulty getting your daughter home. I just need to warn you that you might not want to look at your daughter—she was pretty severely injured. Also, given that she was murdered, we have to do an autopsy."

Madeline was quiet for a long time. "Inspector, you have been very kind. Thank you. And, just so you know, I have asked my husband to find a new place to live other than with me. I don't ever want him back in my life. I'm not sure what I'll do now, but I must do something to make up for my lack of courage over the past fifteen years. I will be in touch."

They disconnected. Madeline sat still in her chair for a very long time.

When Jillian awoke from her unintentional nap, Chad was busy putting away the leftover food. "Oh, I didn't mean to fall asleep. Is it time to go?"

"We should try to leave within fifteen minutes. We can walk to the restaurant—it shouldn't take longer than a half hour. It's a new French one I want to try. I think it's little cold outside so you might want to wear a warm coat."

"Always the considerate one. Remind me again why you are my EX-husband?"

She and Chad enjoyed a great dinner Saturday night, although it was bittersweet because Jillian wanted to share memories of events with Lisa. She recalled meeting her in Vermont one summer, when the four of them rented a place on Lake Champlain. Chad wore one of his silly sailor hats the entire time, which was most appropriate when they were on the lake in the rented sailboat. Chad, Lisa and Beverly all loved sailing. Jillian not so much. But the memory of that vacation was a particularly happy one.

Unfortunately, Chad had to go home to pack for an early flight the next morning. She watched him drive away surprised at how lonely she felt. Normally she enjoyed being alone, but a day with Chad filling the void left her feeling empty when he departed. As she entered her building and headed to the elevator, she also felt apprehensive. She seldom was scared in her own building, but she seemed to be feeling a variety of emotions as a result of Lisa's death. She proceeded quickly to her flat, and entered, again relieved that her lights were off. The rooms were still filled with Chad's presence—adding to her loneliness—so she went directly to her bedroom, turned on TV, and, most likely thanks to the wine, promptly fell asleep.

When she awoke on Sunday, she decided to stay home and catch up on reading and maybe even watch a little TV. She didn't want to do anything, and her intuition told her that was a good idea. The only interruption was a call from Beverly, who was now ready to talk. Jillian gave her as much information as she could, promised to send the inspector's contact information, and also reminded Beverly to let her know if she thought of anything that might be helpful.

Beverly said that Lisa's mother had called her earlier in the day. "We had a long conversation. I think that Madeline is really hurting. She didn't seem to have any life left in her. She truly regrets how they treated Lisa, and she wants to get to know me better."

"I just wish her revelation had occurred before Lisa's death. Will you spend any time with her?"

"Yes. I want to. I owe it to Lisa. I really loved her, you know. I just couldn't stay committed to one person."

"I'm sorry. I thought that the two of you were well matched. You both enjoyed doing many of the same things together."

"Perhaps." Beverly seemed to be thinking over their compatibility and decided to change the subject. "Madeline is planning a memorial service and asked me to be there. She also asked for a list of Lisa's friends, so I'll copy you on my list, and if you can think of anyone else, let her know. I guess Harry is having no say in the matter. I agree with you, however. Pity it took Lisa's death to move her mother to action."

The pain of Lisa's death was less raw for Jillian as the day wore on. Also, talking with Chad the night before and Beverly that day had helped. However, Jillian discovered she was becoming more and more angry at the idea that someone had deliberately killed Lisa. She spent a lot of Sunday thinking and remembering their last night together, and decided to write down everything she could recall in case the information might prove important—like the name of the restaurant, the time she arrived, what they ordered, what they talked about, the time she went home, and picking up her car the next day. This took some extra emotional energy, but her anger fueled her.

In the middle of this effort, she began to feel strong enough to go to Inspector Sherwood's office and sign her statement. He had said any time, so she grabbed her purse and a jacket and headed out. She opted to hail a cab, rather than drive and have to hassle with parking. She entered the police building and asked for Inspector Sherwood's office, explaining she was there to sign her statement. She was directed to what appeared to be a conference room, where she sat and waited. Eventually a young woman in a police uniform brought some typed pages and asked her to review them and sign each page if the information was accurate. Reading through the discussion from the day before was painful, but with only one minor exception, everything seemed very accurate and very consistent with the list she had just prepared. So she signed the document, and waited patiently for the officer to return. She still couldn't believe it. Everything still seemed so surreal.

19 ⋈⋈⋈⋈

onday morning arrived far sooner than Jillian wanted. She slept restlessly Sunday night, and had almost forgotten about Bill Vulkjevich and his urgent package. She remembered as she was getting ready to leave her flat, and put the package in her briefcase. She had not looked at the material since Friday morning just prior to learning about Lisa, but had left several messages for Bill with no response. She would give it to Phil Montgomery this morning, and let Brynn and Phil deal with it.

Pete had her car waiting for her. She greeted and tipped him, and again appreciated the normalcy of these simple events. She headed for the freeway, this time almost relieved that the other drivers were not aware of her friend's death.

Although traffic was slow, she arrived at the office before Brynn or Tim. She did a quick read of her company e-mail—which she had uncharacteristically not checked over the weekend—and was surprised to see a message from Bill Vulkjevich. He was checking in to see if she had had a chance to review his package. What a flake! Jillian truly doubted his judgment. She forwarded the message to Brynn mentioning she had left Bill several messages and would give the package to Phil for his review.

She had not heard from Dan Harrington over the weekend so assumed Brynn had gotten in touch with him. She decided to call back the online broker who had left her a message regarding a reference for Dan Harrington to see what that was about. She pushed the number he'd left and waited for his answer, but received a recorded message. She left a message and returned to the more mundane tasks of her workday.

Brynn arrived at about 10:00, explaining she was late because of a dental appointment. Jillian doubted she had been at the dentist since Brynn never used work time for preventive or non-emergency health appointments, but decided to just accept the cover story. After asking how Jillian was doing, she said she had spent the weekend catching up on sleep, so didn't have any new projects for her. She also suggested that Jillian take time off if needed. However, Jillian preferred to be at the office. The two of them met and discussed the two main short-term projects—the communications symposium later in the week, and the financial conference the following week. Jillian noted her tasks. Brynn also let her know that she had been in touch with Dan and to keep her in the loop regarding Bill Vulkjevich's data, which Jillian had dropped off with Phil earlier.

About that time, Jillian got a call from the online broker who asked if she knew Dan Harrington. Jillian was familiar with the company, although she was reticent to give out any information about Dan. She responded, yes, she knew him, and asked what the broker needed to know. Again this inquiry seemed strange to Jillian, so she asked for additional information from the broker. He said Dr. Harrington had electronically opened a new account and, in response to the company's request for references, he had listed her along with several other people. So he was checking with everyone on Dr. Harrington's list for security and to prevent possible fraud.

Jillian again thought this was strange. She knew Dan Harrington and described him to the broker, and he agreed that that sounded like the man who had opened the account, who he had subsequently met that morning to finalize the details. The broker then thanked her and said he had opened the account earlier that morning given that he had corroborated the client's forms of identity—like his social security number, passport number, drivers license number, date and place of birth etc. Since there were no funds involved yet, he was sure everything was fine. Jillian joked silently with herself, citing her vast experience as a reader of mystery stories as the reason for her suspicion. Nonetheless, if he had already opened the account, then what did he need from Jillian? She decided not to answer any more questions until she spoke with Dan.

"I think we're O.K. I called others on his list and everything seems all right."

Jillian thought this whole conversation was a little strange, but about that time Phil Montgomery, the CSO, entered with the data package from Bill Vulkjevich so she told the broker to call back if he had any other questions. She quickly disconnected and turned her attention to Phil. "I don't know what this is, but it is not the data from the latest lupus trial. It has a different number of patients; it lists different responses to the drugs—in fact, it lists different dosages of a drug and it doesn't even say which drug. Who is this guy?" Phil seemed genuinely annoyed and angry.

She looked at Phil with relief. "I'm glad it's not the latest lupus data. I couldn't be sure. Bill Vulkjevich is one of the contract financial guys Brynn hired to help us do analysis of various potential products. She seems to think he's pretty good. Bill sent me this, asked me to get back to him with some urgency, but he has not responded to any of my messages since Thursday night. I'll call him again and ask him what this is, and what I'm supposed to do with it. It's helpful to know it's not associated with the lupus trial."

Jillian made yet another call to Bill. This time he answered the phone. "Hi, Bill. This is Jillian Hillcrest. I've been trying to reach you in response to the package you sent me. Can you tell me what it's about?"

"Oh, yeah. I kind of forgot about it until this morning. I was really busy over the weekend and my phone wasn't working. I found that stuff and thought it might be important—it looked kind of like the lupus trial data."

Jillian continued to doubt Vulkjevich's judgment. He was in his late 40s yet he seemed to have the mind-set of a teenager. "Where did you find it?"

"It was in with some other stuff your CFO sent me. I can't remember which folder."

Jillian pondered. "Well, thanks, Bill. However, I believe that Brynn only sent you background information on previous products—not on the current lupus trial. I'm not sure where this data originated. Our CSO is positive that this does not include data from the current trial. However, I will check with Brynn to see what she sent, so we can figure out its origin."

"Great. I have to go now. Bye."

Jillian reflected that she should at least be pleased he said good-bye before disconnecting.

The rest of the day was uneventful. Tim arrived and asked about his CEO presentation for the financial conference in New York the following week. The stock price was responding well to the announcement of the data, and he wanted to be sure to continue the momentum. Although sort of in a fog at this point, Jillian continued through her workday. She sent a reminder message to her panel participants for the symposium on Friday with logistics and a follow-up overview of the panel goals. Phil checked back to see about the strange data package, and Jillian filled him in with an apology for bothering him about what appeared to be a false alarm.

Jillian continued to wonder why Brynn employed Bill Vulkjevich. His judgment was suspect, his analytical skills seemed almost non-existent, and as far as Jillian could tell he had contributed very little to the overall planning process for the products he was assigned. She almost always agreed with Brynn on her people assessments, but she just could not understand this one.

Jillian did not have time to speak further with Brynn on Monday about much of anything. Both of them were busy with their respective projects. Nor did Jillian hear anything more from Inspector Sherwood regarding Lisa's case. The day still felt a little surreal. She had spent the weekend thinking about the details of Lisa's murder. Yet today, she barely even thought about it. It was as if Lisa had returned home to Philadelphia and Jillian was continuing with her life as if nothing had happened. She almost felt guilty about it.

Jillian did receive a call from one of the speakers on her panel for the symposium saying that he could not, after all, participate. When Jillian had met John Bowersox in Geneva at the conference, she had invited him to participate on her panel. She recalled the tall, distinguished looking man in his late 50s. He had said that he would check his calendar to see if he was available, and unfortunately discovered he had a prior commitment.

"Oh, that's so disappointing. I so enjoyed talking with you in Geneva."

"Unfortunately, I just can't be in the Bay Area on that day. I have several commitments here in San Diego that I just can't postpone."

"Well that's very unfortunate. Your insights as a financial advisor for the entrepreneur and investor community would add some depth to the panel. You would provide a unique perspective on the topic of communication ethics."

"I would have enjoyed participating very much. Nonetheless, I'm sure that the other panel members will do a fine job."

She left work feeling like she had had a productive day and arrived at her building at around 7:00 that evening. Pete had the night off so she left her car with his substitute, a fellow student who often filled in for Pete. She pulled out her building key; Charlie had continued to honor his promise of locking the front door. The lobby was deserted, and Charlie was not at his desk, which was unusual, although since the front door was locked, not alarming. Still slightly apprehensive, Jillian picked up her mail and headed for the elevator as quickly as possible just as the door opened and Charlie stepped out. "Oh, hi, Jillian. I was just checking each floor to be sure no one was wandering the halls. Everything seems fine. How was your day?"

"Thanks, Charlie. I had a much better day today. Any problems here?"

"Nope. As far as I know, everything is fine. But let me know if you hear anything, or if you find anything strange in your flat again."

Jillian pushed the button for her floor and looked at her mail, which seemed to be mostly junk and bills. When she arrived on her floor, she was pleased to see that Mrs. Anderson had another new flower wreath on her door—a simple addition that made a big difference. This arrangement was fragrant and colorful, employing some kind of yellow blossoms. Jillian wondered whether the woman made the wreaths or bought them pre-made.

She entered her flat again hoping that her lights were off, and this time they were. Just as she was putting all of her paraphernalia on the table, her phone rang and indicated a call from SFPD, Loren Sherwood. She answered with a bit of apprehension. "Jillian Hillcrest."

"Hi, Miss Hillcrest. This is Inspector Sherwood. I wanted to thank you for asking Mrs. Baumgartner to call me. She actually provided a couple of clues that might help us to identify the person Lisa was scheduled to meet. Also, I wanted to let you know that we received the list of employees and companies affiliated with BIS—that's the contractor Lisa worked for—and we have started cross-checking. By the way, don't you work at Harmonia Therapeutics?"

"Yes, I do."

"Well, apparently your company hires people from BIS—particularly financial contractors. I thought I'd check with you directly to see if you could review the list and verify if anyone works at your company. Maybe someone will stand out."

"Inspector, can you tell me the name of this company, please? I'll write it down. I seem to be in somewhat of a fog, and I want to be sure that I remember it correctly. We do hire financial contractors, so it is possible that this is the company we use."

"Yes, the full name is Biosciences Infrastructure Services, and they also go by BIS. Let's see—your company has used at least a dozen people from here. How about if I e-mail you the list of names and maybe you could check it for me and get back to me? We'll have to do a formal request but I was hoping to get some quick added insight from you."

"No problem, Inspector. Go ahead and e-mail the names and I will get back to you with anything I might know."

In the meantime, she decided to have a light dinner—maybe some salad with some of the roasted chicken that she and Chad had brought home from the supermarket—and watch some mindless TV and not think about work, Bill Vulkjevich's weird data, or Lisa's untimely death. Great idea, but then her phone signaled a call from a personal friend and she saw that it was Lisa's mother. "Hi, Madeline. How are you doing?"

"Hi, Jillian. I was just checking in. I spoke with that inspector. He said I was helpful, which was nice of him. Also, I spoke with Beverly and we're going to have dinner tomorrow night. I haven't spoken with Harry." Madeline was speaking quickly and without taking a breath, as if she had to say everything in one minute. "I am having a memorial service. Is there any chance you could come? It most likely will be early Monday afternoon—about 1:00. I am holding it at the children's museum—you know— the one Lisa loved so much as a child. With the economy, they've had to close two days a week, so I am able to rent it." She made a noise that sounded like a half-hearted laugh. "I am even bringing in grownup chairs so people will have a place to sit. I would really appreciate it if you would share the eulogy with Beverly."

Jillian was touched, but still a little annoyed it had taken Lisa's death to awaken her mother to her daughter's specialness. "Of course, I'll be there. I'll fly into Philadelphia and rent a car, so I can be available to drive others as well. I'll get in touch with Beverly to see what she wants to do."

"Thanks, Jillian. Let me know how much time you'll need for your remarks—although the program is flexible."

"I will. You take care."

Jillian ended the call, and all the separation from the weekend's events she had felt during the workday came crashing down, and she was vividly reminded that her friend was dead. The show on TV was insipid, and that it concerned a medical examiner's investigation of a murder made it even less appealing. Reading the daily papers on her Kindle was not helpful. She lay in bed most of the night tossing and turning wondering why Lisa Baumgartner, a beautiful, sensitive woman from Philadelphia had been so brutally murdered.

20 ⋈⋈⋈⋈

Pete was back at his valet position on Tuesday morning. Jillian was pleased to see him, and provided her usual tip. She sensed that he wanted to ask her something. He didn't move as quickly to get out of her car and turn it over to her.

"Good morning, Pete! How are you?"

"Hi, I was wondering if you could help me with something that is sort of confidential. It's about my brother." Jillian couldn't imagine how she could be helpful, but she really liked Pete. "What can I do?"

"Well, you know the guy Mrs. Anderson said was wandering the halls here a few days ago?"

"Yes. He was on our floor when she found him and she didn't know him so she asked him to leave. That wasn't your brother, was it?"

Pete hesitated. "Yes, it was. He didn't do anything illegal, like breaking into any apartments or anything, but that's not what I wanted to tell you. He was standing outside here waiting for me when a guy drove up and asked Mickey to go into the building and in particular to go to the floor where you lived—except the guy had the wrong floor, I think. He mentioned your name. Mickey checked the mailboxes to get your flat number. I just learned about it this morning—and I'll have to tell Charlie about it without getting my brother in trouble. Like I said, he didn't do anything. He was just hanging around. But I think this guy who asked him to go up there could be the guy who really did break into the other flat. I'm just not sure the police will see it that way."

Jillian was dumbstruck. Her heart rate increased dramatically. Someone had specifically mentioned her name and the floor where she lived? Why? What was going on? "I think we need to let the police know, Pete. I'll do what I can to keep your brother out of it, but I suspect the police will want to talk to him so they can get a description of this guy. Did you see him yourself?'

Pete looked really worried. "No, I didn't. But I believe Mickey. He wouldn't lie. He actually volunteered the information because he felt bad about going up there. Apparently the guy gave him a hundred dollar bill, and that was just too much to pass up. But he knows it could cost me my job now. I'll let Charlie know, and we can call the cops who were here on Saturday."

"O.K. Tell Charlie he can reach me all day on my cell. He has the number." Then Jillian called Inspector Sherwood. When he did not answer, she left him a brief message about this new information. She did not think there was a connection between Lisa's death and the flat break-in, but she was certainly concerned that someone knew her name and where she lived. Her car was double-parked, so she decided to head for work. There was nothing she could do at home. If the police needed to talk with her, Charlie and the inspector both knew how to reach her. She wondered if she should consider additional security? Or if she was over-reacting? She would see what Chad thought.

Pete was worried about his brother. He knew Jillian was right. He had to tell the police. But he was concerned about talking to Charlie. Pete knew Charlie was not exactly the most honest person around. Pete was pretty sure he was involved in something illegal—he had seen Charlie talking to people whose honesty Pete suspected. So he wasn't sure how Charlie would respond when he found out that the kid with the baseball cap was Pete's brother. Also, it occurred to Pete that Charlie actually knew his brother, but had said nothing when he saw him with Mrs. Anderson. That could mean either he just didn't want to get the kid into trouble—or he didn't want him to get caught.

So Pete wanted to be careful about talking to Charlie. One of the other tenants needed a car, so Pete brought it around before entering the lobby. He went up to Charlie, who was busy moving boxes from the reception desk to the back room.

"Do you have the contact information for the cops who were here yesterday? Miss Hillcrest asked me to call them because my little brother said that someone had asked him to check out her flat." Pete thought that Charlie looked scared for a minute.

"I would have preferred to contact them myself, but I guess if Miss Hillcrest wants you to contact them directly, here is one of the officer's cards."

Pete placed the call. He knew that he was risking punishment for his brother, but he believed that he was better off dealing directly with the police than going through Charlie. He just wasn't sure what Charlie would do.

Mickey really had been tricked. That surprised Pete; although Mickey was young, he was street-smart. But a hundred bucks is a lot of money. So maybe Mickey wasn't tricked. Maybe he just couldn't turn down that much cash.

Pete reached the officer who handled the break-in. "This is Pete from the building where there was the break-in yesterday. I park cars there. Miss Jillian Hillcrest asked me to let you know that it was my little brother who was caught in the hallway. Some guy paid him a hundred dollars to check out Miss Hillcrest's floor. He just couldn't pass up the money. He wouldn't have done anything illegal."

The officer thanked him. "Bring your brother to the precinct this afternoon. We'll speak to him then."

"Thank you for being so accommodating. It would have been a

problem to have to take him out of school. I'll bring him no later than 4:30."

He turned to Charlie. "Thanks. Mickey and I will go to the police department after school today. He really didn't mean anything by it." Charlie looked doubtful.

Pete returned to his post pleased he had handled another family situation. His mother need never know. It was one less thing for her to worry about.

21

By the time she arrived at work, Jillian had mulled over the events at her building and pondered whether her flat was the intended one rather than her neighbors' upstairs. Or perhaps Pete's brother was being used as a decoy while the real thief broke into his target flat. Given her knowledge of Pete, it never occurred to her that his brother was the thief. However, it did occur to her that she should call Charlie to be sure he didn't fire Pete. Almost everyone at the building liked Pete and they were all pulling for him to succeed.

As she was entering her office building, she connected with Charlie and let him know her wishes about Pete. He agreed and said that he was a little annoyed with himself for not recognizing Pete's brother. He had met him a couple of times, but said when he looked up from the desk that day all he saw was the Giants hat. He, too, doubted that Pete's brother was a serious threat, and he shared her concern that someone had approached the teenager and asked him specifically to go to Jillian's floor. Charlie said Pete had notified the police, and Jillian let Charlie know she had informed the inspector investigating her friend's murder. Charlie sounded a little surprised, which reminded Jillian she had only told people about the death of her friend—not that she had been murdered. So she briefly filled Charlie in. She also reassured him that she didn't think there was a connection between the two events.

Jillian was not looking forward to a day at the office. Yesterday she had welcomed the diversion. Today she was tired after a nearly sleepless night. Most of the work ahead was routine and would not offer much respite. Also, she needed to review the list of names that Inspector Sherwood had sent to see if she knew anyone; it might help the inspector figure out who Lisa had scheduled that early morning meeting with. She had not looked at the list yet, but noticed that it was in her personal e-mail.

As she reviewed the list, she saw that Bill Vulkjevich was one of the names, in addition to several others Jillian recognized as temporary contract accountants or analysts Brynn or the VP of Finance had hired. She e-mailed the inspector that she did know some of these people and that the ones she knew were who they claimed to be. She wrote that she would follow up with her boss to learn more about the contractors and about BIS and then get back to him.

She forwarded the names to Brynn with an explanation that BIS was the company where her friend worked as a contractor, and asking Brynn if she could confirm that the people listed were all bona fide finance contractors. Also, she asked Brynn if she knew anything of particular interest about any of them. Jillian wasn't sure what this last request might provide, and she assumed that the inspector and his team would contact each person individually anyway, but maybe it could help prioritize the list.

Her desk phone rang; it was Dan Harrington calling. "Jillian Hillcrest."

"Hi, Jillian. I was just confirming our panel on Friday. It sounds like fun. I have some definite opinions on the ethics and value of public relations and companies' needs to be, quote, on message."

"Well, I trust you will speak your mind and not hold back," Jillian laughed. "It should be an interesting panel. One of the guys here at work made a short video to start us off, and I prepared a very brief history on the origin of public relations here in the U.S."

"Do you need anything from me before Friday?"

Jillian thought for a moment. "No, I don't think so. You already sent your bio. However, if you think of anything else you need from me, just let me know. By the way, how are you feeling? Have you recovered from the bicycle altercation?"

"Actually, yes. The doctor released me from the neck brace, and my knee feels almost normal, although it still sends me twinge reminders if I push it too hard."

There was something nagging at Jillian, something she wanted to tell him. "Oh, Dan. I got a strange call from an online broker who wanted me to serve as a reference for you. Something about opening a new brokerage account online?"

Dan sounded vaguely interested, but not overly concerned. "What? I don't think so. I haven't opened any accounts for quite a while. And Lloyd, my assistant, is on vacation so I know he didn't either. Do you remember who called and when?"

"Actually, I had heard of the company, but I was not familiar with the broker. It was such an unusual call that I thought it was probably a mistake. I couldn't for the life of me figure out why a broker would call me about you opening an account. However, I might still have his phone number in my 'recent calls' list. I'll check and send it to you. Maybe that will help."

"Thanks, Jillian. I agree it was a very strange inquiry. Send me the number, and I'll check it out. By the way, can you transfer me to Brynn?"

Jillian forwarded Dan to Brynn with the warning that she might not be in her office.

About then she got a call on her office phone from what appeared to be *The Wall Street Journal.* She answered hoping it was the same reporter who wrote the earlier story about the lupus trial data, and that he wanted to do a follow-up. She was half-correct. "Hi, this is Jake Durham from *The Wall Street Journal*. We spoke earlier when you were in Geneva about the data from your lupus trial. Someone sent me some information verifying my assumptions that there were kidney problems with your drug. Care to comment?"

Jillian was more than annoyed. The most likely source of such documents had to be Vulkjevich, who mistakenly had assumed he had relevant data and probably thought of himself as a whistleblower. "I'm not sure what you think you have, but the information we gave you in Geneva was accurate. However, can you be more specific about what was sent to you? Or, if you like, I can arrange for you to talk directly to our Chief Science Officer, Phil Montgomery, who I think you know. I could also arrange a call with the independent investigator. I'm afraid someone may be sending you false information. Was there a letter with the data? Can you tell who sent it?"

The reporter was quiet for a moment. "I will admit that this package of information and the way the data are presented is atypical; it's not like other data reports I've reviewed. And your company has been straightforward with information in the past. So, yes, I would like to speak to both. Can you set it up for today? I'm in New York so it would be helpful if you could arrange it as soon as possible."

"No problem with our CSO. He's here today. However, I don't know about Dr. Reboto, the investigator. I'll have to get in touch with his office to find out where he is. Thanks for trusting us on this, Jake."

"Well, let's see what happens."

"If you hold on, I might be able to connect you to Phil right now. Also, can you fax me a copy of the information so we can evaluate it? It might be hard to comment on it without having it in front of us."

"Let me talk to Phil first and then let's see where we are."

She put Jake on hold and punched the internal number for Phil. He answered immediately—thankfully. Jillian explained the situation and asked Phil if he would speak with the reporter. She would stay on the line and help if needed. Phil was annoyed and asked if Jillian thought this was the same material she had given him earlier. "It sounds like it, but I think we need to ask Jake to describe it in more detail so we're sure. I asked him to fax it, and he might be willing to do so. By the way, you've talked with Jake before. You gave him some background information on that new AIDS vaccine."

"Oh, I remember him. He's fairly savvy. Good. That makes it easier. Let's do it."

Jillian connected the three of them. "Jake—I have Phil on the line. The two of you have spoken in the past at least once of which I'm aware."

"Yes, hi, Phil. And again thanks for that background information on the new AIDS product. It was extremely helpful—especially since it was impartial. Anyway, about this data, I was telling Jillian that it looks very strange. It's a list of–"

Phil interrupted. "Before you go further, let me tell you what it should look like if it were data from our trial." And Phil proceeded to describe for the reporter in a fair amount of detail how the data would appear; how many patients there were; what the end points should be; the adverse events and the number of patients.

He asked the reporter. "Does this match the data you received?"

Jake laughed. "Not even close. Look, I don't know what this is about, but I want to talk also to your independent investigator for the sake of thoroughness. I have the abstract and presentation printed by the conference, and my research assistant just informed me that this list of data does not match that, either. You'd think if someone were trying to cause trouble they'd at least have the number of patients to the closest hundred. Anyway, after I speak with your investigator, I think I should send this to the FDA and let them know someone is trying to misrepresent data. If there are similar cases, they might investigate."

Jillian was relieved, although she was also extremely angry; she was sure Vulkjevich was the culprit, and it didn't bother her in the least if he was caught. He had set up Harmonia to look bad in the business press and potentially experience a drop in stock value and exposure to FDA scrutiny. "I'll track down Reboto—he's the investigator—and ask him to give you a call. He works independently, which means I won't be able to participate, so if you need anything else, please call me. Also, if you don't mind, we would really appreciate getting a copy of what was sent to you. Can you scan it in and e-mail it, or send us a hard copy overnight or fax it?"

"We'll make a copy and send it overnight. There are lots of pages and it would just be easier that way. If it becomes more time-critical—like if my editor over-rules my decision—I'll let you know and I'll definitely scan and send it, but I doubt that will happen. You guys are not known for pulling fast ones. In fact, quite the contrary. Your investors think you provide too much information." He laughed. "Not possible, by the way."

"Thanks, Jake. We appreciate your thoroughness. We are honestly very excited about the results from the trial, although, as with all product candidates at this stage of research, obviously we won't know for sure until we've done broader testing. I'll ask Dr. Reboto to call you. If you need anything else don't hesitate to call me."

Jillian was more than annoyed with Vulkjevich when she hung up. But, first she had to track down Dr. Reboto. She searched for the number on her contacts list, and called his office. He was not immediately available, so she told his assistant that she would e-mail him the name and number of the reporter who needed to be called as soon as possible. If Dr. Reboto had any questions after reading her e-mail, he should call Jillian or Phil Montgomery. She then wrote the e-mail with the relevant information and asked Dr. Reboto to call the reporter. Then she e-mailed Jake Durham and let him know the status and that if he didn't hear from Dr. Reboto in the next few hours to let her know.

Next she called Vulkjevich, who did not answer. As civilly as she could, she left a message. She enunciated each word slowing and clearly. "This is Jillian Hillcrest. Please call me as soon as possible. I need to talk with you immediately." She only tried half-heartedly to moderate her tone. She hoped that he understood that he had better call her soon.

Although still annoyed, she turned her attention to the other day's tasks. A local Chamber of Commerce needed someone to speak at an upcoming conference regarding the benefits that biotechnology companies received through their community and government relations programs. She checked her calendar and sent a message saying she was available and would be pleased to be able to explain that Harmonia's efforts were geared to "give back" to the community as well as influence local and state governments to appreciate the contributions of biotechnology companies. She also responded to the symposium organizer of Friday's panel discussion, saying she was ready and confirming the room requirements. Since John Bowersox—the financial advisor who she'd met in Geneva—had cancelled, she didn't need to provide his biography, which was regrettable. She had already sent the bios of the other participants. Then she immersed herself in adding the finishing touches to the investor presentation for Tim for the following week. She finalized the additional six slides that provided the recently delivered lupus data, and assured that the concluding slides were on message by summarizing the relevance of the data.

It was just past noon when she realized she was hungry and that she had not spoken with Brynn yet. She noticed Brynn was not in her office and checked with her assistant who said Brynn had left the office just after her morning staff meeting. "Oh my God, I forgot all about it. Why didn't someone call me?" Jillian was supposed to attend all of Brynn's standing meetings. The assistant said it turned into a very brief meeting with most of the updates postponed until the next day, so there was really no need for Jillian to be there. However, Tim had also been looking for Brynn. She had been expected to return to the office by 11:00 at the latest. It was about then that Brynn arrived—very apologetic and looking a bit harried.

"Sorry. I got caught up doing some research for Dan Harrington, our favorite hedge fund who-we-hope-will-invest-in-us, and totally lost track of time. Fill me in. Where are we with everything?"

Jillian followed Brynn to her office, wondering what kind of follow-up for Dan Harrington would require Brynn to be off-site. "Well, I just got off the phone with *The Wall Street Journal*. Apparently someone sent some data claiming to be from our lupus trial that made it look like there were problems. Phil talked with Jake, the reporter, and I also arranged for Reboto to call him. The data were bogus, and I think it came from your friend, Mr. Vulkjevich. It may be that same data that Phil reviewed that we talked about yesterday. At any rate, what's important is that Jake also thinks that it's bogus, although he is following up with Reboto to be sure."

It seemed to Jillian like Brynn appeared deeply concerned for a moment before turning on her inscrutable face. "That's hard to believe. That Vulkjevich would send false data to a reporter. He isn't the type. Nonetheless, good job handling it. I assume you're following up?"

"Yes, I think it's handled. But I also want to HANDLE Vulkjevich. I spoke with him yesterday and told him it wasn't data from the trial, but it seems like he sent it anyway. Jake is going to send us a copy, and I'll compare it."

"Did you let Jake know you thought it was from Vulkjevich?"

Jillian thought there was an edge to Brynn's voice. "No, because I don't know that for sure, and it could lead to another story—one that I don't think we want to see."

Again, it seemed to Jillian like Brynn was relieved. Or maybe it was just all that was happening with Lisa's murder. Everything seemed like intrigue! "Oh, and Tim was looking for you, and Dan called as well." Brynn said she had spoken with Dan, which was why she had left the office. Jillian continued, "And I received a couple of e-mails from two more investors who will be available next week to meet with you and Tim at the conference. I added them to the schedule. I think I'm ready for you to look at the presentation—I added the new data and updated our milestones. The new data definitely help to confirm and reinforce our key messages. It's looking pretty good."

Brynn looked relieved. "Thanks, Jillian."

"I'm heading out. I have a lunch date with Miles Smith—you know, the reporter from our county paper. He just wants to discuss the upcoming benefit they're doing to raise money for the new youth center. Of course, I promised nothing, but we do have some employees who might enjoy helping out. I'll see you later. I sent you the updated presentation, so let me know what you think."

Jillian was almost out the door when she remembered the list of BIS contractor employees from Inspector Sherwood. "Oh and one other thing—the inspector in my friend's murder case is investigating all of the local employees of BIS. We have apparently hired about a dozen of their finance contractors. He asked us to take a look at the list to see if there is anything that stands out about any of them. They'll interview everyone individually, but he was trying to see if we might know something to help him shorten the list. I e-mailed it to you."

Brynn seemed to dismiss this relatively quickly. "I doubt any of our contract employees is a murderer, but I'll be glad to look at the list. Have a nice lunch."

"Is everything all right with Dan? He seems to be contacting us a lot lately. Is he planning to buy?"

Brynn shrugged. "Who knows? He certainly is asking a lot of questions. I might need your help getting some additional information for him—maybe tomorrow. By the way, are you ready for this symposium on Friday? Dan mentioned he is looking forward to the panel discussion and hopes he doesn't cause you too much pain."

Jillian laughed. "Yes. Everything is lined up. Oh, by the way, Bowersox cancelled—you know, the financial advisor I met in Geneva who was so impressive. I believe he is a CPA, also. I have enough speakers, so it's no problem. Disappointing, though. If you need anything for your panel, I have time tomorrow to help. See you this afternoon."

Jillian's phone alerted her to a call from Inspector Sherwood, and her respite from the events of Lisa's murder ended. "Miss Hillcrest, have you heard anything more about the guy at your apartment building?"

"No, not really. Charlie, our concierge, was going to notify the police who were investigating the break in, but I thought I should let you know about it in case there is some connection to Lisa's death. I can't imagine what it would be, however."

"Have you had a chance to study the list of BIS employees?"

"I sent the list to our CFO, who hires financial contract employees. As of a few minutes ago, she had not reviewed it but she promised to get to it as soon as possible. She is skeptical that any of them could possibly be a murderer."

"I understand. However, it's just a bit of a coincidence that your company hires people from the same company as where your friend worked. There might be a connection—maybe not a direct one, but something. We just haven't made it yet. We've started interviewing the BIS people, by the way. We're about half-way through the list."

"Anyone stand out?"

"No, not yet. Can you give me the number of your CFO and I'll give her a call to make it official? She might be likely to respond more quickly that way."

"Sure. I'll e-mail her contact information. Let me know if you need anything else."

"Is your ex-husband staying with you right now?"

"No. Actually he's traveling, although he is certainly keeping in touch. He's called me several times since he left on Sunday morning."

"I would feel better if someone were with you, but at least the building is locked now, and people are alerted so maybe everyone will be more careful. Until we know why your friend was killed, we need to assume that you could be in danger also—as remote a possibility as that might seem. In the meantime, thanks for your help.

I'll let you know if we make any progress."

Jillian's mood dipped again. In addition, she now was concerned that her life could possibly be in danger. She really hadn't considered it a real possibility. However, the inspector's words echoed in her head.

Normally she might resent an interruption in her task-filled day, but today she was relieved to be meeting someone totally unrelated to anything she was working on. Miles Smith was currently a stringer for the local paper and he also had a blog that focused on city, county, and state government. He had a history of investigative journalism that fascinated Jillian. Among other stories, he had uncovered a county assessor's officer who basically charged for property value assessments that neither he nor his assistants had ever performed, resulting in inflated bank accounts. And she always enjoyed lunch at one of the many restaurants in downtown San Carlos several miles from her office, where she was meeting the reporter.

$\bowtie\!\!\!\bowtie$ 22

Brynn sat at her desk staring out the window. She had rushed out of the office that morning after she got a call from her husband. He had not been home for several nights, although he had let Brynn know he was staying at a San Jose hotel to think things over. He had decided he wanted a divorce but was willing to talk with her about it, if she wanted to meet him right then. It was unreasonable, but Brynn was available so she drove to San Jose and met him at his hotel coffee shop.

He had sensed her infidelity, but the problem went beyond that. Even now when they needed to talk about their relationship, neither of them could find the words.

Brynn sat at the small table nursing a glass of wine and nibbling at her chicken Caesar salad. "I guess I don't understand why you are behaving this way."

Her husband looked at her for a long time before responding. "I think we both know you have given up on us, Brynn. It's obvious you are not sharing anything with me. It's not just that you're sleeping with someone else, which I suspect you are. You just don't care about being with me, or sharing lunch or dinner with me, or going to a movie together, or even watching TV together. We're just co-existing in the same house. We're not a couple. We're not even friends. I'm not sure at this point that we qualify as roommates."

Brynn physically felt lifeless. She wanted to say she didn't want a divorce, but part of her didn't care. "I don't think I want a divorce."

"You don't think so? Well, you didn't deny any of what I said, which means you really don't care and you are sleeping with someone else. If you really don't want a divorce, we probably need to spend some time talking things over before moving forward with at least a trial separation. Beyond that, I'm not sure what to say."

Brynn's thoughts turned to Tim, and the joy they had felt at their clandestine meetings. She basically didn't want to talk about it at all, so she was glad her husband didn't have more to say. When either of them spoke, they tended to say the wrong thing. It was their pattern. Brynn said she didn't see what the problem was, and her husband wanted her to ask what could she do to make things better. They seemed to bring out the worst in each other, not the best.

Brynn had enough energy for one more attempt—a delay tactic. "I don't have time to talk right now. I have to get back to the office."

"No way. It's now or not at all. You have been postponing this for a long time, and things have now reached a point of no return, Brynn. What do you want to do?"

Brynn looked at her husband, desperate to feel love, or even like, but there was nothing. She looked at him, and he knew.

Her husband sighed. "All right, let's wait before we hire our respective attorneys, and try to talk things over again. Maybe we can engage the same marriage counselor we used last time."

"That sounds good; I'll check to see if she's available and let you know about scheduling something."

They parted with heads down, not looking at one another or feeling much of anything—the tall, beautiful, shapely blonde and the taller, handsome, athletic husband. Others stared at them. They were an incredibly handsome couple. Today, however, the attention was unwelcome, and Brynn, for the first time in her life, was unsure of what she wanted or where she was going.

23

The rest of Tuesday moved quickly for Jillian. Her lunch meeting with the reporter was pleasant, and she enjoyed the Italian cuisine at the small, intimate San Carlos restaurant. The reporter wanted to involve her company in an upcoming charity event, so Jillian discussed Harmonia's donation criteria, which she had developed and cleared with the executive staff and the Board. As she and the reporter were leaving the restaurant, she was surprised to see Dan Harrington—the hedge fund manager was becoming ubiquitous! He was departing another restaurant across the street with a familiar-looking man who turned abruptly and both of them went back into their restaurant. Jillian was sure it was her company's VP of Business Development and Strategy, Archie Linstrom. However, she saw him only briefly and the reporter was still asking her questions so she finished up with him, then headed to her car, and back to the office.

Jillian returned to her office about 2:00 ready to attack the rest of her "to do" list. She received an e-mail from Reboto saying he had no problem calling the reporter, and wondering who was sending false information and why. He said he would send whatever he could to the reporter without divulging confidential patient information to set the record straight. She also received a voicemail from the reporter letting her know he had spoken with Dr. Reboto and thanking her for her help. He was convinced now that the information was a hoax, and said he had sent both her and the FDA a copy. He would let her know if he heard anything back from the regulators.

24

"I have a dinner reservation for two for Madeline Baumgartner."
Lisa's mother was on autopilot as she greeted Lisa's ex-partner, Beverly, with a hug. She recalled the first time that Lisa brought Beverly home and introduced her as her partner. Madeline was too stunned to say anything. Unfortunately, although initially surprised, Harry screamed at them. "Get out! No daughter of mine is homosexual. You did this to her." He pointed at Beverly. "This is your fault. We raised her to be a good Christian woman. Get out of this house."

Madeline had been too surprised and dismayed at her husband's response to say anything and stood there as Harry pushed them both out the door. Although she had spoken with Lisa since then—on the phone mostly—, she had never really gotten to know Beverly. As they followed the hostess to their reserved table, Madeline again regretted not spending more time with her when she was together with Lisa. However, Madeline quickly pushed the regret down. Despite her current state of listlessness, she had vowed to move forward and not be mired in the past.

"Beverly, first of all, I want to thank you for meeting with me. I can't imagine what you must think of me and my family, so I really appreciate this."

Beverly looked at the older woman with compassion. "I'm truly sorry about Lisa. I still had feelings for her, and I wish that we were meeting under different circumstances."

Madeline said she wanted a glass of wine. Although she was not accustomed to drinking, she hoped that it would give her the strength to do what she intended. Beverly recommended one of her favorite Merlots. Madeline agreed and Beverly asked for two.

"Beverly, thank you for agreeing to speak at Lisa's memorial service. I am arranging a non-religious service—because Lisa was not religious, I know that—at the children's museum. She enjoyed it so much as a child and continued to support it until recently, I'm told. So I'm pretty sure she would appreciate having the memorial there. I hope all of her friends will come. I've asked Jillian, too, and she is planning to make the trip. The two of you might want to discuss what you'll say."

"I'm honored. When are you planning to have the service?"

"Well, I was originally planning to hold it this Monday, but the following Monday is better for the museum, so I've scheduled it for then. Will that work for you?"

"Actually, the following Monday is much better for me."

"Thanks, Beverly, you can't know what that means to me."

Madeline hesitated. It was obvious she wanted to say something else, so Beverly waited patiently. She noticed that Madeline was speaking tonelessly, without inflection—probably part of her grieving. "Also, I want to do something. I want to make a contribution. I know I can never make it up to you and especially to Lisa, but I want to move forward and try to help others. There must be other parents like Harry and me who just don't understand. What can I do to help?"

"I think that's an excellent idea, Madeline. Lisa would have been so pleased. I'll get you in touch with some organizations. They can work with you and help you along so you are comfortable with what you're doing. Some are not as aggressive as others, but they make a significant contribution nonetheless. They helped my parents understand."

Madeline looked like she might cry, so Beverly started to talk about the menu, but Madeline quickly guided the conversation back to Lisa. "Can you tell me about you and Lisa? What did the two of you do together?"

"We lived together like a couple. We enjoyed going to movies, plays and symphony concerts."

"What was Lisa's favorite movie?"

"Lisa really liked 'The Foot Locker.' My tastes are more along the lines of the Harry Potter series."

"Where did you go on vacation?"

"Well, we spent a week in Vermont one year with Jillian and Chad—"

Madeline interrupted. "On Lake Champlain in South Hero?"

"Yes, did she tell you?"

"No. We used to go there every year as a family. Oh, how I wish we had gone with you!"

Beverly quickly added, "We also spent time in New York with Chad and Jillian seeing plays and eating at some of the fine restaurants. As you know, Jillian really enjoys fine restaurants."

"Yes, she does. Lisa didn't used to, but Jillian taught her how to eat. She was always so thin, you know."

"She overcame that. She started to exercise to build muscle, and that made her hungry, so she ate more." Beverly laughed, trying to lighten the discussion.

"That's good."

"She really appreciated your talking with her. You need to know that."

Madeline bit her lip. She wasn't sure where she got the strength, but she continued to ask questions about Lisa's everyday life. After another 15 minutes of grilling Beverly, her energy was depleted. Beverly gently changed the subject to the latest restaurants in Philadelphia; TV shows; movies—anything she could think of to help Madeline. By the end of the evening, Madeline guiltily admitted to herself that she enjoyed this evening more than any in a long time. She knew it was just a first step, but it felt good to have made the leap.

25

Jillian was home before 7:00. Pete greeted her uneasily, saying the police only questioned his brother, gave him a warning, and let him go. His description of the person who had approached him was so vague it was useless. Apparently the guy had pulled up in his car and spoke to Mickey through the car window so he didn't even get a feel for how tall he was. Given that Mickey was a teenager, Jillian asked if he had noticed the model of the car.

"All Mickey remembered is that it was some kind of white car—he said it looked like something a geek might drive. And that the guy was old—which could mean anywhere from twenty to eighty."

Jillian froze. "He's sure the car was white?"

Pete looked startled. "Yes, as sure as anything Mickey remembers. Why?"

"Oh, nothing. I'm sure it's just a coincidence. The car that murdered my friend was also white. Did he happen to notice if the car had any dents or scratches?"

"I'll ask him, but he didn't mention it. We're talking about a sixteen-year old, you know. I'm not sure how great his observation skills are. Do you think there's a connection between this and your friend's murder?"

"I don't know. But I'm certainly glad Charlie is locking the front door now."

Pete looked concerned, but was distracted by the traffic jam building behind Jillian's double-parked car. Jillian entered her apartment building, looking in all directions to be sure no one was following her. Charlie was at the desk; otherwise the lobby was empty. "Hi, Charlie. Anything new on the break-in?"

"Just what Pete's brother told the police. The kid was really scared. I don't think he'll do that again. The police now think maybe the guy meant to break into your flat and he used the kid to check it out. Maybe the other apartment was a mistake. They might call you. I gave them your number."

"Thanks, Charlie. I seem to be spending a lot of time with the San Francisco Police lately."

On her way to her flat, she pondered whether the newest theory regarding the break-in suspect was even plausible. Why would anyone want to break into her flat? She had few possessions of value.

She barely noticed Mrs. Anderson's empty door and was relieved her lights were off when she entered her flat. Just then Mrs. Anderson opened her door and greeted Jillian. "I took down my wreath in case someone else comes up here looking to steal something. Are you all right?"

"Oh, hi, Mrs. Anderson. Yes, I'm fine. It turns out that someone hired the kid who was up here. He's actually Pete's younger brother and is very sorry for what he did. The police think maybe he was sent up here as a scout for a future crime or something."

"Well, I'm not sure that is reassuring."

"I wish you would put your wreath back up. It is so nice to see it when I walk by. I doubt that anyone will be breaking in again, especially since Charlie is now regularly locking the front door."

"Do you really like my flowers?" Mrs. Anderson seemed genuinely pleased. "I actually make them myself. I'll put it back up right away. I don't know why this has spooked me so. I'm not usually so skittish. My son tells me I should be more careful than I am. He wants me to come live with him and his wife in Fresno. Can you imagine? Live in Fresno?"

Jillian smiled. No, she could not imagine living in Fresno. She had met Mrs. Anderson's son just once, and he seemed nice enough. The older woman visited him on holidays, but always seemed relieved to return to San Francisco. As far as Jillian knew, he had been to the City only once since Jillian moved in a year ago and that was because he was on a business trip. Jillian had never met his wife and Cynthia's two toddler grandchildren.

Mrs. Anderson came back out of her flat and hung the fragrant wreath on the door. "There. I've put the wreath back up. Thanks for making me realize how silly I was being."

"My pleasure. Good night."

Jillian closed her door just as her phone played "Once Upon a Time." Chad was definitely keeping an eye on her. "Hi. Where are you?"

"I'm just heading to the airport to return to Oakland. I'll be back in Alameda tomorrow morning. How are you?"

"Believe it or not, I'm a little nervous. It turns out that the kid who Mrs. Anderson encountered here in our hallway was Pete's brother. Someone asked him to check out my floor. The guy even gave him my name."

"That's not good. Did you call the police?"

"Pete contacted the police directly. He seems to have some misgivings about talking with Charlie. Then he took his brother into the police station this afternoon after school, where he gave them a statement. I think he's harmless. It's the guy who approached him that concerns us all."

"How did the guy approach Pete's brother?"

"Apparently he was in a car. He called him over and offered him a hundred dollars. Of course, he couldn't turn down that much money."

She almost didn't tell him that Pete's brother had described the car of the person who had approached him as being white. However, he asked her if Mickey had described the car, so Jillian told him.

"I think that you should call Inspector Sherwood and let him know. I agree that, yes, there are lots of white cars, but the coincidence makes it worth mentioning."

"All right. I'll call him. When will I see you again?"

They ended the call making dinner plans for Wednesday night, which put Jillian in a much happier and secure state of mind.

She made a quick call to Inspector Sherwood and left him a message. Her phone alerted her to a voicemail; it was from Dan Harrington. She assumed that his call had something to do with his continuing investigation of Harmonia or with the upcoming panel discussion, since Brynn was handling the request contained in the folder Jillian had given her from Dan. "Hi, Jillian. Did you ever forward the name or phone number of that broker who called you? I need to check on my accounts—there does seem to be something strange happening. I want to be sure. Give me a call." He seemed more concerned than he was earlier when she had mentioned the call to him.

Jillian had checked earlier and she had the number of the broker who had left her a message on Friday morning when she was on her way to the hospital following Inspector Sherwood's fateful call. She promptly called Dan and gave him the number and asked how his investigation into Harmonia was going.

"I am very excited about its potential. I am having lunch with Tim tomorrow to get some additional information. Brynn has been helpful—with that and with some other companies I'm researching. Anyway, thanks for all your help. If I don't see you before, I'll see you Friday."

Jillian acknowledged that they would be seeing each other on Friday for the conference panel and then disconnected. She then turned her attention to fixing an easy-to-cook light dinner in anticipation of the next night's dinner with Chad, which would be full of lots of delicious calories.

She awakened Wednesday morning having actually slept better than the previous nights, but still restlessly. Although still tired, she certainly felt better than any of the previous mornings for the past week. It seemed difficult for her to believe she had returned from Geneva less than a week earlier.

Unfortunately, she was running late and needed to be at work in time for Brynn's 9:00 a.m. meeting. It was close to 8:00 when Pete brought her car around, and she needed to do some preparation prior to the meeting. Today was one of the days when Pete worked two hours in the morning only, so she would not see him that night. She checked with him again about his brother, who was extremely relieved he was not in jail. Pete was sure the teenager had learned his lesson.

Traffic was not cooperative and Jillian arrived at work with barely five minutes to spare. She went directly to the meeting carrying her computer, and quickly turned it on to locate the information she needed. Fortunately, Brynn was also late so Jillian had time to formulate what she would report.

The meeting lasted an hour, during which time Jillian silenced her phone. As she headed back to her office, she checked it and discovered that both Inspector Sherwood and Dan Harrington had called. She called Harrington back first but there was no answer so she left a message. Then she checked in with Inspector Sherwood. He, too, appeared to be out, so she left him a message as well.

Tim was waiting for her in her office wanting to see the updated presentation he would be delivering the following week to a room full of investors and a significant audience listening via webcast. Jillian had not had an opportunity to get Brynn's input and told him that, but he wanted to see it anyway. He viewed it quickly while in her office, and asked her to send it to him; he had time to look at it just then. She did that, letting Brynn know also by way of copying her. Apparently Tim had just learned about Lisa's murder. He seemed concerned about Jillian and asked her how she was doing.

"I'm much better today than over the weekend. It was a real shock. I'll be heading to Philadelphia this weekend for the memorial service on Monday. I might go directly from Philadelphia to New York and meet you and Brynn there."

"No problem. Let me know if there is anything that Stephanie and I can do. We're planning to go to New York together. Stephanie has been alone a lot lately with all my traveling, and we both enjoy New York. So we decided she would come along. And by the way, if you would prefer not to go, I'm sure Brynn and I can handle everything."

"Thanks, Tim. It's tempting, but I've been working on the itinerary and there are several investors and reporters I want to look up in addition to those who are already scheduled to meet with you. I may need to arrange some additional meetings for you and/or Brynn as a result. I want to communicate the data as much as possible."

"Not a problem. It's entirely up to you. Again, I'm sorry about your friend."

"Thank you. Oh, I understand that you're having lunch with Dan Harrington today. Do you need anything for that meeting?"

"No. He just has some follow-up questions. I hope he finally buys a bunch of stock. We've certainly spent enough time briefing him."

"Well, if you change your mind, I'm in the office all day."

Tim left Jillian's office wishing he could be more enthusiastic about the recent success of his company and the potential investment by a leading hedge fund. However, he had been preoccupied with trying to make up to his wife over his infidelity with Brynn. Of course, he was pretty sure Stephanie did not know anything for certain and that she did not suspect Brynn. Or if she did suspect Brynn, she was trying very hard not to acknowledge it. However, she knew her husband and sensed something was amiss.

Tim appreciated and enjoyed the life he had with his wife. Their son, Tim Junior was studying electrical engineering at MIT, and their daughter had just been accepted to several liberal arts colleges, including Stanford. Stephanie and he enjoyed participating in local events and had season tickets to the 49er and Giants games as well as San Francisco Symphony and ACT theater events. They enjoyed each other's company. So he wasn't sure why he decided to pursue an affair with Brynn. But he could not deny that he truly enjoyed it. She made him feel young and vibrant.

However, Stephanie's abrupt appearance in Geneva awakened him to the realization of what he was risking. As devoted as she was to him, she would not tolerate continued infidelity. She was doing what her intuition told her by being at his side. He knew that and strangely appreciated her presence while simultaneously resenting it. He was a risk-taker in business, but he typically had a limit to what he would risk in order to achieve results. He wasn't sure what the results would be if he continued his affair with Brynn. He didn't even believe there was a future, just a joyous present. So, although he should have been filled with enthusiasm and excitement about the current success of his company, he was mostly preoccupied about the choice he had to make between his wife and his mistress.

26

Jillian was concerned about Tim meeting with a major investor without her being there to take notes to assure that the meeting was properly documented. However, her experience over the past year was that Tim tended to err on the side of caution and was usually very careful about disclosing only public or non-material information. It occurred to Jillian that Tim was actually extremely ethical and again it crossed her mind how unlikely was his affair with Brynn.

Jillian was thankfully busy the rest of the day. She chaired another meeting on the progress of the plans for the promotion of the partnered product. She was mildly pleased that Vulkjevich provided a summary of his market analysis intended to help guide their messages toward groups that might be most interested in the product. The partner had also done some analysis and luckily the results were similar. So Brynn's faith in Vulkjevich was momentarily reinforced. However, Jillian asked Vulkjevich to wait on the line when the others had disconnected. She queried him again about the data he had sent her and asked if he was now satisfied that it was not from the lupus trial.

"Oh, I hadn't thought much more about it. I need to go now." And he disconnected.

Jillian was speechless. She continued to wonder that Brynn had engaged this person. He was rude at best. Admittedly this last piece of research would be helpful for the launch of the partnered product. But if, indeed, he had sent the bogus data to *The Wall Street Journal* in some purist belief that he was serving as a whistleblower, well, Jillian really wished she didn't need to deal with him. Not only was this kind of behavior harmful to Harmonia Therapeutics, it was also a dangerous game of crying wolf. Eventually, the public and the media could start to think that whistle blowing was just a play for attention.

Of course, now that Vulkjevich had sent the data, it would look particularly bad to remove him as a consultant. In fact, if they fired him, it would appear they were trying to hush him. Jillian began to wonder if that had been his goal all along. By presenting what appeared to be information detrimental to their trial, he was somewhat assuring his employment under the whistleblower concept—at least from a PR perspective.

Turning her attention to other issues, Jillian was surprised she heard nothing more from either Dan Harrington or Inspector Sherwood. However, she assumed whatever they needed they had found through alternative sources.

She finished her tasks for the day—including her first pass at a communications plan for the partnered product—and headed for home anticipating a great dinner with Chad at his newly discovered restaurant. She dropped the car off at her building with Pete's substitute, ran up to her flat to drop off her laptop, and then went downstairs to wait for Chad, who arrived in his Porsche momentarily.

Their dinner was more than pleasant. In fact, it was outstanding. The ambience resembled a small French bistro themed with the blue Provence motif from the large blue and yellow urns to the dishware and napkins. Jillian also had asked that there be no discussion of anything serious, like Lisa, or anything work-related until after dinner. She knew that Chad would grill her about possible danger, and she just wanted a respite from thinking about Lisa, her flat, or work. Although concerned, Chad was obedient, and he mentioned nothing serious throughout dinner.

"This is certainly a great place. How did you find it?"

Chad smiled, and raised his eyebrows. "That eeez ze secret, madam." His French accent was atrocious.

Jillian started with warm goat cheese on roasted garlic croutons; then she had a Cassoulet white bean stew with duck confit and lamb.

"Will Madame be having ze dezzert tonight?" Again with the bad French accent. "I have heard from zee friends that the tarte tatin is ze best in ze City."

So Jillian finished with tarte tatin, one of her favorite desserts, topped with French vanilla ice cream. She also had a glass or two of the house red wine.

By the time she and Chad returned to her building, it seemed very natural for Chad to turn over his car to Pete and enter the flat with her for a nightcap. Chad opened a bottle of cabernet—something Jillian always preferred to any of the liquors that might have been more standard as an after-dinner drink. They discussed the latest musical in town and planned to see it together. San Francisco was not a big theater town so they both appreciated the touring companies. They talked about the San Francisco Symphony and how much they continued to appreciate Michael Tilson Thomas and especially his interpretations of Mahler's symphonies. They pondered about the latest oil spill. Both of them were huge proponents of alternative sources of energy as a way to mitigate the impact of Middle Eastern political upheavals.

Jillian was reminded of her last evening with Lisa. It was time to turn to the real world. "You know, Lisa and I were saying some of these same things. I still can't believe she was murdered."

"Can we talk about it now? What's the latest? Are the police making any progress?"

"Not much. At this point, they are pretty sure she had her meeting that morning, went to the garage to head for the airport, and was run down by a white car. They don't even know for sure if the driver was a man or a woman. Her mother talked to her the day before and said Lisa told her she was meeting with someone who might have a job for her. She said it sounded like Lisa had done some research for this person. I still think the list of biotech companies they found in Lisa's luggage with the information attached to it was what she was working on. Oh, damn—I forgot to give it to Brynn today to see if she recognized anything. Anyway, if that was the case—if Lisa met with someone—it seems strange that that person hasn't stepped forward . . .unless he or she was the murderer."

Chad mulled that over. "Maybe. But it could be that the person she met with just isn't aware of her murder. Perhaps he is traveling and didn't see the news—it wasn't highly publicized—or he was just in town to meet with Lisa and then left. It sounds like there's no proof the meeting had anything at all to do with her murder."

"You're right. But I can't think what else it would be. I mean, look at her situation. She wasn't wealthy, so money couldn't be a motive. Her family was not supportive but I can't imagine them doing anything to hurt her. They would be more inclined to kidnap her and send her to some sort of rehabilitation center to get her to, quote, 'choose' a different lifestyle—theirs. No, she must have been murdered because she knew something. So it was either from that last meeting or from one of her clients—or maybe she just saw something. And if she saw something that was suspicious, she didn't mention it to me. Regardless, I sure hope the police are looking at more than just that meeting. And I must remember to give that list of companies to Brynn tomorrow."

Their conversation flowed as naturally as it had in the early days of their marriage. Chad looked at Jillian, and cocked his head to one side. "Tonight iz ze night."

Jillian laughed. "You really do need to improve that accent, or preferably, not use it."

It was natural that they ended up in bed together, and that Chad stayed the night. Their lovemaking was more passionate than in the recent past, and they both were happy to share themselves with each other. Jillian was particularly grateful, and snuggled appreciatively until she heard her alarm playing its programmed song at 7:00 a.m.

27 ⋈⫶⋈⫶⋈

Jillian's Thursday morning began somewhat lazily as she tried to continue to recapture the magic from the previous evening and snuggle more with Chad. Unfortunately he had to get across the Bay to Alameda to work by 9:00 and he had not brought a change of clothes (not very optimistic on his part, Jillian thought). He headed out almost as soon as he awoke, with a promise to call her about the weekend. He also reminded her to be careful, exhibiting concern over the latest events in her life. She had asked if he wanted to come to Lisa's memorial service, but he had other plans for the weekend so was not sure. He wanted to make sure she felt up to going. She did; it would just be nice if he were to go along.

She dressed somewhat leisurely and had time for oatmeal in addition to her freshly ground and brewed coffee before calling for her car. She continued to marvel what a great luxury it was to have her car waiting for her! She picked up her laptop—still in its case and precisely where she'd dumped it before dinner—and her purse and headed downstairs.

She arrived at work before 9:00. Brynn had sent her input about the presentation. Tim joined her in her office and also made some suggestions. "By the way, did you hear from Dan Harrington yesterday?"

Jillian thought. "He called me in the morning, but I was never able to reach him. How was your lunch with him?"

"Well, that's the problem. He never showed up. I called him but he hasn't returned my call either, and his assistant appears to be on vacation. I think Harrington is in town this week—you know he has a flat in Pacific Heights in the City in addition to his Napa spread."

"I assumed he probably did. If he calls, I'll let you know. Strange that he missed the meeting."

"Especially since he was the one who asked for it. Maybe he just got tied up, but you'd think he'd let me know."

Jillian didn't think much more about Dan Harrington—she was busy finishing the presentation. She wanted the corporate attorney to review it before sending it to the conference staff in New York next week. She completed the revisions by noon and sent it to the attorney for final review. Before lunch, she sent a reminder to her panel participants about the time they should arrive at the local San Jose symposium the next day and reminded them of the room number and location of the hotel.

Lunch was leftovers from the previous night's dinner. Afterward she reviewed the New York itinerary for the following week and was pleased to see that Brynn's assistant had added a few names to the list of meetings. She also spent time practicing her own presentation for her local symposium the next day. Jillian wrapped up her workday by refining the communications plan for the partnered product. She reminded the receptionist and her assistant that both Brynn and she would be out of the office the next day, as they were attending the symposium.

There was no dinner with Chad to anticipate so Jillian was not in a hurry to get home. She decided to do some food shopping in Redwood City; parking was less painful there than in San Francisco. It would also allow time for traffic to thin out. She reached home after 7:00, dropped her car off with Pete after unloading it, and headed to her flat nagged by a bit of anxiety about tomorrow's panel. Although she was prepared and had practiced, she always got a little nervous before an actual event. She prided herself on her presentation skills, so wanted to be sure things went flawlessly in front of her peers and any participating investors. She was therefore a little preoccupied and did not see the person standing in the doorway of her building until she was almost on top of him. Since the door was locked, she had to set down some of her packages to unlock it. Fortunately her keys were already in her hand and she was able to open the door quickly and enter without letting the man in. She yelled for Charlie, and he hurried across the lobby. But by the time he re-opened the door, the man was gone.

"Did you recognize him? Did he threaten you?" Charlie was genuinely concerned.

Jillian was not sure what she had seen and was a little embarrassed. The man was probably just some poor homeless guy. Charlie handed her the groceries and she headed for her flat. She noticed Charlie was calling someone—he was probably letting the police know. She felt even more embarrassed.

When the elevator door opened on her floor, she saw Mrs. Anderson outside her door fiddling with her wreath. Jillian smiled. She must have been anxious because Jillian was late.

"Hi, Jillian. I was just fixing the wreath. It seemed to be a little loose."

"Hi, Mrs. Anderson. How was your day?"

"Well, it was a little better than usual. My son is visiting this weekend and plans to stay with me. That will be nice. What about you?"

"Well, I have a conference tomorrow. Then I'm headed to Philadelphia on Saturday for my friend's memorial service, which is on Monday. Then I need to go to New York for work. Oh, damn—oh, sorry—I forgot to pick up my mail. Well, I might as well put these down first."

Jillian dropped off the bags of food, her computer, and purse inside the door and then headed back down to the lobby to get her mail. She waved to Charlie and opened the box to find mostly catalogues but also what appeared to be a card from Lisa's mother. Jillian dropped the catalogues into the recycling bin next to the mailboxes, and went back to the elevator to her apartment. She was surprised to see Mrs. Anderson coming out of Jillian's flat when she arrived.

"Oh, Jillian. You left your flat unlocked so I just stepped inside to make sure no one got in. I wasn't sure you'd taken your keys. I really like how you've decorated your flat. Where did you get that beautiful table?"

Mrs. Anderson was beginning to intrude a little too much on Jillian's privacy and was making her uncomfortable. "Oh, I could have sworn I locked my door. I have my keys to get back in. Thanks. The table came from my ex-husband. I don't know where he got it. He has a lot more interest in decorating than I do."

Jillian went into her flat with a somewhat curt "see you later," and turned to her mail. The card from Lisa's mother was a notice for the memorial service. However, Jillian saw that it was scheduled not for this Monday but for the following one. How had she gotten that date confused? Although that was actually a better date, Jillian was sure Lisa's mother had told her the service was this Monday. She could easily re-book her flight to New York and go there first and then to Philadelphia after. Maybe by then Inspector Sherwood would know more about what had happened to Lisa. She would let Chad know—maybe the following week would be a more convenient time for him.

There was a knock on her door. Jillian saw that Mrs. Anderson was outside, and opened the door to a sheepish but determined neighbor. "I'm sorry to bother you, Jillian. You must think me a busybody, but really, your door was not locked. Maybe you could check your lock to be sure that it's working? Your door was even ajar."

The woman was obviously concerned, so Jillian pushed the lock and closed the door—to discover that indeed the door had not locked. She re-opened the door. "You're right! It didn't lock. I'll let Charlie know right away. In the meantime, I'll be double sure to use the bolt lock inside. I can't believe it. I wonder how long it's been that way?"

"You might want to call the police directly. What if Charlie is in on this?"

"Oh, don't be silly. I can't believe he would . . . " Jillian thought about her lights being turned on and considered how it was possible that Charlie, who had a passkey, could have been the one who had entered her flat. "Do you really think so? It really doesn't make sense for Charlie to break the lock—he has a pass key and can get in anytime he wants."

"Yes, but that would make him look guilty. So maybe he needed to create a way for someone other than him to get into the apartment."

"But why my apartment? I don't have anything worth stealing."

Mrs. Anderson's face filled with concern. "Well, you are an attractive young woman. Perhaps robbery wasn't the motive."

Jillian truly hoped that Mrs. Anderson was overly worried, but now she shared her neighbor's apprehension.

"O.K. I'll call the police first and then let Charlie know, since he is the one responsible for getting it fixed. This is really disturbing. It means my flat has been open to anyone who knew it was unlocked. I usually use the inside dead bolt when I'm here, but you can bet I'll be sure to use it now."

"Do you have the police number?"

Jillian checked in her bookcase, and quickly located the card the police officer had left. She called the number and was relieved to connect almost immediately. She asked for the officer in charge of the break-ins at her building and was connected. She relayed what had happened and, to Jillian's surprise and further concern, was told not to report it to her concierge, as the police were investigating him as a "person of interest" for a variety of reasons. Mrs. Anderson saw Jillian's eyes open wide, and she seemed to suck in the air around her. When Jillian explained she would be unable to secure her flat when she was absent unless she reported it to Charlie, they recommended contacting the landlord directly and provided the number to call. This seemed somewhat strange to Jillian, but she did as they requested.

Jillian hung up and called the landlord's number; she listened to a recording telling her to leave a message, which she resignedly did with Mrs. Anderson listening. The older woman was watching with a concerned expression. "Again, I apologize for interfering, Jillian. You probably don't know that I was a police officer for many years, and I guess I continue to be suspicious."

Jillian was flabbergasted. Mrs. Anderson appeared to be a kindly maternal woman with no indication of the toughness that Jillian thought all police must possess. "Really? You were a police officer?"

Mrs. Anderson laughed at Jillian's expression. Her eyes and mouth were wide open. "Yes. For twenty years, although I did mostly desk duty as a community liaison officer. Nonetheless, I saw enough to be more suspicious than your average retired senior."

Jillian continued to ponder this new information. "Well, I am grateful you noticed. As you heard, I left a message for the landlord. I still can't believe Charlie might have had anything to do with this. But then if you had asked me whether I would see my best friend murdered, I would have definitely doubted it."

"Your friend was murdered?" Mrs. Anderson seemed startled. "Why didn't you tell me? You just said you had lost a friend. What happened? Who is the inspector on the case?"

Jillian had mistakenly assumed Charlie had informed everyone. So she filled in Mrs. Anderson, who listened attentively. "Well, first, I'm glad that Inspector Sherwood is involved. He has a great reputation for solving cases, along with his partner, Joe Sodini. And, although he isn't a maverick, he won't let procedure get in the way. Do you think the break-ins here have anything to do with your friend's death?"

"I honestly don't know. We can't figure out what the motive was for killing Lisa. She wasn't wealthy, and as far as we know, she wasn't involved in anything—unsavory. She was just a marketing consultant trying to earn a living and live her life. Inspector Sherwood and I are trying to establish a connection between what she was doing and what I'm doing, but until we do, I can't believe there is a connection."

"So you're headed for Philadelphia this weekend?"

"No, I thought I was but I must have gotten the dates confused. It's not this weekend but next weekend. So I'll be here this weekend and will probably leave for New York on Monday, as I have work to do there for most of the week. Then I'll go to Philadelphia after New York, instead of the other way around."

"Oh, good. That means you can meet my son. Would you be able to join us for dinner Saturday night? I'm cooking. And what about that nice young man I've seen here?"

Lisa smiled. She should have known Mrs. Anderson would have witnessed Chad's visits. "Actually, that would be nice. I don't know about my ex-husband, however. I'll check with him and let you know."

"Oh, he's your ex-husband. He is very handsome."

"Indeed he is. He has been very supportive through all this."

"Does he live far away?"

Jillian couldn't believe the questions. "He lives in Alameda, so it's not that far although, of course, sometimes bridge traffic can slow the trip. Anyway, I'll let you know if he is available."

"Well, in the meantime, please be careful. I'll be particularly vigilant and will watch for Charlie."

Jillian's phone rang and she was relieved the call was from a locksmith. He said he would be there within a half hour and confirmed her flat number and said he would call her when he arrived so she could buzz him in. Jillian relayed the information to Mrs. Anderson, who returned to her flat with a last word of caution to Jillian.

ynthia Anderson returned to her flat more concerned than usual about her neighbor. She decided to get in touch with some of her friends still on the job, and find out more about Jillian's murdered friend. She didn't want to alarm Jillian any more than necessary. However, it wouldn't hurt to find out whether the inspectors considered Jillian a suspect or a possible victim. Cynthia doubted Jillian was a suspect. Even though she had known her for less than a year, Cynthia trusted her own instincts.

Cynthia Anderson had been modest about her contributions to the San Francisco Police Department. Although she did indeed do desk duty as a community liaison during the later years of her service, she had been an officer in the field during a time when female officers were not common. Her harmless appearance and unassuming nature caused both peers and perpetrators to underestimate her—until they got to know her. She could assess people more quickly than most, and this insight coupled with her quick thinking enabled her to defuse potentially volatile situations before they ignited. Over the years, she earned the respect of most of her fellow officers, and had the reputation of being a resourceful and competent officer. However, her career had taken a dramatic detour one night when she and her partner responded to a domestic violence situation where the wife was the violator rather than the husband. When the officers intervened, the wife stuck a kitchen knife into Cynthia. Fortunately Cynthia's partner responded quickly, and was able to pull the angry wife off Cynthia before she did more damage. Although Cynthia recovered from the wound, she was restricted to desk duty for the remainder of her police service.

Therefore, her senses were tuned into Jillian's situation. She knew Jillian was not involved in any criminal activity, and she also knew Inspector Sherwood's reputation. If he believed there was a connection between Jillian and her friend's murder, there probably was. So Cynthia Anderson sat in her chair mulling over what she knew and formulating questions to ask Jillian the next time they saw each other.

29

Jillian awakened to her phone alarm at 5:00 a.m. She needed to stop by the office on her way to today's symposium, and although her panel discussion was not until 11:00, she was hoping to arrive for registration at 7:30 or at least in time for the first presentation at 8:00. Since it was being held in San Jose, she estimated an hour and a half from her flat to the hotel allowing extra time to stop at her office to pick up the handouts. So she dressed quickly. To save time, she had decided to forego her usual freshly ground and brewed coffee and get some at the conference.

The locksmith had replaced the hardware on her door, and she carefully made sure that the door locked behind her. Pete had her car waiting for her—as she had pre-arranged. Given the early hour, traffic was light and she arrived at her company building fairly quickly.

She went to her office and found the handouts on the chair by her door where she had left them the previous night. She noticed there was a folder in her in-box that hadn't been there when she left yesterday. It appeared to be the one Dan Harrington had left for Brynn with a sticky note from Brynn asking Jillian to review the contents and supplement the information Brynn had provided. Just in case it was urgent—and also because she was curious—Jillian hurriedly opened the folder and saw the list of company names the inspector had given her from Lisa's luggage. Somehow it had gotten mixed in with Dan Harrington's folder.

Then Jillian looked more closely. She went to the stack of folders on her desk and pulled out the one containing the list Inspector Sherwood had given her from Lisa's car. It was still where she had left it, and it appeared that the same list was also in the folder provided by Dan, who had written a note on it asking Brynn to check out these companies—excluding Harmonia, of course. What? How did the same list end up in Lisa's car? She looked through the rest of Dan's folder. It contained Brynn's summary of each company and her perspective of its potential. Jillian momentarily forgot she needed to be in San Jose shortly. Her mind was racing. She looked again at the list. It was even in the same format as Lisa's with the same headings. It was definitely an exact copy.

Jillian felt an incredible sense of urgency to speak to Brynn immediately and called her, but got no response. She calmed herself by realizing she would be seeing both Brynn and Dan shortly at the conference and could ask them then where this list had originated. She took the folder with her in addition to the handouts and headed for her car. She continued to think about the two lists. It seemed like too much of a coincidence for the same list of names to be in the possession of two people Jillian knew. What was the connection? Could Dan Harrington be connected to Lisa's murder? Was he the person Lisa met on that last day? She told herself there was no way he could be involved. Why would he? The more she examined the possibilities, the less sense they made.

Jillian didn't notice if traffic was heavy or not. She simply responded to the commands of the voice from her GPS navigator and arrived at the downtown San Jose hotel, parking her car in a city lot behind the hotel. She picked up her computer—she needed it for the presentation—stuffed the handouts and folder in her soft briefcase, and headed for the meeting. She was relieved to see signs in the lobby to help her find the conference rooms quickly. It was not quite

8:00 a.m. yet. She saw people milling around the registration area. She looked for Brynn, but did not see her, nor was Dan Harrington anywhere. She picked up her registration kit and headed for the coffee and breakfast table. Maybe the caffeine or some fruit would give her the jolt she needed to think more clearly.

One of the meeting organizers approached her and asked if Jillian was ready. She responded that she was and that it should be a great panel discussion. She liked the way her panel was presented in the program—it included a quote from Warren Buffet: "If you lose money for the company, I will be understanding. If you lose one shred of the company's reputation, I will be ruthless." Jillian hoped others in her profession were as interested as she in exploring the foundation of the ethics of their field. Most of the presentations focused on "how to" instructions for a specific function, so her discussion was unique in that it was intended to serve as a catalyst to think more broadly and deeply about the role of public relations in today's world of accelerated communications.

She continued to look for Brynn and Dan as the first general presentation commenced. Brynn might be with the rest of her panel; it was scheduled second on the agenda at 9:00. Jillian decided to wait for Brynn outside the room so she wouldn't miss her. Her apprehension was growing rather than abating. After 15 minutes of standing outside the conference room, she decided to go back into the room in case Brynn entered from another door.

The first presenter ended to thunderous applause—apparently he'd been humorous and entertaining, although Jillian had had difficulty paying attention. The panel in which Brynn was participating was announced, and she, along with three other CFOs from local companies of various sizes and product offerings, entered from a door on the side of the room and took seats on the raised stage. Damn. Where had she been? The panel discussion was scheduled for an hour—one of the longer hours Jillian had ever experienced.

During that time, she again compared the two lists of companies and again confirmed it was the same list.

She blamed herself for not giving Brynn the list from Lisa's car earlier. If she had given it to her sooner, she would now know the answer about why the two identical lists existed. There must be some explanation; maybe some broker had published it online and that's why the lists looked the same.

Finally, the CFO panel finished. A breathless Jillian rushed to the front of the room to talk with Brynn, who was taken aback at her brusque approach. "I need to talk to you right away."

An investor acquaintance of Brynn's was speaking with her, so she motioned to Jillian to wait. Jillian tried to be polite but was sure this was an important lead and was concerned it could even be dangerous. The past week had heightened her apprehension and stretched her sense of reasonableness to its fullest extent.

"What is it, Jillian? Did I say something I shouldn't have?"

Jillian was momentarily confused. "No, no. I need to talk to you about this list you left me from Dan Harrington. Where did he get it?" In response to Brynn's quizzical expression, she said, "It's the same list that was in my friend's car—the one who was murdered."

"Oh. That's the list you gave me from Dan—on Monday, I believe. He just wanted some background information because he is looking to do some major investments and was hoping to narrow down his investment opportunities or at least prioritize them. He has a financial advisor checking into it, but he wanted us to do an independent overview as well, for comparison."

"So Dan gave you this list. Or actually, he gave it to me, and I gave it to you, not knowing it was the same list as the one the police found in Lisa's luggage. But why would he want us to review it? Who is the advisor? Do you know? Maybe he was planning to use my friend, Lisa."

"I—excuse me" Brynn said after accidentally bumping into someone. "Let me think a moment. I will think about this, but maybe you might be over-reacting a little. I'm sure there is a logical explanation." One of the other CFOs approached Brynn and the two of them walked away from Jillian toward another group who appeared to be waiting for them.

Brynn's response seemed evasive to Jillian, although admittedly she was preoccupied with the panel discussion and meeting with any investors who might be there. Regardless, Jillian was in too much of a rush to pursue it with her boss. She was convinced that she needed to contact Inspector Sherwood. Thankfully he answered his phone. "Inspector Sherwood, I need to tell you something. I wish I had noticed this earlier. You know that list you gave me from Lisa's car? Well, a hedge fund guy named Dan Harrington gave that very same list to my company. You might want to check with him about it. He has an office down here on the Peninsula—his firm is called Biotech Investments. I should be seeing him shortly; he is scheduled to appear at a symposium I'm at in San Jose."

Jillian started to calm down now that she had done what she could do. Inspector Sherwood said they would check into it, and he would prefer she not say anything to Mr. Harrington regarding the matched list. In the meantime, the next presentation was underway in the general conference room, and it was time for Jillian to gather her group and check their conference room to be sure it was arranged properly. They were in one of three breakout groups presenting next, and so were scheduled in a different, smaller room.

When Jillian arrived at their assigned room, two of her participants were already there. She connected her computer to the projector, opened a browser, and downloaded the video they were using to introduce the discussion—a series of clips showing various presidential spokespersons saying the same exact words to convey a key message at various venues across multiple geographic areas. Then she made sure she had quick access to her presentation on the history of public relations so she could display her brief introductory PowerPoint presentation. She arranged the participants' nametags on the speakers' table and waited anxiously for the arrival of the others.

When it was time for the meeting to start—the room was so full they had to bring in more chairs—all of the participants except Dan Harrington had arrived. Where was he? He had missed the meeting with Tim on Wednesday, and now was late for this conference. It was not like him, and he had seemed excited and interested in the topic. Jillian had called his cell number but received no answer. She tried his assistant and listened to a message that said he was on vacation and would be returning next week. Leave a message and someone would return the call. The secretary at his office was not available. Jillian could wait no longer, so she started the discussion almost 10 minutes late without her representative institutional investor. By this time, Jillian was feeling too frazzled to do anything other than start the discussion.

She did her best to focus on the panel. The video clip was a success and described the issue at hand in an amusing and demonstrable manner. Surprisingly not a lot of practitioners were aware of the history of the discipline of public relations. Her presentation described how it grew largely out of business and political needs and for many years had no academic coverage to standardize practices. Edward L. Bernays, who was Sigmund Freud's nephew, is credited with one of the first forays into the field of public relations as he combined the theories of crowd psychology with that of his uncle's psychoanalysis. He formed one of the first agencies in the 1920s and Bernays essentially served as a public relations officer for Woodrow Wilson and Calvin Coolidge in addition to the American Tobacco Company, General Electric, Alcoa, the American Dental Association, Dodge Motors, and the NAACP. In the early days, the discipline was referred to as "propaganda." However, in the late 1920s and throughout the 1930s proponents of the field changed the term "propaganda" to "public relations" as it had acquired a negative connotation with its use by the Germans and then the Russians for totalitarian control of the masses.

The practice of modern public relations still uses crowd control and behavioral theories, as reiterating key messages and staying "on message" plays an important role in publicizing companies and their products. Most of the attendees of the conference understood the importance of staying on message, as they were communications experts. They developed key messages and worked them into their press releases, presentations, and interviews. Repeating these key messages enabled them to reach their audiences and familiarize them with the value of their companies' offerings.

At the end of this seven-minute presentation, Jillian started the discussion with the basic question "What is public relations?" After all of the panel members had finished their responses, she posed another question and the representative members again responded. The group divided much as anticipated—investors and reporters believed companies were trying to hide something when they repeated themselves or their messages. Those two constituencies only needed information; the reporters and investors could interpret it themselves.

Companies believed they were providing context so investors and customers could better understand the value of their offerings and their potential. They pointed to the need for confidentiality based on competitors and partner or customer contractual restrictions. The discussion was heated, but did seem to make both sides aware of the others' perspective. Most important, it made everyone think and evaluate why and how information was shared in the age of accelerated communications. In a time of change, there is always value in "going back to basics."

She had to wind down the animated discussion to allow everyone to attend the luncheon, which featured a scheduled keynote speaker. So she thanked the panelists and audience, made sure they had the handouts—fortunately she had made extra copies because there was more interest than anticipated—and offered to answer questions during the mid-afternoon break.

Jillian was still concerned that Dan Harrington was not part of the discussion. Whatever had she or her company done to annoy him and prevent him from attending the conference—or from having lunch with Tim? Maybe he got called out on a family emergency. And since his regular assistant was on vacation, perhaps that was why he hadn't notified anyone. Despite all that had occurred, Jillian was still looking for reasonable answers.

During the lunch hour, she called Inspector Sherwood to let him know Dan Harrington had not appeared. She also told him the investor had stood up the CEO on Wednesday, and said she found this behavior strange as Dan Harrington had always had excellent meeting etiquette. Sherwood had not had the opportunity to follow up on Harrington, so she located and gave him Harrington's mobile and work phone numbers as well as the address of his office, and said he had homes in Pacific Heights and in the Napa Valley. She also said it would be useful to know whom Dan was using as a financial advisor, since it was possible that he was looking to use Lisa to help him do market research on the companies. Or that could be a far-fetched supposition. At that point, she remembered how Brynn's response had seemed evasive when asked if she knew Harrington's analyst. Jillian felt very uneasy about her concern, so did not say anything to Inspector Sherwood. She would check with Brynn later.

"Can I reach you at this number today?"

Jillian responded that since it was her mobile phone, she would answer and although she would be at the conference for a while longer and her phone was silenced she would watch for his call, or he could text her and she would call him. "Oh, and I'm not going to Philadelphia this weekend. It turns out the memorial service is next weekend."

"Thanks. I'll get back to you. It sounds like we really need to talk to this Dan Harrington."

nspector Sherwood disconnected from Jillian's call with a sense of anticipation. He was open to the idea that Dan Harrington could be involved in the Baumgartner case. He might even have been the person she had met that morning. He was mildly pleased that his idea that Jillian Hillcrest would make the connection had paid off. Without her, it was unlikely he would have gotten this lead—or at least not this soon.

He checked in with his partner, Joe Sodini, who started the search for Harrington with a phone call to his office. The receptionist did not know where Dr. Harrington was, and was surprised that the police were calling again so soon. She said she had just spoken to someone from law enforcement that morning. Inspector Sodini asked if she had the name of the person who called. She said of course and provided the name. She asked to please be kept informed, as they were beginning to worry about Dr. Harrington; he had not been at the office for two days and had not alerted them of any business trip or any other reason for his absence.

Inspector Sodini was now very interested. What if the guy had left town? "Is it unusual for him to take trips without letting you know?"

The receptionist was quite emphatic. "Dr. Harrington has absolutely never done such a thing. He even calls to let me know whenever he is putting his phone on silent mode, like when he goes to a movie or a concert. He is usually on time for his meetings—or lets us know why not. I called the police yesterday because we are all so worried about him. The other officer said they were going to check his homes in both Pacific Heights and up in Napa. I hope nothing has happened to him. He is one of the good guys."

Inspector Sodini placed a quick call to the police officer who had left her name with Harrington's office and learned they indeed were on the way to both of Harrington's homes. She promised to call him as soon as they learned anything.

Inspector Sodini walked to Sherwood's desk with the expression of someone on the verge of discovery. "You're not going to believe this: That Harrington guy has disappeared. We're looking for him."

"That's very interesting. I've been doing some research on him. He's quite successful and appears to be very wealthy. Of course, you never know. I don't get the connection between him and the Baumgartner girl, but apparently he was looking to invest in Jillian Hillcrest's company and has been spending time investigating them. The list we found was his, and he asked Hillcrest's boss to provide information about those companies—most of which are public. It isn't like he was looking for any inside information—or maybe he was. Maybe that's what this is about. Getting inside information in order to make a—killing." He arched his right eyebrow in recognition of his pun.

Sodini agreed it was a plausible explanation. "Maybe Baumgartner got onto him, and he had to take care of her. Maybe she met with him and he realized she knew too much. And he needed a couple of days to arrange a trip to the Caribbean or Brazil and is now on his way."

"I wonder if Jillian Hillcrest's boss is involved?"

The two were still speculating when they received the call that caused them to change their theory.

Jillian returned to the main conference room and tried to eat the broiled salmon lunch. She had been looking forward to the speaker, a nationally known CNN financial news broadcaster. However, she was only half-listening, and could not make herself focus. She decided to call Lisa's mother to confirm the memorial service, not believing she had misunderstood the date. She found a quiet place in the hallway with a comfortable chair.

Madeline answered almost immediately. When Jillian asked her about the date of the service, she apologized. "Oh, I'm so sorry, Jillian. I did change it, because the later date was more convenient for the museum. Also, Beverly had another commitment with her mother, I believe. So, yes, now it's the following week. I had it in my head that I had talked to you about it. I hope the new date works for you?"

"Actually, it's a little better for me. I also need to go to New York next week and having the service after rather than before will make traveling easier. I can even come earlier to Philadelphia and help with arrangements, if that would be useful."

"It would be great to see you, although you certainly don't need to do anything. I would love you to just visit. I've convinced Lisa's brother to come—it will be helpful to have you here to talk with him and Harry.

I still don't even know if Harry will go. By the way, will Chad be coming with you? I know you two are no longer married, but you all seemed to have such a nice time together, and I know Beverly would be glad to see you both."

"I haven't heard from Chad since the time got changed. I'll let you know. He's been traveling a lot lately, so I really couldn't blame him if he decides to stay home."

"Have they learned anything more about what happened?"

Jillian hesitated. "Not really, but they may be making some progress. The inspector was going to contact me later today. I'll let you know."

They disconnected, and Jillian was now reassured that neither she nor Madeline had the wrong date for the memorial service. She was a little concerned about Lisa's brother attending. He had been particularly unreasonable and had said some very nasty things to Lisa and Beverly. Well, if Lisa's death were to mean something, maybe it could sway this family to comprehend and accept Lisa for who she was.

Inspector Sherwood phoned her. She was surprised he was calling again so soon. She answered apprehensively and at the same time with anticipation. The inspector seemed very abrupt, "How well do you know this Dan Harrington?"

"Why? What's happened?"

"Answer my question, please."

Jillian was a little intimidated, because the inspector was usually cordial, or at least civil. Her reaction was to tell him more than he needed to know. "Basically, I would say he is a business acquaintance. He has visited the company several times, and we have visited his office; he has met with our CEO and CFO. We talk on the phone. I respond to him as much as to any of our investors. He has always been friendly enough. I couldn't imagine him as a murderer. He has plenty of money. He started and now runs his own fund. He grows grapes at his place in Napa—and has brought us wine made from his grapes. Is that what you want to know?"

"How long have you known him?"

"I've only known him for about six months. He knew our CEO, Tim Wharton, at a former company years ago. In fact, as I told you, he was scheduled to have lunch with Tim on Wednesday—he had some follow-up questions about the company. I think our CFO met him about the same time as I did. But, again, I just can't imagine any reason why he might murder Lisa. Did he tell you where he got the list that was like the one Lisa had? Did he know Lisa?"

"I'm going to need to talk to you in more detail, but I can't leave here. Although this is not consistent with police procedure, can you come to Pacific Heights?"

"Pacific Heights? That's where Dan lives when he's in the city. Have you talked to him? What does he say?"

"I'm afraid he's not saying much of anything right now. He's dead. It's possible that he's been strangled."

Jillian wasn't sure she heard correctly. "What?"

"Mr. Harrington has been murdered. I need to talk with you, and I'll also need to talk with your CEO and CFO." The Inspector was now quite brusque. "It would help speed things up if you could provide their phone numbers. I'll send someone to meet with them. I don't want you speaking with either of them until I have. In fact, please don't speak with anyone. We are also looking for Harrington's assistant, by the way, who apparently is on vacation. Do you have his number?"

Jillian felt like she was somewhere far away and this voice was coming to her through a very narrow tunnel and it seemed to be echoing. She heard someone tell the inspector that he already had Brynn's number, and then realized it was her own voice. She automatically gave him Tim's number and said she had no knowledge about Dan's assistant, other than the office number she had already provided. "Where do you want me to be now?"

"You don't have to do this. It is not typical for me to bring a civilian to a murder scene. But it could speed things up, I think, if you could come to Mr. Harrington's flat. The murder of your friend and Harrington are connected. I'm not sure how or why, but I think the answer is in your head somewhere. So if you could, I would really appreciate your getting here as soon as possible. I'll text you his address when we hang up—I need to get it from someone. How long will it take you to get here?"

Jillian responded without protest. "Of course I'll come. I don't know. I think maybe an hour or two. It's almost 2:00 now. I'll get there as soon as I can. What is going on?"

"I might know more by the time you get here. I've barely just arrived myself. When you called earlier, we learned Mr. Harrington had been missing and that local police were on their way to locate him in Pacific Heights and in Napa. Several other people had reported him missing, so there was already an alert about him. The police officer here talked with the concierge at his apartment building, who said that his car was in its parking place. They decided to check his flat, and when he didn't answer, the concierge unlocked the door and found Mr. Harrington. It looks like he's been dead for a day or two."

Jillian was trying to think what it was she had wanted to ask, but her mind was not functioning. She could not remember anything at the moment. "I'll try to leave here in the next five minutes. It will probably take me an hour or two—I'm in downtown San Jose. I'll get there as soon as I can."

"Thanks. I'll see you shortly. Oh—and bring that list of names that your CFO gave you—the one that's the same as what we found in your friend's car. Miss Hillcrest, I'm sure you can appreciate that this is just too big a coincidence for these two murders not to be related."

"Of course. I'll bring the list."

"Again, please do not talk with anyone or inform anyone of Mr. Harrington's death."

Jillian was stunned. She didn't know what to think, and even doubted that she could think. She went through the motions of preparing to leave the conference. She gathered her purse, computer, and other things she had accumulated that day. She remembered Inspector Sherwood had asked her to do something, and then recalled he wanted the list of companies Harrington had given to her, so she checked her briefcase to be sure she had the folder with the list, and then headed for her car. When she got there, her phone indicated the text message from Inspector Sherwood with the Pacific Heights address. She added it to her GPS navigator, and let the robotic voice talk her out of downtown San Jose onto the freeway north to San Francisco.

Why did the inspector want her to come to the place where Dan had been—did he say—strangled? What could she provide? Was she a suspect? Oh, that's absurd. Why would Jillian be a suspect? And if she were a suspect, surely Inspector Sherwood would not be asking her to come to Dan's flat. Maybe he thought Jillian knew something more than she was telling?

Then the actual reality of what had happened hit her. Someone had strangled Dan Harrington. His life had been abruptly stopped, as had Lisa's. Both of these vibrant people no longer existed. She reflected on her last meeting at the company when Dan had proudly given her a bottle of wine made from his latest grapes. He was so very much alive.

Nonetheless, unlike Lisa's death, Jillian could quickly imagine motives for killing Dan. He was worth tens of millions—if not hundreds of millions—of dollars, and that amount of money could fuel avarice to cross the line into criminal activity.

Jillian's mind began to reel with questions and possibilities. If it had happened in his flat, did that mean he knew the person who killed him? How likely was it that Dan would let someone in that he didn't know? Then Jillian remembered what it was she had wanted to ask Inspector Sherwood. It was about the broker who had called, asking her to identify Dan because he was opening a new account. But when Jillian had mentioned it to Dan, he had said he hadn't touched his accounts or opened anything for weeks. And Dan's assistant was on vacation—or was he? Did he possibly open an account in Dan's name and then disappear? For what reason? Was it possible the assistant was able to transfer funds from one account to another in Dan's name? Could he have killed Dan when he found out? If so, what did that have to do with Lisa and the list of biotech companies?

Had Dan already been killed on Wednesday when he was supposed to meet Tim? Jillian tried to remember when she had last talked to Dan, which was when he told her that he was meeting Tim and also that he had not recently created any new brokerage accounts. She recalled getting a message from him Wednesday morning while she was at Brynn's staff meeting between 9:00 and 10:00. She had called him back but there was no answer. It seemed to her he had called the night before asking for the number of the broker who had called. That was when he told her he thought something strange was happening to his account. He was scheduled to have lunch with Tim at 1:00 on Wednesday. So something could have happened to him between 9:00 and 1:00 on Wednesday. Good—she was organized enough to share all of this with Inspector Sherwood when she arrived.

Jillian considered calling him to let him know about the broker and the new account and the timeline vis-à-vis her communications with Dan, but then decided she would be seeing him soon enough. He was most likely busy at the crime scene and a phone call would be more of an interruption than anything. She tried to focus on driving, but her mind continued to wander. According to Brynn, Dan had asked her to evaluate the companies to corroborate the work from the financial advisor he had hired. That seemed a little strange and why Brynn? And why had Dan seemed so anxious about it? As Jillian recalled, he had contacted her several times to be sure Brynn had received the folder. If he had someone else doing research, surely corroboration of the analysis couldn't be that urgent—unless he needed to invest quickly to take advantage of specific future events, like an FDA Advisory Committee Meeting or product launch.

Jillian had not had a chance to carefully review Brynn's comments on the list nor compare her comments to those from Lisa. Brynn's comments appeared to be more thoughtful with multiple references, while Lisa's were basically downloads from the Internet. Regardless, Jillian had not compared the output to see how close the two were. She would recommend to Inspector Sherwood that someone compare the two analyses to see if there were any glaring differences. She wasn't sure if that would matter, but it seemed like something someone should do just in case the differences might offer a lead as to why both Lisa and Dan were murdered.

Traffic on Highway 101 on Friday afternoon was definitely slowing Jillian's progress, so she decided to cross over to Interstate 280 where sometimes traffic moved faster. She was not sure why the inspector wanted her to come to Dan's flat. It was going to take at least two hours to get there. She decided to let him know her status so she put on her headset and pushed the "most recent call" button. He answered almost immediately.

"I just wanted to let you know that it's very slow, and it will take me longer than I originally estimated."

"O.K., thanks for the call. Just get here when you can."

"Also, I remembered that the last time I spoke with Dan Harrington was Tuesday night. He also called me and left a message Wednesday morning. I remembered something else that might be important. I got a call from an online broker asking me to verify Dan Harrington's identity. The broker said that Dan had set up a new account, although no funds had been transferred. He wanted me to verify that I knew Dan, although by the time I got back to him he had received all the necessary pieces of identification. However, when I mentioned this to Dan, he said that he hadn't opened any new accounts. I gave him the broker's contact information, which I can give to you as soon as I arrive."

She was hoping Inspector Sherwood would say, "Thank you," and that she didn't need to come to Pacific Heights after all, but no such luck.

"That's very helpful. Thanks. I really appreciate your coming here. I really believe that you can help expedite pursuit of the killer. Again please don't talk to anyone."

She disconnected, after repeating it would be a while before she arrived, but she would be there as soon as she could. About that time, traffic thinned out somewhat and she was able to speed all the way up to 50 mph. She tried to empty her mind of the murders and focus entirely on her driving; going faster in rush-hour traffic with its frequent stop-and-go cycles can lead to more serious accidents than just fender benders.

Although she continued to mull over everything that had happened between her company and Dan Harrington, she was paying more attention to traffic patterns and exits and arrived safely to the street where the investor had lived. The GPS had been unable to find the exact location Jillian had entered so she was searching for the number in the semi-dark of a late stormy March afternoon. However, she did not see the address and decided she must have missed it so drove back to the original location—and still did not see the address. Nor did she see any police cars or flashing lights. She was tired and hungry, so she could have missed it. However, after driving back and forth and still not seeing the address she decided that perhaps the inspector gave her the wrong address. She had no choice but to call him one more time. "I'm sorry, Inspector Sherwood, but could you please check the address you gave me? I can't seem to find the house. I'm on his street here in Pacific Heights."

He repeated the number, and Jillian realized he had juxtaposed the two numbers in his initial message.

"Let me try this address in my GPS. If it works, you'll see me shortly. If not, I'll call you back."

Jillian entered the corrected number into her GPS, and it told her she had two miles to go, which turned out to be strictly uphill, as so many streets are in San Francisco. She arrived at her destination, an ornate multi-story building with a fountain in front and an incredible view of San Francisco and the Bay itself. There were several police cars parked in front and people coming and going. She finally located a parking spot almost two blocks away and parked her XB, picked up her briefcase and purse, locked the car, and walked toward the front of the building. As she was entering, a police officer stopped her and asked to see her identification and explain why she was there. She responded that Inspector Sherwood from the San Francisco Police had asked to see her. The uniformed policeman asked her to wait, and called someone on his handheld communicator.

As she waited, she noticed a much more ornate lobby than that of her own building, with what appeared to be velvet wallpaper, two over-stuffed down sofas, three Louis XIV style chairs, and heavy marble tables with two- to three-foot tall bouquets of exotic flowers. There was also a fire in the stone fireplace at one end of the room. Her admiration was cut short by the return of the police officer, who asked her to follow him to the elevator (which she hadn't noticed because the wood panels of the doors blended with those of the walls). He pushed the button to the fourth floor and smiled only briefly—he was definitely all business. When the door opened, Inspector Sherwood appeared just outside the elevator and greeted them abruptly.

"Hello, Miss Hillcrest. Thank you for coming. Also, do you have the name and number of that stockbroker?"

"Yes, of course." As they were entering the flat at a rapid pace, Jillian pulled out her phone, pulled up the phone number from her "recent calls" list and gave it to him. He, in turn, called someone and relayed the information to him. Jillian was exhausted and somewhat numb. She had been up since before dawn and had eaten almost nothing. She was having difficulty focusing on what the inspector was saying. He seemed to be repeating himself as he guided her.

"Let's go in here. Could you please put these on?" He handed her a pair of paper booties, which Jillian placed over her shoes. "Follow me."

Jillian was aware of a modest entrance to what appeared to be a two-story flat. As they entered, she noticed the tape outline of a body apparent on the floor of a doorway from the entrance hall to what appeared to be a dining room. She assumed that was where they had found Dan Harrington. Fortunately the body had been removed, but the impact of the tape on Jillian caused her to start shaking and reminded her that Lisa's body, too, probably had a tape outline. Images of Lisa at the morgue forced themselves into Jillian's mind, which she pushed down with difficulty as she followed the preoccupied Inspector Sherwood into another room.

This room appeared to be a library since there were floor to ceiling bookcases filled with books next to a large stone fireplace. Inspector Sherwood noted her condition, motioned for her to sit, and asked for the list of companies. Jillian obediently pulled the two out of her briefcase and showed him both lists pointing out the obvious—the two lists were the same. She also said she thought it might be helpful if she spent a few minutes reviewing the printed remarks prepared by both Brynn and Lisa to compare them. It might not mean anything, but it seemed like something she could do.

Inspector Sherwood asked her to review again the timetable of when she had last spoken to Dan. She repeated what she had already told him on the phone adding the conclusion she had reached that Harrington had left her a message between 9:00 and 10:00 on Wednesday, and had not gone to a lunch meeting that day with her CEO, so it was possible he had been killed Wednesday morning.

Inspector Sherwood produced a tired half-hearted smile at her amateur sleuthing, and then nodded. "When did you get the original call from the broker asking about Harrington?"

"Actually it was when I was on my way to meet you at the hospital after you called about Lisa last Friday. I didn't talk to him that day. I thought it was a mistake and as you can imagine I was distracted. I believe I did finally talk to him Monday, which is when he told me Dan was opening a new account, although there were no funds or stock involved. He said he was double-checking Dan's references, although everything seemed above board. This seemed really strange to me, and I told him that. He backed off, then said he was feeling more comfortable about the transaction since all of the correct passwords and information had been provided."

"And when did you mention this to Harrington?"

"I think it was Tuesday. At first he thought it was a mistake, too. But, he called back later and asked for the number of the broker who had called me, which I sent him that evening, I think. Then he phoned again Wednesday morning while I was in a meeting and left a message to call him back, which I did. But he didn't answer."

"Yes, we have that message on his phone, and a lot of others as well."

A young man in a suit entered the room urgently. "Inspector, I need to speak with you right away."

The two went out to the hall, and Jillian heard the inspector exclaim, "How much?! Holy shit!!!" Then she couldn't hear anything else.

Her phone was playing "Once Upon a Time," which caused Inspector Sherwood to look in on her. She looked questioningly at him but he shook his head "no," so she let the call go to voicemail. Since she couldn't hear what the inspectors were saying, she studied the room. Someone had spent a lot of money and thought decorating it. Chad would enjoy seeing this place. The antique desk (Chad would know its origin) was the focal point of the room. Almost as impressive was the stone fireplace, which extended up the wall to the 12-foot high ceiling. Jillian surmised that the chairs and settee were stuffed with soft down as she sank into the chair deeply and comfortably. There were no drapes— just some kind of deep mulberry fabric drawn into knots over an elegant brass rod on either side of the window to allow people to see as much of the view as possible. It was approaching 5:00 p.m., and the lights in the Bay Area made for an incredible view.

Inspector Sherwood came into the room. Jillian noted that he was animated and feared that something else bad had happened. "Tell me again exactly what Mr. Harrington said when you told him about the call you had from the broker."

Jillian thought for a moment. "At first he didn't say anything. He seemed to agree with me it must have been some kind of mistake. I think I told him I would send him the phone number of the person who had called, because when he called back . . ."

"And when was that call?"

"I believe it was late Tuesday morning around noon. I had sent the logistics to the people participating on the panel regarding the conference that happened today—via e-mail. Dan was supposed to be there. Anyway, I sent an e-mail confirming everything, and Dan called. It was then I mentioned about the broker. Oh, I think he said it must have been a mistake because there had been no activity in his accounts for quite a while. Oh, and that his assistant was on vacation, so he was pretty sure he hadn't done anything either. As I recall, I transferred him to Brynn, that's our CFO and my boss, although I don't know if she talked with him or not."

"Don't worry about her. We'll talk to her separately. Then when did he tell you that he thought something was wrong? Again exactly what did he say?"

"Well, I think he called me that night, so that would have been Tuesday. He asked me to send the phone number of the broker, which I did. And I think he said he needed to check his accounts because there was something strange about them."

"He used the word 'strange'?"

"I think so, but it could have been 'unusual' or some similar word."

"You also said that he called you Wednesday morning and left a message. What time was that?"

"It was during a meeting between nine and ten. I noticed it as soon as I left the room and tried him back by ten-fifteen at the latest. All he said in his message was to please call him."

The inspector looked pensive. "And that was the last you heard from him?"

"Yes. Then that same day Tim, our CEO, came back from lunch and said Dan had not shown up to a meeting he had requested. At the time, I wondered if he'd had a setback from his bicycle accident."

"Bicycle accident?"

"Well, apparently Dan did a lot cycling and had had an accident. He arrived at our company last Friday with a neck brace, a cane, and some bruises. He made light of it, although it looked like he was in pain."

Inspector Sherwood made some notes. "Again, we'll get that information from your CEO about his meeting with Harrington. How did you know Mr. Harrington's assistant was on vacation?"

Jillian thought for a moment. "Well, I think Dan mentioned it. But also I called Dan's office when he didn't show at the symposium this morning. His voicemail said his assistant was on vacation and to leave a message and that someone would return the call. Do you think he had something to do with this?"

"We're looking at all possibilities. We don't know how much his assistant was involved with his affairs, but it's logical to assume he might have had knowledge of Harrington's passwords and accounts." He checked his notes. "His name is Lloyd Jenkins."

"Yes, that sounds right. I've only spoken with him a couple of times. He has always been helpful at arranging meetings."

"Have you ever met him?"

Jillian remembered meeting a young man when Brynn, Tim, and she first visited Harrington's office six months ago. "It's possible I met him. When we visited his office, there was a young man—in his mid-twenties, I'd say—who sat in the meeting and seemed to be helping Dan. That could have been him."

"Can you describe him?"

"As I said, he was in his mid-twenties, about six feet—I remember that he was not a lot shorter than our CEO who is about six-three. He had dark hair—no facial hair. I couldn't guess his weight but he seemed to be in pretty good shape—maybe he weighed about two hundred?"

"Is there anything else you can remember about him? Did Harrington happen to mention where his assistant might have gone?"

"No, I don't recall hearing anything other than that he was on vacation. And I barely knew him. He just seemed like an efficient MBA type who was working as Harrington's assistant to learn about the world of finance. He seemed bright, and certainly personable, very efficient. He was very good at keeping Dan's calendar. I assumed the reason we didn't hear from Dan on Wednesday and today might have been because he was on vacation. Why would you think he'd have anything to do with this?"

The inspector was studying Jillian, and seemed to make a decision. "Well, we think Harrington's death might have something to do with the eight million dollars worth of stocks that were transferred out of his accounts into this newly created account—yesterday—a day after his death and with all the proper passwords. And his assistant might know something about that."

"What?! Wow! Someone transferred eight million dollars out of his accounts after he was already dead?" Something clicked in Jillian's tired mind. "Maybe the financial advisor who was helping Dan evaluate the stocks on that list—maybe he knows something."

"We're trying to identify him. Do you have any idea who it might be?"

"No, none whatsoever. Given that both Harrington and Lisa had the same exact list of companies, I was thinking maybe Lisa was working with him, although she was a market—rather than a financial—analyst. However, she would have been valuable at assessing the competitive positioning of the companies. But certainly his assistant would know. Also, Brynn—our CFO—might have some inkling. She had talked to Dan about that list and was the one working on it. Have you been able to reach her?"

"Someone is speaking with her right now. And we are also talking to your CEO. Was there anyone else at your company who knew Harrington besides the three of you?"

Jillian tried to remember who had spoken with him. "Well, we're the main people. Our CSO—sorry, that's Chief Scientific Officer—he's one of the founders—also met him and did a presentation, but I don't think they met outside our office. Oh, and I'm not positive, but I also think one of our executives, Archie Linstrom, met with him at a local restaurant a few days ago. I wasn't sure; I only saw the person briefly. That would have been Tuesday, I think, but you might ask him. I can't believe it—eight million dollars! Wow. Now that you know about it, you'll be able to retrieve it, won't you? That certainly is a motive for murder, isn't it? I mean, whoever did that won't be able to get away with it, will they?"

"Not if we can help it. We are in the process of freezing all of Harrington's assets. He was divorced, so I'm not sure who will inherit his estate. His ex-wife, by the way, lives in Vancouver, British Columbia, and has not left there for at least the past six months. Although the stock was transferred to a different account, it was still in Harrington's name, so whoever made the transfer knew his codes and passwords, and will still need to sell it to get any equity. That's why we want to talk to his assistant. We're trying to keep the discovery of Harrington's body quiet, to tempt the thief into trying to sell or transfer the stock. He'll still need to use Harrington's identification, as the new accounts are in Harrington's name."

Jillian was trying to process all of this, and despite being upset over Dan's death, the mystery was reinvigorating her. "So maybe the stock got transferred last week or early this week. Dan didn't know about it nor suspect anything until I told him about the broker contacting me. Then he asked his assistant about it, and maybe his assistant killed him? And then left? Or something like that?"

"Maybe. We're not sure exactly when the assistant left. But it's not out of the question. Eight million dollars is a lot of motive. The medical examiner should be able to tell us more about how Harrington died following an autopsy. He might have been subdued prior to the actual strangling. There have been cases recently of a victim being tazered and then strangled. Also, there could have been more than one person involved."

"Given his injuries from the bicycle accident, he might have been easier to subdue than usual. But how does this involve Lisa? And why is the list of companies relevant?"

The inspector was again thoughtful. Jillian considered the obvious: that being an inspector in charge of solving murders required a keen sense of puzzle solving. "I don't know. It's possible that your friend picked up on this somehow. That's why I wanted you here. You knew your friend and you knew Harrington. As of now, you are the only person who knew both. So I'm hoping that you'll notice something common to both of them that no one else might see."

"The only connection I am aware of is that list of companies. If you give those copies back to me, I'll review what both Brynn and Lisa said about the names to see if there is any connection there. Also, I don't quite get where that list fits in, unless they are the same companies whose stock was transferred out of Dan's accounts? Is that possible?"

"We're checking on that. We're just in the process of tracking down the actual broker who received the stock. We plan to freeze the stock and if anyone tries to access it, we have a way to track him or her. We're using that to try to pull in whoever is responsible. In the meantime, it would be helpful if you could review the two lists and the analyses to see if there is any information there. I'll get you a copy of what your CFO provided; here is the copy back that I gave you earlier from your friend, Lisa. Of course, it is possible that the two murders are not connected, but all my instincts say otherwise."

Jillian still did not understand the connection between her friend Lisa and the investor Dan Harrington. That Dan had been killed for a large sum of money at least made some sense. But Lisa had little money. Somehow, however, she might be connected to Dan. But why was she killed? Had she overheard something that would lead police to whoever had been planning to kill Dan? Was it possible Dan Harrington was the person Lisa met on that fateful morning? Harrington had asked Brynn to review the list of companies. Perhaps he had also asked Lisa to review the list. Maybe he had told her something that concerned his killer. And, if Dan's assistant had also attended the meeting, he too would have heard the conversation and, well, who knows?

It still seemed hard to believe someone had murdered these people whom Jillian knew. She enjoyed murder mysteries and cop shows as fiction—she liked the puzzle of figuring out "whodunit." However, she was definitely sure she did not appreciate being part of a real one.

Why Lisa? Lisa was basically a market analyst who did research to assess the potential market for new biotech products. Due to the approval cycle, there was such a long time from development of a product until its marketing that companies needed detailed background information to determine market potential and the competitive landscape. Given the percentage of products that made it to market—the biopharmaceutical industry spent more than $65 billion on drug development in 2008 with only 24 drugs approved by the FDA—a successful company was careful to conduct as much research as early as possible to minimize the failure rate. Lisa's expertise had been in assessing the market potential of new drugs and in ways to market them.

One of the officers brought Jillian a copy of the research Brynn had done. Jillian opened both folders—the one with Brynn's work and the one from Lisa. Because there was no identification on either except for the outside folder, Jillian was careful to keep the contents separate. Brynn had obviously had more time to consolidate and prepare her list—she had summarized information with the pertinent facts. Lisa's folder, on the other hand, just included printouts of information from various sources on each company. That made Jillian wonder if Lisa had prepared a similar summary of each company and given it to her mysterious recipient that morning. It was likely Lisa would provide only the end-research to whomever she was meeting. So whatever else she found would have been summarized in a report that was most likely on her computer. Where was her computer? Did the police find it? Like Jillian, her friend seldom traveled without it. She would have used it to take notes if she was having a meeting with someone that morning. It might also have a lead about whomever she was meeting. She made a note to ask Inspector Sherwood what they had found on Lisa's computer.

Jillian next looked at each company and compared the information from both Brynn and Lisa. It looked like Brynn was able to add some extra input beyond what was available on the Internet. As Jillian noted when she first reviewed Lisa's folder, the printed material appeared to be downloads from various websites. There was no additional analysis. Given Lisa's knowledge of the industry, Jillian assumed that Lisa, too, would have produced additional information about each company or at least added her analysis of the potential of each company. Jillian was familiar with about half of the companies on the list, and agreed with the conclusions reached by Brynn. However, she did not have access to Lisa's assessment so could not compare them. There were several companies on the list with no corresponding printouts in Lisa's folder. Jillian checked Brynn's review and saw a notation about those companies that there was no printed information about them. Brynn had contacted several of her analyst friends to learn about them, and had summarized what she had discovered. These companies were very young and were looking for seed money.

Jillian theorized that the folder in Lisa's car was most likely just her original research; she hadn't needed to give it to her client. Maybe the killer was not aware it existed. The police really needed to examine Lisa's computer and briefcase. However, Jillian suspected if there had been any information on Lisa's computer or in her briefcase the police would have found it by that point.

Inspector Sherwood entered the room and asked if she was making any progress. Jillian inquired if they had examined Lisa's computer and briefcase. The inspector said they had not found a computer or a briefcase—just her purse. "Well, she was probably carrying both with her, so maybe the killer took them. I've been thinking about things and have some ideas I'd like to run past you.

"First, I think this list is a clue to why she was killed. For some reason, the killer did not want anyone to know he knew about it. Maybe it connected him to someone, or something. The killer probably didn't know Lisa had additional information in her car. However, I truly believe he or she didn't want a connection made between Lisa and this list. Basically, this folder just contains the raw research Lisa downloaded. Her final report would have looked similar to my CFO's printed report—it would have been an analysis, although more about the competition and market potential. But that report isn't here, so she most likely gave it to whomever she was meeting, but did not give this downloaded information to him because she incorporated it into her report. The fact that her computer and briefcase are also missing reinforces that theory—again, the killer wanted to remove any evidence or connection between the list, Lisa, and him.

"Point number two: this list is the same one Dan Harrington gave to me for Brynn to review. He wanted Brynn's input specifically to compare to that of his new analyst. He told her this was a list of companies he was investigating for the purpose of investing. Therefore, we can assume this was his list, i.e., that he created it. So how did Lisa get it? Did Dan Harrington also give it to Lisa? That doesn't seem likely because he wouldn't care if anyone knew he had given her the list. And I truly believe that the person who killed her did so to keep anyone from knowing he was associated with that list. Therefore, Lisa's killer was not Dan Harrington. Rather the person who gave the list to Lisa did so clandestinely and did not want anyone to know he or she had the list. Once he got the information from Lisa, she became dispensable and a liability because she could connect the killer to that list and Dan Harrington. So, bottom line, my conclusion is that the list was prepared by Dan and holds the key to at least Lisa's murder."

"Thanks." Inspector Sherwood smiled appreciatively. "That's some good sleuthing. We are also working on the stock angle. We are sure that it's a big part of all this, specifically Dan Harrington's murder. Of course, it's always the money. We have gotten in touch with the receptionist at Harrington's office and she gave us the contact information for his assistant. According to her, he's in Puerto Vallarta at his sister's place. She e-mailed him to get in touch with us as soon as possible, as he apparently did not take a cell phone (given the high roaming charges in Mexico) and the house where he's staying does not have a telephone—hard to believe. Also, he doesn't have a computer with him. He is using an old computer in the house."

Sherwood checked his notes. "She said that she had no knowledge of any stocks being transferred for Harrington, and was surprised to hear that it had happened. Also, she was not aware of anyone working with Harrington other than his staff, although she did say that he had been doing a lot of research into your company lately. Given that she had just heard the news about Harrington's death, she was fairly coherent, but I will talk to her again."

Jillian absorbed this information, but was not sure what to say. "Do you need me here any more tonight?" It was close to 7:00 and Jillian had not eaten for hours—she had barely touched breakfast and lunch. Chad had called again, and she really wanted to let him know what was happening. "Also, can I call my ex-husband and let him know about all this?"

"Yes, you can talk with him. We checked him out pretty thoroughly and, as far as we can tell, he has no relationships to your company or to Mr. Harrington. We are still interviewing your CEO and CFO, so I would appreciate it if you do not contact them until you hear from me."

Jillian was curious, but assumed this was due to some sort of police procedure. She probably wouldn't be seeing them over the weekend anyway, although they were all scheduled to be in New York together in a few days. "Oh, by the way, the three of us are traveling to New York next week. Tim, the CEO, is scheduled to give a presentation. I assume that won't be a problem?"

To Jillian's surprise, the inspector looked like it would be a problem. "When are you scheduled to travel?"

"I'm in the process of re-booking my flights—as you'll recall I thought I was going to Philadelphia first, now it's reversed—anyway, I plan to fly Monday to New York for several days and then to Philadelphia returning most likely the following Tuesday or Wednesday. At a minimum, Tim needs to be there on Wednesday for his presentation. If necessary, we could re-book the meetings scheduled for Tuesday, but the current plan is for Brynn and Tim to arrive late Monday and return mid-afternoon Thursday. You don't really suspect them in any of this, do you?"

"Well, I can't restrict them from traveling. Only a judge could do that. Regarding whether they are involved, it is too early to say. We don't know." Jillian sensed there was something more, but she was too tired and hungry to try to figure out why Inspector Sherwood's reaction caused her to think that. "At any rate, I want them to have a fresh perspective without anything else influencing their memory of events."

The same policeman who had been in and out of the room most of the evening entered and asked Inspector Sherwood to step out for a moment. Although Jillian truly appreciated the situation and the inspector's desire to solve what now appeared to be a double homicide, she really wanted to get something to eat and she wanted to talk to Chad and she wanted to go home. She was relieved she didn't have to travel to Philadelphia tomorrow as originally planned. Maybe Chad and she could spend some time together. My God! It had been a week since Lisa and she had met at the wine bar. Jillian was at least glad she didn't have to go to the hospital to identify another body. She assumed someone else had that duty for Dan Harrington.

"Miss Hillcrest, as I said, we're still in the process of interviewing your boss, Brynn Bancroft. And your CEO. However, to answer your question, you can call your ex-husband, but I would really appreciate your not discussing the case. Tell him that I asked that you not talk about it. You can tell him about Harrington's murder, because I must confess I'm a little worried about you—so would like him to be aware of the possible danger. Ask him not to tell anyone else so that we can continue executing our plans to attract a possible killer. Do you have somewhere you could go over the weekend?"

As tired and hungry as she was, Jillian had become more and more apprehensive as the inspector described his concern for her. However, she really wanted to go home, so she decided to ignore it. Maybe Chad could come over. "I'm probably safe in my flat, Inspector. There are people around, and there is always someone at the front desk. And my lock was just changed. Also, thanks for letting me tell Chad about Harrington."

It took Jillian about two seconds to call Chad. She was incredibly disappointed when he didn't answer. She left a message asking him to call her, and then she headed out to her car. The view was breathtaking. Ah—it must be nice to be rich. Well, maybe not so nice if it invited murderers into your house, but the view was outstanding.

She got in her car, and asked her GPS to take her home. What an event-packed day. She could not even remember how it started, but she knew it was a long time ago. She hoped the conference had finished well. She should have been there to greet people and answer questions, but she had to tend to a murder—the second one in a week—instead! Hopefully at some point her colleagues would overlook her sudden departure. At the moment, though, she was as hungry as she was tired. She tried to remember if she had anything at home to eat. Tiredness won out, and she decided she could find something at home, if only an English muffin and a fried egg, or some cheese and crackers.

Her thoughts quickly returned to the events of the day and Dan

Harrington's death specifically. Where did his assistant fit into the puzzle? And if it had been Archie Linstrom meeting with Harrington on Tuesday, why were they meeting? If they were meeting to discuss the company, Archie should have talked with Jillian first—or at least with Tim. Maybe he did. Also, who else had reported Harrington missing? What did they have to do with this? Jillian continued to believe the connection between the two murders was the list of companies Dan had apparently created. Maybe he had asked Lisa to investigate the list—and then went to Brynn for a comparison. Maybe it was as simple as he was planning to hire Lisa. But then why would someone have killed her?

When Jillian arrived home, she handed her car over to a new person who introduced himself as Tom, who said he would be working the night shift and offered his cell phone number. She wearily thanked him. Remembering she had arisen at 5:00 that morning, she allowed herself to be tired. She pulled out her key, opened the front door as quickly as possible, grabbed her mail, and headed for the elevator. The night clerk was at the desk and he was also new. She again unenthusiastically introduced herself and welcomed him. As the elevator door was closing, she noticed he was talking on his cell. She wondered if the inspector was keeping an eye on her.

She passed by Mrs. Anderson's door remembering she owed the woman her RSVP for dinner the following night. Strange—she had not heard back from Chad. Maybe he had a function tonight. He often had to entertain customers and partners.

She had difficulty unlocking her door, and then remembered that she had changed the lock, so searched for the new key and entered her dark room—so no one had been there to turn on her lights. Just as she closed the door, her phone played Chad's song. "Hi, Chad. How are you?"

"Good. How was your conference? Are you O.K.? Your message sounded strange."

Jillian laughed and her tone was almost a shriek. "Strange? Is that all? You won't believe the day I've had. I'll tell you about it in a minute, but first, can you join me for dinner at Mrs. Anderson's tomorrow night? She invited you, or I should say she invited 'that nice young man who visits' me. I would appreciate it. I need to let her know right away."

"Sure, but I want to know what's going on." Chad had detected the shrillness in Jillian's voice and the rapid pace of her speaking.

"Good, I'll let her know. As for everything else, I hardly know where to start. But I guess the best place is to tell you that there has been another murder, which might be related to Lisa's."

"Who? Who has been murdered? And are you sure you're all right?"

"Yes, I'm fine. The person who was murdered is a hedge fund manager who was investigating Harmonia Therapeutics as a possible investment. I only knew him as a business colleague. He was supposed to speak on my panel at the conference today, but he didn't show up. Oh, and remember that list of companies Inspector Sherwood gave me at the morgue—the one from Lisa's luggage? Well, Brynn was working on that same list that the second murder victim, a man named Harrington, had given to me to give to her. I hadn't even looked at it. Which is why there might be a connection. Anyway, Inspector Sherwood said I could tell you about the murder, but no one else, because they are setting a trap for the killer." Jillian had spewed these words at a very rapid pace.

Chad was quiet for a second. "Does the inspector believe that you are in any danger?"

"Maybe, although I feel pretty safe here. And I think they have added policemen to the staff, because we have a new person parking cars and a new concierge. Of course, that could just be coincidence. Also, did I tell you I had the lock changed? I can give you more details about everything when you come over tomorrow."

Even as Jillian was telling Chad how safe she felt, she was double-checking her front door to make sure it was securely locked.

Chad was not convinced. "I think I should come over tonight, and—"

Jillian interrupted. For some reason, she resented his protective gesture. "Chad, really, I'm safe here. I've even locked the sliding glass door to the balcony. There is someone downstairs, and the front door is locked. I'll be fine. I won't let anyone into the flat. I promise. Just come over tomorrow afternoon and we'll have a nice dinner with Mrs. Anderson and her son, and then we can go out for breakfast on Sunday . . . oh, did I say breakfast?"

Chad laughed. "All right. I want you to check your door right now, and call me in the morning when you get up and no later than 8:30. I need to do some stuff in the morning, but I will be in constant touch with you, and I'll let you know what time to expect me."

"Sounds good. Oh, and by the way, you won't believe it, but Mrs. Anderson—you know my neighbor with the wreaths—used to be a police officer. Cool, huh? Hard to believe."

"That's interesting. Maybe we can get her to tell us some cool stories. See you tomorrow. Bye."

With that Jillian disconnected, undressed, and fell fast asleep uncharacteristically forgetting her hunger.

32

Jillian awakened to her phone ringing—and it wasn't her alarm. She realized she hadn't charged it but fortunately it still had some battery left. It was about 8:00, which seemed early for someone to be calling on a Saturday morning, but with all that was going on in her life, Jillian did not hesitate to answer the "private caller." "This is Jillian Hillcrest."

"Miss Hillcrest? This is Dan Shell. You don't know my name. I am working with Inspector Sherwood on the Lisa Baumgartner case. He wants to see you as soon as possible this morning in the Woodside area. He said to tell you to meet him at Buck's of Woodside, the restaurant, and the two of you could go from there. He has something he needs to show you."

"What?" Jillian was barely awake.

"Do you know where that restaurant is?"

"Sure, but what could he possibly want to show me up there?"

The caller was not forthcoming. "I don't know, ma'am. I just know that he asked me to phone you and to get you there as soon as possible. When would that be?"

"I guess it will take me at least an hour."

"I'll let him know." And before Jillian could ask any questions the voice disconnected.

Jillian was annoyed. She had been traveling a lot to help Inspector Sherwood. Why did he need to show her something relevant to Lisa's death up in the hills? And it looked foggy outside. Of course she would go, but she felt the need to complain about it.

As she was getting dressed, she called downstairs to have her car ready. Then she called Chad—who did not answer—and left him a message that she needed to leave to meet Inspector Sherwood about Lisa's case, and she would let him know when she expected to return, but hopefully it wouldn't take too long.

She knocked quietly on Mrs. Anderson's door. She wasn't sure how early the retired woman started her day, but was hoping that since her son was arriving that morning, she would be up. Indeed she was.

"Good morning, Jillian. So will you and that hunk of an ex-husband of yours be coming for dinner? I do hope so."

Jillian laughed. "Yes, we are both coming. And we are both looking forward to it. When does your son arrive?"

"Well, he said he would arrive right after lunch, so I expect he should be here by 2:00 or so. Can you and your young man—I forget—what's his name?"

"His name is Chad Bradbury. We've been divorced for a year or so—but we're still very good friends."

Mrs. Anderson smiled knowingly. "Well, why don't you and Chad come over about six o'clock for drinks; then we'll start dinner around seven. That should work. Are you headed out for shopping?"

Jillian had stopped being either surprised or annoyed at the woman's curiosity about her whereabouts. "No, I'm meeting the inspector at Buck's of Woodside. Something to do with my friend's case. I'm feeling a little annoyed about it—I would prefer to be going to Buck's for breakfast at this time of day—but if it helps solve her murder, well, I feel like I have to go."

"Well, be careful up there. It's foggy today. And I'm really looking forward to dinner tonight and meeting your EX."

Jillian said good-bye and headed for her rendezvous. Buck's was a well-known Silicon Valley restaurant and meeting place, and she wished she were going there with Chad to have a traditional breakfast rather than to help with a murder case. Traffic was light, but it took her almost an hour to get to the restaurant, whose parking lot was quite full of Saturday morning breakfast diners. However, she found a place and just as she was walking into the restaurant, her phone rang and displayed "private caller." Again, it was the same policeman who had called earlier. He apologized on behalf of the inspector and said that he wanted to meet Jillian somewhere for which he had to give her directions. Jillian tried to interrupt but he seemed intent on getting the directions correct and he seemed to be in a hurry; his abruptness did not allow her anytime to comment. She had dug out a pen and an envelope with a to-be-paid bill in it and wrote down the directions. The voice didn't give her an address, just directions with landmarks to the destination.

So she got back in the car, and as the directions seemed fairly straightforward and, given that she didn't have an actual address, she didn't even turn on her GPS. She drove down the road and turned where she had been told. She crossed several roads and continued to climb higher. It had always amazed Jillian how there could be these deserted, winding roads surrounded by thick forest within an hour or so of San Francisco. The higher she climbed, the denser the fog became. She was beginning to be concerned as well as annoyed. She decided she needed to double-check with Inspector Sherwood about the directions, but realized she had no cell signal, not even a single bar. And right about then, although it was difficult to see, a deer ran out in front of her car—just a little deer—but Jillian swerved to avoid it and that was the last thing she remembered.

33

She was still behind the steering wheel of her XB. Something was bing, bing, binging. Her head felt enormous. Was that a branch in the passenger seat? What happened? Where was she? She tried to move—ouch! The air bag had deployed and her chest felt it. She was beginning to panic—she couldn't open the car door. She had to get out of the car. Where was her phone? She had to call someone.

Where was she? There was her phone—on the floor. Or was that the roof? No, that was the floor. She was right-side-up. Why couldn't she open the car door? She tried to look out and saw a tree lodged against the front of the car. What about the back door? No, there was nothing blocking the back door. Jillian tried to release her seat belt to climb into the back seat, but her fingers were not cooperating. At least two of them seemed to be just sort of dangling from her hand. Her left arm or shoulder also hurt and she tried very hard not to move them in order to avoid pain. She finally found a digit that would move and pushed the button on her seat belt.

Obviously she had been in an accident. What is it you are supposed to do first? Turn off the engine—at least it would stop the insufferable binging noise. Jillian reached out as best she could and turned the key in the ignition. Mercifully, the binging stopped.

She realized that crawling into the back seat was more an ideal than a possibility. She had to carefully avoid the pieces of glass from the windshield that covered her and the seat. The branch intruding into the passenger seat made it difficult to move. Or was that the pain that she now felt everywhere—especially her ribs. Nonetheless, her panic was driving her, and she reached down for her cell phone, anticipating that it would be her salvation. She grasped it with some effort, but was disappointed to see there was no cell coverage.

The significance of not being able to phone for help was overwhelming. The effort of picking it up had used all the energy Jillian had, so she sat back in her seat and took deep breaths to handle the pain. Why was she here? Oh, yes, Inspector Sherwood had something to show her about Lisa's murder. Why up here? What on earth could be here that was so important? He'd better be looking for her. At least he would have some idea where she was driving.

How long had she been here? Her watch said 9:45. And where was here? All she saw looking out the window was lots of brush, and leaves and tree trunks, and what appeared to be a steep hill. It seemed to Jillian all she had to do was to climb up the hill and she would be on the road—and surely then someone would drive by and rescue her.

Chad would also be looking for her. She had told him she would call when she was finished with the inspector. And he expected to meet her for dinner at Mrs. Anderson's. And Mrs. Anderson would be looking for her, also. Jillian started to feel less isolated as she realized all of these people would notice her absence.

However, if she couldn't get up the hill—she realized movement would not come easily—could they see her car from the road? Could they tell there was even a car down here? Well, surely they would have a search party. But Jillian began to worry that it would be difficult to find her, and she wasn't sure how badly she was injured or how long she could last. She needed to get out of the car and figure out a way to get up the hill or somehow call attention to herself.

Again, she focused on moving to the back seat and opening the rear door on the passenger side. She tried to push her seat back to give her more room to move and actually succeeded in moving it an inch or so. Somehow she got her knees under her and turned her back to the smashed windshield. She gripped the seat as the pain shot through her, leaving her breathless. She steadied herself and then crawled over the branch, half-falling and half-rolling into the back seat. Then the spinning started and it seemed like she was drifting off to sleep.

She had no idea how much time had passed before she was awake again. She was relieved to see she was somehow in the back seat. She pushed on the door handle and was ecstatic that the door opened, although not very far. She worked her way through the half-open door, falling into a clump of wet, green foliage. As Jillian was hardly an outdoorswoman, she had no idea if she was rolling into poison ivy or oak or whatever grew in California. She knew, however, that she was now not only in pain, but was also wet and very cold—in fact, she was shaking. She assumed that she was probably in shock, although it could be hunger since she hadn't eaten for 24 hours.

She continued to clutch her cell phone, as if it were her lifeline— and kept checking for cell coverage. The fog was still very thick and it was difficult to see very far. She tried to find the path her car must have created when it plunged down the hill. By backtracking its path she hoped to get back up to the road. She thought she heard a car passing, but couldn't be sure. The hill was quite steep, and she could barely move.

She decided to rest, but woke up even colder than before. She tried to recall if she had anything warm in the car, and remembered regrettably she had just had the car cleaned inside and out. She had been very proud of this, as she tended to collect things in her car. The gods were against her on that one.

She crawled a few more inches, intent on getting to the top of the embankment. However, at her current rate she realized it would take her hours to go even a few feet. She needed to use her brain. O.K., so she wasn't a survivalist. She could hear her mother's voice, "Jillian, you are a bright, healthy, young woman who ought to be able to figure a way out of this." What about a walking stick? Or something to help pull her up the hill?

She looked around for any kind of aid—a stick or vine—there probably weren't any vines in the California hills. What was in the car? The thought of crawling back to the car was not pleasant, but it occurred to Jillian there might be some tools in the back with the jack, which could be useful. However, she took one more look around first just in case she had missed something, and decided she needed to rest again for a few minutes.

After a while, Jillian checked her watch to see how long she had rested. It was now 11:00. She again checked her cell phone and grew even more panicked. She had forgotten to charge her phone the previous night, and was so rushed this morning that she had not plugged it into her car charger. The battery was getting low. She decided to save the battery by turning off the phone. She would turn it on only periodically.

It was so cold! Maybe the car was actually the best place for her right now. She started to crawl back to the car and realized she did not even have the energy to work her way inside through the half-open door. So she decided to crawl to the trunk. Unfortunately, it occurred to her she could not unlock the trunk because her keys were in the car, and she could not get into the car.

Even crying didn't help.

34

When he had not heard from her, Chad called Jillian just before noon. He was ready to start for her flat and wondered if she was home. It was unusual for her not to have called him back as promised. He was surprised when the call immediately went to voicemail, but left a message saying to call him as soon as she was available, and that he was on his way to her flat. If he arrived before she did, he would have lunch at that Mediterranean restaurant where they had had breakfast last week.

When he still didn't hear back from her, Chad had the new attendant park his car at Jillian's building and headed for the restaurant. Although a little anxious—but more annoyed at the inspector because Jillian had not returned yet—he thoroughly enjoyed the lunch and splurged by eating both spanakopita and moussaka. However, when he still had not heard from her by 2:00 p.m., he started to worry. He decided to call Inspector Sherwood to see when they would be finished, since for some reason Jillian was still not answering her phone. Unfortunately he did not have Inspector Sherwood's direct number, so it took a few calls to track him down.

"Hi, Inspector Sherwood, this is Chad Bradbury—Jillian Hillcrest's ex-husband. We met at the morgue last week when Jillian identified Lisa Baumgartner's body. I was wondering when you expect to finish your interview with her. She thought–"

Sherwood interrupted. "What do you mean? I've been trying to reach her all morning. We had a couple questions for her, but she hasn't called me back."

Chad began to feel very queasy. "You didn't contact her this morning for a meeting?"

"Absolutely not. What gave you that idea?" The inspector's apprehension was alarming.

"Oh, damn. She left me a message saying you had contacted her to meet and that she would call me as soon as she finished. We were scheduled to have dinner at her neighbor's flat tonight and when she didn't show—oh, Jesus, what's happened to her?"

Sherwood was already calling someone. "Tell me everything you can remember about her message. I've just sent a car over to her flat. Can you meet him?"

"Yes, I can meet him. I'll wait outside since I don't have a key. She said she had to go somewhere to meet you—she didn't say where. Just that someone had called her."

"I have her cell phone number. I'll see if we can trace whoever called her. In the meantime, introduce the officer to the concierge, the parking guy, and even the neighbor. Find out if Miss Hillcrest said anything to them this morning. Oh, and by the way, the new concierge is O.K., and he has a pass key to get into Miss Hillcrest's apartment."

35

Jillian spent several hours lying by the car hoping that someone would come. Surely they would start to look for her, and the inspector and his police helper had some idea of where she was. She listened for any sound that might be human but she was not sure she was even awake and conscious most of the time. She tried to move a few times, but found it far too painful. Nonetheless, as the day wore on, she realized she had to do something. She did not relish a night lying on the ground in the forest. She had tried to close her mind to the possibility of any kind of dangerous critters, and could not even envision what they might be.

She started to check out her injuries. One of the reasons it was so difficult to move was that her right leg appeared to be broken—she couldn't put any weight on it and it was swollen. Maybe if she put some kind of splint on it and found something to use as a crutch, she could make better progress climbing the hill. She had a jacket, a shirt, her jeans, and her bra—and it seemed to Jillian that the bra was the most logical tie for a splint. She looked for some sticks or twigs and saw a possible branch within crawling range. She headed for it, understanding it would not be easy to break it from its tree. However, it was low enough that Jillian thought she could break it by sitting on it. She pulled herself up and was pleased that her plan actually worked. The branch was easily two inches thick and about two feet long.

Next, Jillian took off the bra, which was painful given the excruciating pain from her bruised ribs. She did so as quickly as possible—not out of modesty but because it was very cold. She hurriedly re-dressed holding her breath against the rib pain and was grateful that she had worn her jacket. Now she needed to figure out how to jury-rig a splint with a bra and a tree branch. As she recalled, normally there are two parts to a splint, but Jillian decided to try to make it work with just one branch—the likelihood of finding another seemed unlikely. She gingerly fitted the branch to her leg. It would have been better to have two pieces of bra so she could tie it at the top and bottom, but no matter how hard she tried, she could not tear the bra in two. So she did her best to lash it to the thick part of the branch, taking some time to remove the outgrowth branches so they wouldn't scratch her through her jeans.

Jillian was now beginning to worry about sundown. It seemed to her it must be imminent. This concern helped to drive her to pull herself toward the hill. First, she made sure her cell phone was secure in her pocket. After moving several feet, she reached the steepest part of the hill. She looked for the best path to the top—places to hold onto to pull herself up—then started to drag herself up. The pain was unbelievable, especially in her ribs, and she had to stop frequently.

As she lay on her back trying to catch her breath after crawling a few more feet, she again reminded herself she was an intelligent human being who could figure things out. So she focused on the problem, studied the hill, and wondered if she could make better progress by going up backward, that is, by sitting and pushing with her good leg, dragging her bad leg while she used her arms to pull herself up using whatever holds were available. Experimenting with this approach resulted in doubling the distance for each push she made, and it seemed to take less effort. She continued to push her way upward, holding tightly to every branch, tree, root, or stone that offered support—she knew if she fell back down the hill, she would not have the energy to try again.

She did not reach the top before dusk, but she had checked the hill carefully and knew approximately where each handhold was located, and as the sun was setting, Jillian kept creeping up backward, ever closer to the top. She decided to check her cell phone one more time to see if she had a signal, but still there was none. However, she realized that the light from her phone was helpful, so she briefly used it like a flashlight to help guide her. Her progress was encouraging, and she was now less afraid of the dark than she had been earlier. She had grown somewhat accustomed to the pain. And she was angry. Even though she knew it wasn't Inspector Sherwood's fault— how could he know Jillian would hit a deer?—she was still upset he had gotten her into this mess. And as soon as she blamed him, she felt guilty because he wasn't the real bad guy—it was whoever was responsible for Lisa and Dan's deaths.

Jillian continued her slow upward progress. As she reached for the next handhold, she was dismayed to find there was nothing to grab hold of, so she pulled out her phone for the light, and collapsed on the highway.

She had made it to the top.

36

C had waited anxiously at the front door of Jillian's apartment building for the officer, who arrived within ten minutes. The two men rang the bell, entered the building, and checked with the concierge to see if Jillian had said anything to him that morning. However, they had only said good morning to each other, before Jillian left. She had called for her car between 8:00 and 9:00. The concierge called the parking attendant from that morning, but he had no additional information, either.

In the meantime, the police officer got a call from Inspector Sherwood. They were unable to track her phone's GPS signal. Inspector Sherwood suggested they go up to Jillian's flat to see if they could find any information at all—perhaps she had written down an address or directions. He also suggested they check in with the neighbor.

Chad asked the new concierge to open Jillian's door. The policeman nodded to the man—which is when Chad's suspicion that the man was an undercover cop was confirmed—and the three of them headed for Jillian's flat. As they were opening the door, Mrs. Anderson stuck her head out. "What are you doing? Where's Jillian?"

Chad walked over to her. "Hi, Mrs. Anderson. I'm Chad Bradbury. We haven't met officially. I'm Jillian's ex. She's missing. Someone called her to come to a meeting—we don't know where. Did you happen to see her this morning?"

Mrs. Anderson looked very concerned. "Oh, no. I told her to be careful. She said she was meeting someone—I think she said Inspector Sherwood—at Buck's to help with her friend's case. And it was so foggy—I told her to watch out for those roads."

The policeman was already on the phone to Inspector Sherwood. "She was headed for Buck's."

"Did she say anything else?" Chad turned to Mrs. Anderson, who was looking alarmed and thoughtful at the same time.

"No, just that she felt she had to do anything she could to help find her friend's killer. She is very conscientious, you know. Of course you do. Anyway, she said she was meeting an inspector at Buck's and she wasn't sure why."

Chad wasn't sure how much to tell her, but he recalled Jillian had said she was retired from the police force. "Unfortunately, the call was not made by the police. Apparently it was an attempt to lure her somewhere, and we are very concerned for her."

The woman's look hardened, and now Chad believed she had been a policeman. "What can I do to help?"

The policeman took charge. "Let's go into her flat to see if there's anything here that might give us some clues. It's very helpful to know she went to Buck's. Thank you for that. There are police on their way there. Mr. Bradbury, do you have a photo of Miss Hillcrest we could use? Send it right to Inspector Sherwood. Here's his e-mail address."

Chad pulled out his cell phone, showed the officer a photo, and then e-mailed it to Inspector Sherwood. Then they all began searching Jillian's flat.

37

Inspector Sherwood got to Buck's in record time, arriving about 3:00. He blamed himself for Jillian's disappearance and assumed it was the killer who had called her. He had been correct: Jillian held the key to the murders. But he had underestimated the resolve of the killer to eliminate that link.

Buck's was busy. The staff was very co-operative and looked at the photo of Jillian, but no one had seen her. One of the waiters suggested checking with a busboy who had been there since 7:00. He frequently went outside to smoke, and it was possible he had seen her in the parking lot.

Inspector Sherwood tracked down the young man and showed him the photo. At first, he did not recognize her. However, when Sherwood said she would have been alone and would have arrived between 9:00 and 10:00—maybe someone had met her?—he recognized her. "I remember because it took her a while to find a parking place—you know it gets pretty busy here on Saturday mornings. Anyway, she finally parks the car and gets out and is headed into the restaurant when she gets a call. She looks kind of annoyed and gets back in her car and heads in that direction." The busboy pointed down the foggy road.

"Thanks. That helps a lot. I'll let you know if we find her. You guys have been very helpful."

Sherwood contacted his partner telling him to start a search on the road indicated by the busboy. At least it was some place to begin. He told Sodini he would start driving slowly, but it would be helpful to know what was on that road for the next five to ten miles. Were there any abandoned buildings, like hunting cabins or campsites? In the meantime, they needed to get the appropriate law enforcement teams to join the search. Also, it was time to let the TV stations know Jillian was missing.

Sherwood hung up feeling very uneasy. What was this guy's game? He had told Jillian he would meet her at the restaurant. Then when she had arrived there, he had called her to tell her. . . what? And given the timing of his call, he must have been in the parking lot to know she had arrived. Did he know her by sight? If so, was he someone Jillian knew? Did he follow her? Why would he follow her? To force her off the road? Sherwood called his partner again. "Joe, let's assume that she was pushed off the road somewhere. Tell the searchers that they need to look for a car wreck. Also, I assume you got the make and model of her car so be sure to let everyone know that."

"Yeah—we've got this under control. They're investigating several abandoned places along that road. Also, you should be hearing and seeing a helicopter soon. They wanted to get it in the air as soon as possible—before it got dark. However, the fog is still pretty thick, so they're not promising much. And they've got patrol cars out."

"Jesus, Joe. I screwed this up pretty bad, didn't I?"

"Hey, this isn't your fault. Don't blame yourself. This is the bad guy's fault. We're going to find her."

38 𝕏𝕀𝕏𝕀𝕏𝕀

J illian lay by the side of the road. She was thirsty, and her lips were dry. She knew she should be hungry, but mostly all she was feeling was pain. It was very dark, and it occurred to her in her dark clothes she could be hit by a car if she didn't do something to make herself obvious. She did not see any signs of the deer, so she surmised she had not actually hit it. The fog was even thicker now than earlier. Jillian checked her phone. She still had no coverage, but there was still enough battery life to let her use it for the light.

She considered her options. She could not walk. She could try to crawl back the way she had driven. At least she knew what was there—not much of anything for several miles. Or she could stay where she was with the hope that a car would come by. If she stayed here, however, she would need to find a better place to face traffic. She realized that although the climb up the hill had been painful, the exercise had helped her to stay warm. So she decided to crawl back down the road the way she had driven realizing that it was unlikely she would reach any civilization for miles—but at least the activity would keep her warm.

It only took a few pushes with her good leg to let Jillian know that her plan was foolhardy. She needed a better plan. So she looked around for a place that would help improve her visibility and help her to do something to call attention to herself. She vaguely remembered a clearing shortly before she encountered the deer. Maybe she could crawl there—at least that was a goal. Once she got there perhaps her cell phone might have some bars, or at least enough power that she could wave it or something to draw attention. Well, at least it was a plan. She should have grabbed the flashlight from her car, but it was too late to think about that at this point.

It was now close to 8:00 p.m. Jillian was sure Chad and Inspector Sherwood and Mrs. Anderson would all be looking for her. She had to do whatever she could to help them, so she dragged herself toward the clearing. It was all she could think to do. But, she only managed a few feet before dizziness overcame her and the spinning road rose to meet her.

39

ynthia Anderson and her son, Fred, waited anxiously with Chad in Jillian's flat. Cynthia had contacted some of her fellow police friends who kept them updated. They knew that helicopters and patrol cars were searching the Woodside and Portola Valley hills, but the fog was thick and it was difficult to see anything. They also knew that Inspector Sherwood himself was out looking. Chad, too, wanted to be out there, but Inspector Sherwood told him that they had plenty of people searching, and that since he was a civilian the officers would feel obliged to keep an eye on him, which would only detract from the effort to find Jillian.

Chad thought about notifying Jillian's mother, but knew she had recently had a mild heart attack. He considered calling her, but decided there was nothing she could do except worry. He really liked Vivien Hillcrest and still had a humor-filled, give-and-take relationship with her, despite the divorce. Chad also had a lot of respect for her, given that she had worked her entire life to improve access to education in California, having taught and promoted the arts and sciences with the same amount of intense passion. Her contributions were unheralded but Chad and Jillian were both convinced that without her, today's youth would be less aware of the value of the arts and less understanding of the role of science in confronting modern problems. In addition, she had reared Jillian as a single parent after her husband had been killed in Vietnam, never having met his daughter.

She would be angry at Chad for not contacting her, but he decided that at least for the moment he would wait until there was some news. He rationalized that if he were not involved, the police would not know to notify her.

He also wondered about whether to check in with Jillian's boss. People at Harmonia might know something. He decided Inspector Sherwood would probably be the better person to contact them so he made a quick call to him, just in case. Sherwood said he would handle any communication with Jillian's company, and to please not contact them. Chad also let him know about Jillian's mother. Sherwood agreed with Chad that it was too early to contact her. Nonetheless, Chad felt better—like he had done something.

It turned out that Cynthia Anderson's son was a financial advisor. Chad decided to ask him if he knew any of the companies on Harrington's list. He remembered a couple of the names—including Jillian's—and was not surprised when the financial specialist commented that although the biotech space was not his area of expertise, those companies were indeed considered potential investment targets.

Chad then asked him if he knew Dan Harrington and his company. Fred responded that indeed he did know him. He was considered a true financial leader and many analysts followed his choices carefully. He was also reputed to be one of the more ethical investors and although he operated a hedge fund, he typically invested for long-term growth and the success of companies, rather than short-term profit. If he was interested in Jillian's company, it was a good thing and many others would probably follow his lead.

It was about 10:00 p.m. when Chad's phone played an old-fashioned ring. He was ecstatic to see that the call was from Jillian.

He screamed her name. "Jillian?! Where are you? Are you O.K.?" He held the phone out so Cynthia and her son could hear.

"Chad—on road—phone dying—forgot to charge battery—inspector—don't know—left Buck's—then turned left—avoided deer—crashed—leg broken, I think. . ."

"Jillian, hang on. You're breaking up. Tell me where you went after you left Buck's."

But all he got was static. "Shit!!! Goddamn it!" He was frantically pushing her number to get her back.

Cynthia was immediately on her phone calling her contact. "We just heard from her. She was able to make a call—then her phone died. It sounded like she is on a road somewhere with a broken leg. Something about a deer so maybe she hit a deer? The best we could tell is she went left after leaving Buck's. Can you locate her cell phone?"

Chad continued to try to call his ex-wife's number, but there was no answer. He looked anxiously at Cynthia to find out what she had learned. She shook her head.

"Well, at least we know she's alive."

"Can I borrow your phone, Fred? I want to keep mine available in case she tries to call back, and your mother should keep hers clear to talk with her police contact. I want to call the inspector to let him know I heard from her. Thanks."

Chad punched in Inspector Sherwood's number. He answered immediately. "Who is this?"

"Hi, Inspector Sherwood. It's Chad Bradbury, Jillian's ex-husband. Jillian just called me. We let the police command post know, but I thought you'd like to know, also. It was a weak connection but she said something about a deer and broken leg and that she is on a road somewhere. Also, it sounded like she turned left after leaving Buck's."

"Thanks, Chad. I can't tell you how relieved I am to know that she's alive. We know that she turned left from the parking lot, but maybe she meant that she turned left from Woodside Road. Just a second—I got another call. Let me get back to you."

40

Jillian must have slept for a while. She awakened on the side of the road, very cold and very wet. The fog penetrated her clothes. Her leg and ribs were throbbing, and she also realized several of her fingers were very swollen. She tried to move but just could not. She decided to turn on her phone—it was very dark. She was amazed to see a bar even though there was also a low battery message. She quickly punched in the easiest number—which was Chad's. He answered immediately, although she could hardly hear him. It was so incredibly good to hear his voice. She tried to tell him where she was but realized she didn't really know. She managed to get out Buck's and that her leg was broken, and that she was on the road. But her phone was now completely dead. The battery had finally given up. She didn't even have the light for comfort anymore.

Again she tried to move. She decided she needed to be on the other side of the road so she would be facing oncoming traffic. That seemed safer, so she managed to drag herself across the road. Then she again reminded herself that she was a smart, intelligent, resourceful person. What could she do to enhance the likelihood of her rescue?

First, she needed to stay alive. To do that, she needed to be warm. So she planned to move for about ten minutes—or until she counted to 6,000 slowly. Then she would rest. While she was dragging herself, it occurred to her that if she could be waving something it could help cars and/or planes to see her better. Also, that might be better exercise to keep her warm than dragging herself along the road. So she looked for a branch or whatever. Unbelievably there was no litter of any kind along the road. She pondered whether she should sacrifice her leg splint and use her bra, but then it occurred to her that perhaps she could make a sign in the road using twigs and branches.

She grabbed all the branches she could and dragged them to the middle of the road to form a giant X, extending the letter to the sides of the road. She completed this feat at the side of the road in one of the few places that offered a fairly wide shoulder. Having used all the energy she could muster, she allowed herself to fall asleep, using as many leaves and pine needles (she surmised) as she could find for warmth. She had no idea what time it was, but suspected it would be a long night.

nspector Sherwood finished his call with the rescue helicopter. They had decided to ground it until morning. Even with their large spotlight they could see little through the thick fog. If it cleared later, they would go back but for the moment it was fruitless. The patrol cars would continue, and in the morning they would start to comb the area with hikers and again send up the helicopter. Sherwood knew this was probably the right decision, but he tried to talk them into continuing for just a bit longer since they had received a phone call from her indicating she was on a road somewhere. The temperature was dropping into the 30s, and the fog made it very wet as well, so they were all concerned. However, the helicopter was to remain on the ground until daylight.

In the meantime, Sherwood's team was working to locate Harrington's assistant. He had still not responded to any of their e-mails. They had contacted the Mexican police in Puerto Vallarta. The young man's sister was sure he had been headed there; she had sent him directions, a key, and a packet of information for the area. But the Mexican police had been unable to track him down so far.

Although they had kept the death of Dan Harrington quiet, the online broker where the stock was transferred had not received any additional messages from the faux Dan Harrington. Sherwood's team had not yet located Harrington's laptop computer, which his secretary said he took with him everywhere. So they assumed the embezzler/murderer must have it and was planning to use it to sell the stocks. It appeared he had changed all the passwords and relevant information regarding "Dan Harrington" when he transferred the stocks. Therefore, the embezzler would know the necessary user identifications and passwords and would have full access to the $8 million worth of securities.

Of course, there was a slight possibility the embezzler and the murderer were two different people, but no one on Sherwood's team believed that. They were very sure whoever had access to the funds also was responsible for Harrington's death. It was almost always about the money.

Sherwood had learned a lot about Harrington in the last 36 hours, and, although he typically resented the very wealthy assuming that they had to have committed some crime or hurt someone to be so rich, he had a begrudging respect for the man. He seemed to have earned his wealth honestly, and also to have given back a considerable portion of it, particularly to various foundations focusing on the diseases whose therapies had earned Harrington substantial payback. Sherwood really wanted to catch whoever had shortened Harrington's life.

Sherwood was also sure there was a connection between Lisa Baumgartner's vehicular murder and Harrington's strangling, and was equally committed to catching whoever had run her down. He believed the victims were two really decent human beings who had deserved longer lives. And now there was the possibility of a third victim, if they didn't find Jillian Hillcrest in time. All so that someone could steal $8 million and get a bigger house and several cars and become an affluent member of society. Certainly Sherwood could understand and comprehend how greed could entice embezzling or robbery—he had encountered enough of it to know that it did. However, as many murders as he had solved, he could not comprehend how greed could push people to take the life of another human being, particularly if done face to face.

42

Jillian awoke to the sound of a helicopter overhead. She was disoriented and barely able to move. It was daylight, but still foggy. She was wet and cold. She could not think what was happening or why she was there. She could not think why the sound of the helicopter was so important. However, she tried to drag herself toward it. She was glad it stayed there for a while because she could not move very rapidly. She was very stiff. The helicopter seemed to hover for a very long time.

The next thing Jillian was aware of was the sound of voices. They seemed to be nearby. Again she knew that these voices were important but she still could not focus on why. She tried to move, and then she tried to speak. "Hello—I am here!" It sounded like a squeak to Jillian, so she tried again. "Hello? I am here." That sounded much better. They were saying something about an "X." Jillian thought that was important, too.

"There she is." Two men in some kind of uniforms ran toward her. Jillian again said, "Hello. I am glad to see you, I think."

"We found her!"

43

When Chad's phone sounded he answered it anxiously—fearing the worst and hoping for the best. "We found her. She is on her way in an ambulance to the hospital. She was not totally coherent, and she has some broken bones—but she seems in pretty good shape. We're still looking for her car. She had somehow made an "X" with some branches on the road near where she was lying. The guys in the helicopter spotted it. We might have missed her otherwise. I'm not sure how she did it."

Chad's entire body morphed from dejected to excited. He started pacing, and quickly informed the others in the room, and then asked the voice when he could see her. "You can meet her at the hospital. She should be there within ten to twenty minutes. I'll let them know you're coming. By the way, she was pretty resourceful out there. I take it she's had survivalist training?"

Chad almost laughed out loud. "No, officer, I can assure you she is not a survivalist. If she had her way, she probably wouldn't even go outside—especially in the woods. Why do you say she was resourceful?"

"Well, she managed to make a splint for her leg using her bra to tie a strong branch on it. Then she got to the road somehow, which we think required her to climb up a very steep hill with a broken leg and probably broken ribs. And she made a big X on the road with branches and twigs so that we'd find her. Plus she covered herself with leaves and tree needles to stay warm. I'd call all that pretty resourceful."

Chad couldn't help himself. His sense of humor and new sense of euphoria took over even as his concern for her well-being grew. "Officer, can you please save that bra and be sure that we get it? I think that it needs to be given its proper accolades."

The voice on the other end chuckled. "I'll be sure to get it to you. Check with the hospital."

"I can't thank you enough. We're on our way."

Chad, Cynthia Anderson and her son, Fred, headed for the hospital. As they walked toward the elevator in Jillian's building, Chad contacted Inspector Sherwood, who was already on his way to the hospital as well. He didn't know much more than the search and rescue person had already told Chad. They still did not know if Jillian was all right. The voice on the phone had said she was incoherent and appeared to have broken bones. What did that mean? And what had happened? Where was her car?

They decided taking a cab to the hospital would be faster, and given that they found one almost immediately, that plan seemed correct. The hospital had been alerted and the receptionist directed them to the area where they could meet the ambulance, warning them to avoid getting in the way of the emergency crew. They knew they were in the right place when they saw Inspector Sherwood. He greeted them hurriedly; the ambulance had just arrived.

Chad and Inspector Sherwood proceeded anxiously to the vehicle as the paramedics opened the back door and professionally and quickly moved a bundled, dirty, and bruised Jillian toward the door. Both men tried to speak with her but the paramedics pushed them back. "Let us get her inside and have the docs look at her. I can fill you in a little. She had a car accident—something about hitting a deer. She said she was on her way to meet an inspector, and that we should let him know that she'll be missing that meeting. Also, is one of you Chad? She wants to be sure you know that she is O.K. So just give us a minute, all right?" The paramedic was brisk; it was obvious that his primary concern was his patient.

The four of them sat uncomfortably in the waiting room. They all looked apprehensive and un-reassured by the paramedic's words. Mrs. Anderson suggested to her son he might want to contact his family to let them know why he would be late returning to Fresno. "This was not exactly the visit I had anticipated."

Inspector Sherwood's phone rang and he quickly answered it with an abrupt "What." He listened intently. "I'm at the hospital. I haven't had a chance yet to speak with her. As soon as I do, I'll let you know. Keep looking for the assistant. Try the sister again. She may have some idea of where he might have gone after Mexico. And I'll want to talk with the CFO myself. Call me back and let me know where I can meet her later today, unless you think we should bring her in. Either way let me know."

As the inspector disconnected, he appeared very thoughtful. He looked at Chad. "How much do you know about the people at Jillian's company?"

"Almost nothing. She got her current job after we divorced. Unless Jillian contacts me specifically about a work-related question, we never discuss her work. And I am only peripherally aware of the executives and their backgrounds—more from what I read than from Jillian. Why? Is someone from there involved in all this?"

"Maybe. I need to speak with Jillian. I'm going to go see if the doctors will let me talk with her briefly. Stay here. I'll try to get you in as soon as I can."

Sherwood was mulling over several theories. He was more certain than ever the embezzlement and the murders were connected. They still couldn't locate Harrington's assistant, their most interesting person of interest. The police in Mexico said, according to a neighbor, he had left Puerto Vallarta several days ago, but he had not yet returned to the Bay Area, so they were searching for him—he was the most likely person to know the accounts and their passwords in order to embezzle the funds. That put him at the top of the list of suspects.

While the dramatic rescue had been taking place, Joe Sodini had uncovered a new lead. It seemed Brynn Bancroft and Tim Wharton had been having an affair. This became apparent during a rather unpleasant interview with the CFO resulting in her request for an attorney, which seemed a little suspicious. Only because of Sodini's experience did he pick up on the secret, but what mattered more was that she might have been blackmailed about it. So far, she had been unwilling to say anything and swore that none of her activities had anything to do with the murder of Jillian's friend.

They had still not informed anyone about Harrington's death. Nonetheless, no one had attempted to place an order to sell any or all of the $8 million worth of stock, perhaps because it was the weekend. Sherwood was considering letting Brynn know about Harrington's murder to see if that would shake her up enough to tell them what she knew so that he could determine its relevance. However, if she were the murderer/embezzler, they would be informing her of Harrington's death and would not necessarily trap her in the act of accessing the bogus account. He understood there would be repercussions regarding the affair, so he wasn't surprised she was reticent to talk about it for reasons other than the crimes being investigated. He might be able to protect her privacy, but would only do so if she co-operated and if her revelations were not pertinent to the murder investigations.

But first he needed to speak with Jillian. It was likely she would be aware of the CEO/CFO tryst. He thought she was extremely sensitive to people's interactions and would have tuned into any out-of-the-ordinary activities. And she might also know if her boss was being blackmailed, although he doubted it. Jillian would have told him when she learned of Harrington's death.

Sherwood reached the area where they had last seen Jillian and searched for a nurse or doctor who could help him locate her. He wanted to know more about the telephone conversation she had had with the person who had claimed to be speaking for him. What had that person said? Where had she been headed? The address could be an important clue to his identity.

"Excuse me." He flagged down a nurse as she came out of an examining room. "I'm Inspector Sherwood of the San Francisco Police Department, and I really need to speak for a couple of minutes to Jillian Hillcrest. She was the one . . ."

"I know who she is. Considering what she's been through, she's doing well. I'll ask them to hold off for five minutes—no more. I can't promise that she is too coherent. She is dehydrated and feverish. We're giving her fluids and antibiotics. Also, the doctor wants to do surgery right away on her leg—assuming the swelling isn't too severe. She's in there."

"Thanks. I really appreciate it. This will help a lot."

"Five minutes. No more."

Inspector Sherwood entered the room as quietly as possible. He didn't want to startle her. However, it was she who startled him. He was not prepared for the bruising and the swelling—her left eye was swollen shut and her face was scraped and black and blue. Her left hand was bandaged, and her injured leg was protruding unceremoniously from under the sheet.

"Hi, Miss Hillcrest. It's Inspector Sherwood."

He wasn't sure she heard him, but then she turned toward him with as much of a glare as she could muster. "Sorry I missed our meeting." Jillian spoke slowly and took a breath of air after each word.

Inspector Sherwood was taken aback that she still seemed to think he was the cause of this. "No, no. Didn't they tell you? I didn't call. No one from the police department called. We're not sure who contacted you. Listen, we don't have much time. For right now I need you to focus just for a minute and tell me everything you remember about the call. What happened when you got to Buck's? Why didn't you meet there? Think, Jillian. It's important."

"I'm relieved it wasn't you who got me into this. I hate those awful country roads anyway. Give me rush hour traffic on 101 any day. Sorry."

Sherwood waited as patiently as possible while Jillian collected her thoughts and took a deep breath.

"The voice on the phone said he was calling for you, I can't remember the name he used. It was a "he," by the way. The phone woke me. It must have been seven-thirty or eight o'clock." Jillian had to stop to catch her breath. "He said he worked with you and that you had something you needed to show me regarding Lisa's murder, and could I meet you at Buck's as soon as possible. I was annoyed, you know, but I agreed because I really want to catch her killer–now more than ever, assuming it's the same guy."

It took her a long time to get these words out between breathing pauses. Then she seemed to go to sleep. Sherwood gently spoke her name to keep her awake.

"Anyway, I got to Buck's and spent a couple minutes finding a parking place, and when I finally got one I was headed into the restaurant when the same guy called back. He gave me directions to a new place and said to meet you there. And that's where I was headed when I swerved to avoid hitting the deer and landed down the mountain."

"Good. That's good. Now do you remember the address?"

"Address?"

"Of the place where the man said to meet me."

"Oh, no, but I wrote it down, I think. He didn't actually give me an address." Jillian was having difficulty staying awake. "I think he just said to look for something. I wrote it down. Did you look in my car? Oh my God, my car. I bet it's a goner."

"Do you remember where you put it in your car? Would it be on the seat or in your purse? They're towing your car to our garage. I haven't seen it, but those who have are amazed that you're alive. I'll look there. Miss Hillcrest, was there anything at all familiar about the voice? Maybe something you thought about then but put aside in your hurry to get there?"

Sherwood thought she had fallen asleep again and was just about to awaken her when she opened her one good eye. "I wrote it on an envelope, I think. On one of my bills." She paused, and again Inspector Sherwood thought she had gone to sleep. "You know, you're right. The voice was familiar; that's why I thought it was O.K. I assumed he was the policeman that was talking to you at Harrington's house. It sounded like him."

"Good. Just one more question. I need to know if you were aware that your CFO and CEO were having an affair?"

"What? How did you . . ." Jillian could not hide her surprise—but it was obvious she knew. "Why does that matter?"

"Well, we think that your CFO was being blackmailed and need to know if it had anything to do with either the murder or the embezzlement. Any thoughts?"

Jillian was not pleased with this question. She seemed to muster some renewed energy from somewhere. "I can't even imagine how there could be a connection. Both Brynn and Tim are incredibly ethical, honest people and would not do anything that would lead to embezzlement or certainly not murder. I can't believe you would even think such a thing."

"Thanks, Miss Hillcrest. But my partner is very perceptive about things like this, and we do believe that there is something going on and possibly a connection. It's possible that your CFO doesn't know how involved she really is. We haven't told her yet about Harrington's death, so maybe she'll revise her statement."

"You're wrong." Jillian paused and seemed to reconsider. "But then it never occurred to me they were having an affair in the first place, so maybe I'm wrong, but I don't think so."

"Of course. I need to go now. Mr. Bradbury—your ex-husband, I believe?—has been waiting for you with Mrs. Anderson all night. By the way, he strikes me as more of a husband-to-be than an ex-husband. I'll see if I can sneak him in before they take you for surgery. Hold on."

At that point, Jillian seemed to really go to sleep.

Inspector Sherwood left and went to retrieve Chad and hurried him back to the room. Again, he gently called her name. When she awoke, the inspector quietly left the room. Jillian seemed very glad to see Chad, although she looked a little taken aback at Chad's reaction when he saw her. Nonetheless, Chad was prepared to cover his concern. "So where is this famous bra that rescued my survivalist ex-wife?"

"Don't make me laugh. It hurts. What can I say? It worked and it was all I had. Remind me never to clean out my car again—if I ever have a car again. Have you seen the XB?" She was again gasping.

"No, not yet. Don't try to talk. We've been waiting to see you, and they're not going to let me stay here much longer. The nurse says they're taking you for surgery on your leg. I'll see you later today. I'm going to call your mom, now that we know you are O.K. How much have you told her about what's happening—with Lisa and everything?"

"Oh, God. Not much. She'd be worried sick. However, let her know that I'm in the hospital. Tell her about the bra. That might help. Oh, she does know about Lisa." It was difficult for Jillian to speak, and her words were a bit slurred, but Chad was relieved at her attitude, which reflected her spirit.

At that point, the nurse arrived and ordered him out of the room. He reached for his cell phone and called his favorite ex-mother-in-law. He knew he'd be seeing her later that day. He was sure that she would rush to be with her daughter, and it was a short flight. He also knew she would be furious with him for not informing her sooner. He looked forward to seeing her.

44 ⋈⊐⋈⊏⋈

Vivien Hillcrest disconnected from her former son-in-law, apprehensive and quite annoyed he hadn't called her sooner. She knew about Lisa's murder, as Jillian had said, but she had no idea Jillian was in any way involved or in danger. And she wished Chad had called her the previous night when Jillian had gone missing. She might have been able to help.

Of course, Chad knew she would worry, one of her key traits that growing older had exacerbated. She had reared Jillian as a single parent since Jillian's father had died when she was only a few months old. His death in Vietnam, coupled with a series of her own auto wrecks, left Vivien apprehensive about accidents, and she still liked to be informed about Jillian's whereabouts, such as her safe arrival to and from Geneva.

Vivien quickly booked a seat on the next flight to SFO, recognizing that she would have to rush to the San Diego airport for the hour flight. She texted the flight information to Chad, who had offered to pick her up at the airport. She stuffed an overnight bag with whatever she could locate, and headed for the airport parking lot. There was no question about whether she would fly to her daughter's side. Yes, Jillian was very independent, but her mother knew there were times when she wanted to cry and be held. She was her mother, after all.

45

Brynn Bancroft sat rigidly in the small conference room at a San Francisco police station. She was angry—perhaps unreasonably— at Jillian for involving her in her friend's murder investigation. She didn't understand why they needed to talk to her again—and on a Sunday, too. Why was it taking so long? Why were the police interrogating her so thoroughly? She had already spoken with them for an hour on Friday at the conference hotel about the list of companies she had researched for Dan. She told them they needed to speak with Dan further about the list. She understood it was the same list Jillian's friend had, but she knew nothing more about it or how it could possibly be related to Jillian's friend. It was absurd to think anyone she knew would have anything to do with murder. It was Dan Harrington's list, and the police needed to talk with him about it.

Further, she was furious with the policeman—Inspector Joe Sodini—for digging beneath her usual stoic surface and discovering her affair with Tim. She wanted to phone Tim to alert him, but they had asked her not to make any calls, and she wasn't sure where Tim was or if he was with Stephanie. She had demanded her attorney and was allowed to call Harmonia's corporate lawyer, who politely said she really needed a different kind of lawyer. He would make some calls and have someone contact her as soon as possible. In the meantime, the best thing would be to say nothing. She was still waiting for someone to arrive, and unless the questions were very benign, she had decided to say nothing more.

As she waited impatiently, a casually dressed man with a shaved head and striking blue eyes entered the room. He placed a small tape recorder on the table and turned it on. "Hi, Mrs. Bancroft. My name is Inspector Loren Sherwood. I am the homicide inspector investigating the murder of Lisa Baumgartner, who is a friend of your employee, Jillian Hillcrest."

"I demand to know why you have asked me here. This is ridiculous. I don't know anything about Jillian's friend. Furthermore—"

Inspector Sherwood raised his hands as he interrupted. "Yes, I'm sure that could be true. And I apologize. What you don't know is that there has been a second murder, which we believe is connected. I apologize for not informing you, but there are circumstances that require that we keep it quiet for at least a few days in order to trap the murderer or at least an embezzler. It's because of your connection to the second murder victim that we asked you down here. And I know that it was an effort for you to come as I understand that you live an hour away in Los Altos Hills."

Sherwood paused briefly to let all this information sink in and to make his next statement a little more dramatic, then continued. "More pertinent, I also need to inform you that someone tried to kill Jillian Hillcrest yesterday." Brynn truly gasped and her face lost its expressionless composure, so he hurried to add, "For the moment, she is all right, but she is undergoing surgery following a very harrowing day yesterday and last night spent in the hills. Maybe you saw the coverage last night on TV saying that she was missing?"

Brynn could hardly speak, but managed to choke out, "No, I don't watch TV news. I find it too depressing."

As the inspector was speaking, Brynn first appeared dumbfounded, speechless, and then concerned. She managed to mouth, "Who else was murdered?"

"I'm telling you all this so that I can impress upon you the importance of your sharing information with me. If you hold anything back, you could be endangering more lives. Do you understand?"

Brynn nodded, not trusting herself to speak.

"The other person who was murdered was Dan Harrington, the—"

Brynn gasped for the second time in a minute. "What?! The investor, Dan Harrington? Oh my God, I know him well. He was looking to invest in our company. But how is his death connected to the death of Jillian's friend?" Brynn absorbed this information and appeared to be thinking quickly to make the connection between the two murders. "Oh, I see, that's why the list of companies that Dan asked me to research is so important."

Sherwood nodded. "We're not sure, but we do believe that the link between the two murders is that list of company names that you reviewed for Harrington. The real motive was more apparent. It appears that someone succeeded in transferring approximately eight million dollars of Harrington's stock holdings—probably the day after his death—to an account created almost a week ago, all under Mr. Harrington's name, using his passwords and identifications. We're reasonably sure that Harrington was initially unaware of the new account that was created and that when he discovered it, he may have guessed who was responsible and possibly confronted him asking for an explanation, resulting in his death. We're keeping news of his death quiet because whoever transferred the stocks still needs to sell them to actually access the funds. We're hoping that if he thinks that Mr. Harrington's death has not yet been discovered, he will be more likely to proceed with the transaction, and we'll be able to identify and arrest him at that time. He still has all of his passwords for the new account. Given all that he has done to get the funds, we consider it a high likelihood that he will continue with his plan."

Sherwood paused to consider what else to tell her. "As to the connection—as you concluded—both you and Miss Hillcrest's friend had the same list of company names. We now know yours came from Mr. Harrington. We're not entirely sure why or how that list is tied in, but we believe that it is connected to the embezzler, who we believe is also the murderer. Why he also killed Miss Hillcrest's friend, we're not sure. Maybe she found out something; maybe she recognized him. Maybe by helping him with that list she could identify him, thereby tying him to Mr. Harrington. However, we are hoping to catch the person responsible when he tries to sell the stock. The broker has been alerted and we will track the person down if he makes any moves toward the account. In the meantime, we are pursuing leads to help us close in on the murderer."

Brynn was still trying to comprehend what was happening. "You said someone tried to kill Jillian? Why? How? Is she all right?"

"Someone called her and lured her up to the hills near Buck's restaurant saying that they represented me and telling her to be there to review something related to her friend's murder. She crashed her car on a foggy road avoiding a deer, and we didn't hear from her for twenty-four hours. They found her this morning, and she is now at the hospital with several broken bones. She is in surgery for her leg right now. I'm not sure what other injuries will require additional attention." Sherwood knew he was repeating himself, but he wasn't sure that Brynn had comprehended his earlier description of Jillian's status.

"Oh my God. What is going on? I'm sorry. I didn't know."

Inspector Sherwood decided on the straightforward approach, trusting what Jillian had told him: that Brynn was a person who on balance chose to err on the side of doing the right thing, and was most likely not the embezzler. Just in case, they had done a background check on the CFO, and had investigated her bank accounts, which revealed that although she was not extraordinarily wealthy, she and her husband could be labeled millionaires. A further check of her phone records over the past six months showed no suspicious calls. All of this reinforced Jillian Hillcrest's assessment of her.

"Look, I know that you and the CEO were having an affair, and that probably is causing you to believe that you need to be secretive. That's why we chose to bring you here rather than talk with you at home where your husband could possibly hear. I don't care about the affair. We'll do everything we can to keep that quiet. But I need to know if you did anything as a result of that affair that might have led to any issues with Harrington or Miss Hillcrest or your company. Did someone see you, maybe, and if someone is blackmailing you, I need to know that. Even if it seems absurd to you that it might involve someone not capable of murder. I especially need to know anything regarding Mr. Harrington."

Brynn looked at Inspector Sherwood for a long time before responding. She had recovered most of her composure, but this discourse was not something that she wanted to have. "Inspector, I can't begin to tell you what the repercussions will be if our affair leaks. However, that is my problem—and Tim's—not yours. And you don't need to worry about keeping the news from my husband—he moved out several days ago. Regardless, we need to stop a murderer first. So I'll tell you everything I know. By the way, you seem pretty certain about this. Does Jillian know?"

"Yes, ma'am. She definitely knows. And she also said that I should trust that you would provide whatever information we need. She has a lot of respect for your integrity."

Brynn almost smiled. "Well, my husband also suspected, so secrets are just not that easy to keep, I guess. For what it's worth, we're ending it and both of us really regret it." Brynn sighed and then continued. "However, the one person who might somehow be involved—although given his lack of intellect, it's hard to believe that he could pull off something like this—is a financial guy named Bill Vulkjevich."

Sherwood interrupted. "Can you spell that for me?"

Brynn complied and then continued. "He works for BIS, which

is the same contractor that represented Jillian's friend. He saw Tim and me a couple of months ago coming out of a room in a hotel in San Jose, and although he never explicitly asked for any money, his company presented him as a candidate for a consultant opening shortly thereafter, and I hired him despite his shortcomings. He also asked me for a recommendation to work at other places as well—and, Dan Harrington's office was one of the places."

"Thanks. We'll look into him. Why do you say that he wouldn't have the intellect to pull off something like this?"

"Well, when you talk with him, it will become obvious. He understands numbers, but not their significance. I can't believe that he could fool Dan, or even Dan's assistant, for that matter. However, he did cause some issues during the past week that involved Jillian. For some reason, he sent what turned out to be some bogus data to her at home, which concerned me that he knew where she lived. In fact, it was the same weekend as her friend was murdered. I remember, because she tried to reach me about both issues. Anyway, Vulkjevich just sent her this data with no explanation and then when she tried to reach him about it repeatedly, he was not available. She gave the data to our chief scientific officer, who verified that it had nothing to do with our current trial results, or any other trial related to the company.

"Then, Jillian got a call from a reporter who said someone had sent the same data to him. Although Jillian straightened it all out, I was really annoyed with Vulkjevich and suspected he was just trying to needle me and let me know he was around and could do some damage to the company if he wanted to."

Sherwood finished making some notes in his notebook. "Well, we definitely need to speak with Mr. Vulkjevich. You may not be aware but there were some other occurrences at Jillian's apartment building that also concern us, and if this guy knew her address, well, he becomes a very likely suspect. You don't happen to know what kind of car he drives, do you?"

"No, sorry."

"By the way, on a different topic, what do you know about Harrington's assistant?"

"Oh, I barely know him. However, he seems bright enough. And he is in charge of Dan's accounts, I believe. You can check with his office to confirm, but I got the sense that he was pretty actively involved in the actual process of buying and selling for Dan."

"Do you know if Vulkjevich did any work for Harrington?"

"No, I'm not sure Harrington hired Vulkjevich. And if he did hire him, I can't believe he would have been able to fool Dan's assistant, even if he did get by Dan. I never checked to see if Dan hired him, but I didn't give him a rave review, just said we had used him and were satisfied. It's possible Dan saw through the recommendation."

"Well, Harrington's assistant has been on vacation. Perhaps he used that as an opportunity. We're still trying to reach him. He seems to have disappeared."

Brynn looked surprised. "Really? That's strange. Have you checked with his office?"

"Yes, and his family. He went to Mexico for a few days, but no one has seen him for almost a week. Can you think of anything else? What about Tim? Did he mention anything?"

"No, I don't think Vulkjevich ever approached him. And if he was approached by anyone else, he never told me. Of course, I didn't tell Tim about Vulkjevich approaching me, either. I know Tim was acquainted with Harrington at a previous company where they had worked together, but they were business colleagues, never friends, I believe. However, I'm sure he can fill you in."

"Thanks. That is all very helpful. Do you have contact information for Vulkjevich?"

Brynn said she probably had information at the office, but he was one of the people listed on the BIS list of contractors—didn't Sherwood have that list?

"Of course. I'll check it. Thanks. I hate to ask, but could you stay here for just a little longer? By the way, I really appreciate your co-operation. Hopefully we can keep your situation quiet—at least until you can work it out."

"Thanks, Inspector. How much more time do you think you'll need today? Also, we're scheduled to fly to New York tomorrow. Obviously Jillian won't be able to go. But it would be a problem for the company if Tim and I don't appear. Is there any reason we can't travel?"

Inspector Sherwood looked thoughtful for a moment, and Brynn's face registered concern. "Actually, I can't restrict you from traveling. However, I would really appreciate your contact information so that I can reach you if I have more questions. Right now we need to speak with Mr. Vulkjevich."

Brynn looked relieved. She asked him if she could check with Harmonia's SEC attorney to assess the need to either issue a press release or file an 8K if there was any concern of the materiality of the events. While Jillian's accident was regrettable, she was sure it would not be considered material, as Jillian was not an officer of the company. Also, since the police had requested that they remain quiet about Harrington's death, there was probably nothing to be said about his investigation into their company. Further, she didn't think there would be a need to divulge it anyway, since they were not involved in his death. However, she wanted to be sure the company was protected. Inspector Sherwood granted his permission to inform the SEC attorney with the caveat that beyond confiding with the attorney, there was to be no disclosure of Harrington's death until he said so. He also asked Brynn to wait for their interview to be transcribed, so that she could sign it before leaving the station. He again apologized and thanked her for her co-operation.

Sherwood left the room as Brynn was connecting with the company attorney. He was headed for another conference room where Sodini was speaking—or not—with Tim Wharton, the CEO. He had been less forthcoming until this point, and had not admitted his tryst with Brynn. However, he had not denied it either. Again, Sherwood decided to trust Jillian's judgment of him and decided to inform him of Harrington's death and Jillian's near-death. The police had also done a background check on the CEO and knew that he and his wife were also well off, although Sherwood suspected that sending two kids to college could greatly deplete the couple's savings.

When Inspector Sherwood entered the room, Tim Wharton appeared to be exercising his position of CEO of a company by refusing to comment on whatever it was that Inspector Joe Sodini had asked. Sherwood noted the tape recorder already running, smiled deferentially, and approached the CEO respectfully. In much the same way he had informed Brynn, he described the circumstances of Harrington's murder and the attempted murder of Jillian. The CEO's demeanor then changed drastically from belligerence to concern, and he immediately offered to help in any way he could.

Sherwood continued. "First, we know about the affair between you and Mrs. Bancroft. Quite frankly, we don't care about the affair and we promise to do everything we can to keep it quiet. However, what we just learned from Mrs. Bancroft was that she recommended someone to Harrington based on that individual's having seen you and her leaving a hotel together. We recognize this as a form a blackmail, if you will, although this guy, er," he checked his notes, "Vulkjevich, never actually said so. What I need to know is if you had anything similar happen to you. Did anyone either directly or obliquely threaten to expose the affair that in any way might have anything to do either with Mr. Harrington's or Miss Hillcrest's events?"

"Inspector, before I answer that, can you tell me if Jillian is all right?"

"We think that she'll be all right. She is at a hospital right now undergoing surgery for injuries from an automobile crash. I am waiting to hear from the hospital."

"Thanks. I appreciate that. You are correct that Brynn and I, unfortunately, were involved. Neither of us is proud of it, and despite what you might think we both respect my wife. Anyway, for what it's worth, we have stopped seeing each other outside of work. However, I was not aware that Brynn had been approached. If I had, I'm not sure what I would have done. No one has said anything to me, with the possible exception of my wife, who appeared in Geneva unexpectedly and is traveling with me to New York—I suspect because she sensed something."

Tim stopped to gather his thoughts (an attribute that Jillian valued as it made him a careful and effective spokesperson). "What I know about Dan Harrington—we worked together more than ten years ago at a company in Philadelphia. He was still married then, and the four of us went out together a few times to work-related events, like management conferences or awards dinners. He was an interesting guy, and I liked him. We just never got to know each other too well because we were working in different divisions.

"When he decided to become an investor and put together his hedge fund, he approached me about our company. His fund focuses on biotechnology companies in early stages such as ours, and it has been growing successfully. I knew he was knowledgeable about the science, which always helps in telling our story. At first he wasn't too interested, but about six months ago, he started becoming more involved—maybe because an analyst started to cover us, or maybe because he learned more about our products. So for the past six months, Brynn, Jillian, and I have been responding to his inquiries by calling his attention to publicly available information, inviting him to the office and labs—with the hope that he would invest. He has become a recognized leader in the financial world, and if he buys our stock, we believe that others will, too.

"He has been visiting the company frequently the past few weeks. All of us have been providing information to him. I believe Brynn also helped him with an analysis of some companies he was investigating."

Sherwood interrupted. "What do you know about those companies?"

"Not a whole lot. Brynn showed me the list, and based on what I know, I would certainly consider them for investment—with one or two exceptions. She said Dan had asked her to provide whatever details she knew so he could compare her information with what his financial advisor was offering. Apparently he was working with someone new and wanted to corroborate his information."

"This financial advisor, did he tell you that he had hired someone new? Could it have been Vulkjevich?"

"I am trying to remember if Dan discussed it or if Brynn told me. I talked briefly with Dan on Tuesday, I believe; he wanted to have lunch on Wednesday. I was encouraged as I was pretty sure he was impressed with the data that we just announced that our Chief Scientific Officer had reviewed with him. Anyway, he asked to meet me for lunch, and then he never showed up, which I told you about on Friday when we spoke. However, I don't think he and I ever discussed his investment advisor or the list of company names, so I must have heard about them from Brynn."

"How well did you know Harrington's assistant, Mr. Lloyd Jenkins, I believe is his name?"

"Not very. As I recall, he was on vacation this week, which is why Dan called me directly to make the appointment for lunch. Lloyd always seemed very professional—and smart. I remember he made a comment once in a meeting that seemed particularly astute. He appeared to be in charge of managing Dan's portfolios, and was becoming very familiar with the financial world of buying and selling stocks."

"Would you say he was someone who might embezzle from Harrington?"

"Well, I'm not sure that's something you can tell from the few meetings I had with him, but basically I would say 'no.' He struck me as someone looking to become another Dan Harrington. I believe he had his M.D. and was looking to grow into Dan's shoes as an expert on biotech or pharmaceutical stocks. He could probably make eight million dollars honestly—or as honestly as you consider stock market speculation—within the next five years. I'm not sure why he would steal from Dan."

"Thanks. That is very helpful. Can you stick around for just a few more minutes so that we can transcribe this conversation for you to sign? I know that you need to fly to New York tomorrow. I would really appreciate your contact information so that I can reach you if we need more questions answered. Also, of course Jillian will not be traveling with you. I advised Mrs. Bancroft also. For the moment, perhaps you could just tell your employees that Jillian was in an automobile accident, and that she can't have any visitors. We want to avoid the possibility of a potential killer having access to her and it is easier to control if we have fewer people visiting."

Sherwood checked his notes in case he'd forgotten anything. "By the way, as your name was on Harrington's calendar for Wednesday, the other inspectors investigating Harrington's murder and embezzlement are probably considering you a person of interest. I'll let them know that I've spoken with you and if you should get a call, offer my name. It might save you another interview."

"Thanks, Inspector. Yes, I can stay for a few more minutes. Is it all right if I let my wife know I'll be returning home within the next hour or so? Also, my wife and I will want to visit Jillian in the hospital. Is that all right?"

"I'm not sure that they'll allow visitors today, but I'll make sure that you and your wife's names are on the list of approved visitors. As you can imagine, we are being careful. Before I leave, can you think of anything else—any other conversations with Mr. Harrington or about him—no matter how unrelated you might think they are?"

The CEO reflected for a moment as Sherwood waited. "Well, yes, there is one other thing but I can't believe it's germane to either a murder or embezzlement. Dan approached me about one of our executives,

Mr. Archie Linstrom. Archie is basically very wealthy—and I do mean very wealthy—and is working for us for almost no salary to learn more about how to run a company. His goal is to start his own company eventually—he actually has a five-year plan for getting there. We are very lucky to have someone with his skill set and connections to help us grow our partnership and customer base. Only Brynn, our attorney, the board of directors, and I are aware of the agreement with him that he is only a temporary employee.

"Anyway, Dan approached me about speaking with Archie, who he had apparently met several times over the years and been impressed with. He wanted to talk with him about becoming the Chairman/CEO of a new startup he thought had huge potential if the company had the right leadership. Given that is what Archie wanted, and that he is likely to leave our company within a year anyway, I said there was no problem on our side. Of course, Dan didn't have to ask my permission anyway, but I appreciated it and let him know. I informed Archie, but don't know what happened after that."

"When did Mr. Harrington first speak to you about it?"

"Oh, about two weeks ago, I think."

"O.K. Thanks. That actually helps us probably lower Mr. Linstrom on the list of potential suspects, because he was seen speaking with Mr. Harrington, and we weren't sure why. If he is extremely wealthy, it is unlikely that he would need to embezzle eight million dollars. However, Mr. Harrington might have said something to him that could be useful—like mentioning something about his assistant or a recently hired financial advisor. Now I need to take care of some things—like track down this Vulkjevich guy. Please, make yourself as comfortable as possible. Can we get you some more coffee?"

"No, I'm fine. It's not the best coffee I've ever had!"

46

Vivien Hillcrest called Chad as she was filing out of the plane to let him know she would be in front of the Arrival area in a few minutes. Several hours had passed since he had first called, and she was anxious to hear the latest news. She hurried to the curb, and arrived just as Chad's Porsche pulled up. Vivien liked the car, but chose not to think about what a huge contribution its purchase price could have made to the arts or to education.

"Hi, Chad. How are you? What's the latest?"

"Hi, Vivien. You're looking great! Good news. She's out of surgery and is in the recovery room. There were no problems. She had managed to splint the leg using a stick and tying it with her bra. She wanted me to be sure to tell you that; she was sure you would be proud of her survivalist skill."

Vivien laughed. "Thanks. I needed that. I'm glad to hear the surgery went well. What's next?"

"I'm not sure. We can find out together. I think she also had some broken or at least bruised ribs—not much they can do for that. And, as I recall, her hand was bandaged—it looked like maybe she broke some fingers. Mostly they will watch for internal injuries. However, I want to warn you before you see her: she looks pretty rough."

"Thanks, Chad. I appreciate that. How are you holding up? And what are you doing these days?"

Chad was relieved to change the topic. Vivien always seemed to sense what to say, and even though she was concerned for her daughter, she knew enough to try to create some normalcy so they would both be better prepared to care for Jillian.

Chad parked the car in the garage next to the hospital, and the two of them walked quietly into the facility. Chad led Vivien to the waiting room where he had left Mrs. Anderson and her son, still faithfully sitting with his mother. Chad introduced everyone, and Cynthia Anderson told them Jillian was still in the recovery room. The hospital staff had not informed them where she would go next. As her mother, Vivien could probably gain more information so Cynthia led her to the nearby nurse's station. The nurse informed the group that they would let them know as soon as a room had been assigned. So they all settled down to continue to wait.

47

Inspector Sherwood hung up the phone following his latest conversation with the sister of Harrington's assistant. If she hadn't been so concerned about the well-being of her brother, she might have been annoyed at the number of calls from the police in Silicon Valley. She repeated that she had offered her brother her house near Puerto Vallarta when she learned he was going on vacation in Mexico. She had been surprised, as he typically did not go on vacations, but he had been doing some snorkeling and was learning to dive, and she assumed that's why he had decided to take the trip. However, it had been sudden, and it was fortunate no one else was at her house, which she frequently time-shared with friends. She had no idea where he was now though, and was very worried.

"You say that Lloyd's decision to go on this trip was sudden? Did he say why he decided to go at this time?"

Lloyd's sister sighed heavily. She had been answering this question over and over. "No, Inspector, he didn't. He just asked if he could stay at my place there for a few days. He was in a hurry the day he called, and we only spoke for a moment. He said he'd explain later, but he never called back."

Sherwood had asked her to think about where else he might have gone, but she had no idea. He just didn't travel very much other than to his job in the Bay Area or to her house in Phoenix. She was the only family her brother had. She had been e-mailing and texting and calling him frequently for several days, since the Mexican police reported he wasn't at her home, but still had not heard from him. She wasn't even sure whom to tell or to ask about his whereabouts. Certainly Dan Harrington's office where he worked was being less than helpful.

Sherwood wished he could see her face to face. He had not told her about Harrington's death. If her brother was the embezzler, he didn't want to alert her in case they were both involved in pilfering the financial savant's funds. If her brother were not a participant, knowing about the murder of his boss would only cause her to worry more. So he promised he would get back in contact with the Mexican police, and also continue to check with Harrington's office. He assured her he had already spoken with the Harrington people who also were trying to get in touch with him. Regardless, he would keep her informed.

After he disconnected from Harrington's assistant's sister, Sherwood sat quietly thinking about what he had just learned. Why had the assistant chosen now to take a vacation? Was he the one who had opened the account and moved the stock? He had the passwords and the authority to make it happen. Or did someone take advantage of his absence to make it happen? And, if so, who had gotten close enough to Harrington to learn of his IDs and passwords well enough to fool bankers accustomed to trading millions and millions of stocks regularly?

Inspector Sherwood found his partner and pulled him into an empty room. "I want to run this by you to see if it makes sense. Either Harrington's assistant arranged all this or it happened now because he wasn't here. We need to find out more about why the guy went on vacation at this particular time. And who else was working with Harrington who might possibly know his passwords. It can't be that easy to move eight million dollars worth of stock. Even in today's financial world, that's a lot of money."

Sodini looked at his partner with that enlightened-look-of-possible-solutions that Loren Sherwood had come to trust. "I wonder if someone helped the assistant go on vacation—either forcibly, which could mean that we might find another body; or financially, like maybe he won a trip somewhere with all expenses paid. I'll get in touch with some contacts I have in Mexico. Maybe they can check further to see when the assistant was last seen—if he talked to anyone, whatever. The sister sent me a photo so I'll ask them to circulate it down there to be sure he was actually there. And, I'll call Harrington's receptionist and see if she knows anything else. She seems pretty sharp, actually, and maybe she's remembered something. You know what else? I think you and I should go to Harrington's flat and really look through his things beyond just forensics searching for clues to a murder suspect. Maybe we'll uncover the name of the new advisor Harrington was auditioning. Who knows? He might have been the one who had access to Harrington's passwords. How about we go there tomorrow?"

"Sounds good, Joe. I hope we don't find another body. In the meantime, did you learn anything about Vulkjevich?"

"Yeah, they're bringing him in now." Sodini looked at his notes. "Also, you wanted to talk to a guy from the Hillcrest girl's company, an Archie Linstrom? I haven't reached him yet. You said Hillcrest had seen him with Harrington at lunch one day, which was unusual, I guess."

"Yes, I think I know what that was about. The CEO just told me that Harrington was looking into him to possibly head a startup. I still want to talk with him, but that can be a lower priority. Since Harrington talked to him shortly before the murder, he might have told him something about this financial advisor Harrington was hiring. I'll see if the CFO has contact information for him. Let me know when Vulkjevich arrives."

Sherwood was closest to the room where Brynn was waiting so he walked in to find her still on the phone. She finished her call, and looked up inquiringly. "All done?"

"Actually, I have one more question. We need to reach Archie Linstrom. Do you happen to have a mobile phone number for him?"

"Sure. He's one of our executives. However, he's probably almost as wealthy as Harrington—not a likely embezzling suspect." She picked up Sherwood's card and typed Linstrom's e-mail address and mobile phone number on her phone e-mail and forwarded it to Sherwood. "Anything else?"

"Did Harrington say anything to you about this investment advisor he hired? I mean why would he hire someone and then have you check up on him?"

"Inspector, I agree. I wondered the same thing. In fact, I asked him, and he said he had just met the guy and although he had references, he, Dan, always liked to double-check new people so he could assess their strengths and weaknesses without losing too much money in the process. You know, he said it in a way that made sense, although right now it seems weak. However, we were anxious for Dan to invest in the company, so we were willing to show off our own talents as an indication of our management strength. When he asked me for my help, I provided it without hesitation."

"But he didn't give you any indication who this guy might be?"

"No, he didn't, which leads me to believe it wasn't anyone I know. Otherwise, Dan would have asked me about him."

"O.K. Thanks. And thanks for coming in. I really appreciate your help. Again, please don't say anything to anyone about Harrington's death. We told your CEO the same." A uniformed officer entered the room and asked Brynn to review and sign her statement.

"Inspector, do you know if it's possible to see Jillian?"

"Probably not today would be my guess. You might want to call the hospital, however. Be sure to leave your name. I'll let them know that it's all right to speak with you, as we want to be careful, given that it's possible that someone might try to reach her again. We're asking that you tell people at work that she was in a car accident and nothing more. Also please tell your employees no visitors for the immediate future. We're not sure that this guy will try again, but Miss Hillcrest is still not sure herself why she was targeted."

"You really think she's in danger? Phew. Thanks. I appreciate your letting me know. We'll at least send flowers, and I'll alert employees that visitors are limited right now."

"Have a good trip tomorrow." He left Brynn reading her statement, reasonably pleased with his decision to inform her of Harrington's death and certain it had provided them with a sought-after lead in the name of Vulkjevich. His respect for Jillian Hillcrest had grown as he had uncovered the integrity of her bosses. He seldom encountered this level of respectability in his world.

Sherwood then went to see Tim Wharton and reminded him also not to say anything. He made sure he had both of their mobile phone numbers in case he needed them. The same officer appeared with a statement for the CEO to sign.

Both Brynn and Tim were gone for at least 15 minutes before Vulkjevich arrived. Sherwood preferred that he did not see the two Harmonia executives, so was relieved they were already out of the building. And it didn't take Sherwood or his partner very long to understand why Brynn didn't believe that Vulkjevich had the intelligence to pull off something as sophisticated as embezzlement.

48

C had, Vivien, and Cynthia Anderson waited patiently in the hospital lounge for news of Jillian. Cynthia's son had received a call from his wife and had decided to return to Fresno with the caveat that he would return if his mother needed him. However, he smiled, as he was rather accustomed to her not needing anyone, so he was actually pleased he had been of use to her and her friends. He promised he would return another time so they could indeed have dinner together and get to know the neighbors under better circumstances. And he invited them to Fresno.

A new hospital volunteer arrived to let them know the room number where they were taking Jillian. Chad was relieved it was not Intensive Care, which meant she was probably not in any immediate danger. The volunteer said to wait about ten minutes and then they could all go see Jillian, but not to stay too long or tire her out.

The mood in the room changed perceptibly. Chad again revived the story about Jillian using her bra to help create a splint. Vivien smiled, but she was still uneasy and couldn't allow herself to become too optimistic. They decided they couldn't wait any longer, and headed toward the wing of the hospital where Jillian would be. There seemed no order to the room numbers—probably as a result of multiple additions or remodels. Chad approached another nurse's station to ask directions. As he approached, he heard her say, "I'm sorry, I can only provide that information to Miss Hillcrest's immediate family. I'm sorry you feel that way, but it is hospital policy."

Chad hurried to the nurse and tried to signal to her to get a name, but the nurse hung up shaking her head. "Some people just don't appreciate our problems. That man wanted me to divulge information about a patient that legally I can't provide."

"Who was that? What did they want? Did they say they knew Jillian?" Chad was very excited and even more concerned.

"Who are you?" The nurse was looking at her list.

Chad thought quickly. "I'm Jillian's husband, Chad Bradbury. Who was that on the phone?"

"Well, it says here that Miss Hillcrest has an ex-husband named Chad Bradbury. So if you are her EX husband, can you please give me your identification?"

Chad managed to look a little sheepish that he had tried to pass himself off as Jillian's husband. "Yes, my name is Chad Bradbury, and here is my I.D. And this is Jillian's mother, Vivien Hillcrest with her I.D. ready for you. And her neighbor Mrs. Cynthia Anderson—also with her I.D. ready. Now can you tell me who that was on the phone?"

"Thank you. That man on the phone said he was a friend of hers and needed to know her room number and how she was doing. He wouldn't give me his name. I had just been warned by the administrator that the police had asked that we note any calls about Miss Hillcrest by people not on this list."

The nurse looked very pleased with herself as she directed them to Jillian's room. "Oh, and by the way, the police also requested someone from hospital security to be by her room until they send someone. One of our off-duty guards is there for the moment, but he's only available for a short time."

As they were walking to the room, Chad heard the nurse speaking to someone to let them know there had been a suspicious inquiry regarding Jillian Hillcrest. Chad didn't know whether to be relieved or concerned that the police were keeping an eye on Jillian. They must be concerned that someone would try to get to her again. Chad hadn't had time to even consider that possibility; he was more concerned with Jillian's recovery. He looked over at Vivien and realized that unfortunately she fully understood the meaning of the encounter and was looking concerned. He didn't have to check Cynthia to know she understood and had probably anticipated the need for the added security.

They were aware that the local news channels had reported finding Jillian, although the police had not provided the name of the hospital where she was taken. If someone were deliberately trying to kill her, he would assume that she was at a hospital and might try to track her down and try again.

The room was at the end of the hall. There was a somewhat corpulent hospital security guard sitting outside her room reading a newspaper. Cynthia Anderson rolled her eyes and whispered to Chad, "I think we should probably think about how we're going to guard her ourselves—at least until Inspector Sherwood can get someone here. I might have some friends willing to help." And she pulled out her phone.

Chad looked at her with more fondness and appreciation than even he anticipated. Then he quietly confided to Vivien, who looked at them inquisitively. "Also, please remember both of you that Jillian was in an automobile accident and looks like it. She has lots of bruises and scrapes."

Vivien pushed her way into the room without listening to the end of Chad's comments. She did stop abruptly when she saw Jillian lying in bed with a face that bore little recognition to that of her daughter's. Cynthia was right behind her and gasped. However, since this was Chad's second visit, he pushed them both aside and approached her bed with a bombastic "How's my little survivalist doing?"

Jillian opened one of her eyes—the other seemed to be swollen shut—and feebly smiled. "Hi, everybody. Thanks for coming to see me. I must look awful. Hi, Mom."

Vivien was determined that under no circumstances would she cry and used an old trick of recalling an incident involving a fellow teacher bureaucrat that made her so angry that it replaced all other emotions and kept her from crying. "Hello, Jillian. What have you gotten yourself into this time?"

And when Chad looked at Cynthia Anderson's expression, he decided that under no circumstances did he ever want to get on her bad side.

nspectors Joe Sodini and Loren Sherwood had just finished an exasperating two hours of trying to interrogate Bill Vulkjevich. They had not informed him of Harrington's death—or the embezzlement—they wanted to see what he knew first and find out if he could lead them to some answers. So they were careful about the questions they asked. He was full of his rights and demanded his attorney, except he didn't have an attorney, so he demanded they release him. He didn't know anyone named Lisa Baumgartner, and he did not do any work for Dan Harrington. And he drove an old light tan Chevy he had for years since he was hardly rich like the people at the drug companies. He could not comprehend why the police were questioning him. He had his rights, and he chose not to answer any but the most basic questions.

Inspector Sherwood got a phone call in the middle of the interview, so Sodini continued without him to learn how he had obtained Jillian's home address, and why he had sent the bogus data to her and then to the newspaper. After a few more minutes, Sodini decided to leave the room to consider a better approach—and to give Vulkjevich some time to think about things.

In the meantime, Sherwood was speaking by phone to one of the officers who had followed up on locating the address given to Jillian by the person who lured her to the Woodside area. They had found the paper with the address, and had tracked it to a closed diner about five miles from where Jillian crashed. Apparently the owner had died a few months earlier, and his descendants had not figured out who was the rightful owner, so no one had been managing it. Although there was a campsite within a mile, there was little else in the immediate area of the diner. They were in the process of tracking down each of the possible owners and would get back to the inspector if they found anything remotely suspicious.

Sherwood disconnected. It was possible, he thought, that the deer and the accident might have saved Jillian Hillcrest's life.

Inspector Joe Sodini re-entered the room where Bill Vulkjevich sat defiantly, looking like he wanted to jump down the policeman's throat at a minimum. It didn't bother Sodini. He had seen far worse, and this 40-something 5 foot 8 inch, round bald guy was hardly physically capable of doing anything to the 50-year-old, 6 foot very physically fit cop. However, Sodini also knew if he wanted to get anything from this guy he had to approach him the right way—by appealing to his over-inflated sense of what was right.

"Mr. Vulkjevich, can you tell me about how you've been helping this so-called pharmaceutical company that makes the drugs I have to pay a fortune to buy?"

"Boy, isn't that the truth. I do not help them." He emphasized the "not."

"Glad to hear that. They really bug me. What—it costs them a couple pennies to make a pill that they charge me ten bucks for?"

"You got that right. I ought to know. I do financial analysis for them, and I can tell you they make huge profits."

"So what did you do to make it right?"

"Nothing illegal, if that's what you mean. I just sent some data to that Hillcrest broad. She treated me like she knew better than me—like she knew better than anybody—so I figured I'd give her something to worry about."

"You sent her fake data? To her company? Didn't she just have someone there figure it out?"

"Naw—first, it wasn't fake. It was from another trial—an older one from years ago. I just didn't tell her. And I sent it to her house over a weekend—that way she had to worry about it for a while."

"Glad to hear that. Did you do anything else—that was legal, of course—that might have caused any trouble?"

"Well, I sent the same data to a newspaper guy who wrote about the company. I never saw anything from him, so they must have convinced him that it wasn't the current trial. I never said it was. I just sent it. So, I caused a little bit of trouble."

Sodini laughed appreciatively. "Good job. Glad to know someone is getting even. But aren't you working for them? Aren't you helping them to market a product?"

"Yes and no. I had to do something so I could stay close, so I asked a guy I met at a conference to help me with some research for them. He didn't know I was getting paid for it, nor who the company was. That way, I could stay close. These people are really bad. I saw the CEO and CFO come out of a room at a hotel in San Jose, and I'm pretty sure they weren't doing work, if you know what I mean. And Jillian Hillcrest, who thinks she's so superior, well, she lives in a hoity-toity apartment in San Francisco and has her car brought to her every day. I know because I followed her one time to see where she lived."

Sodini smiled to encourage him. "Wow, you really have done your homework. What about this fat cat Dan Harrington? What do you know about him?"

"Oh, jeeez. Talk about a rich son of a bitch. He's definitely part of why this country is in the mess it's in. You know—the guy who helped me with the work I did for Hillcrest—well, he and I were thinking about how to get Harrington. We both knew he must have gotten all that money by taking it from the rest of us somehow. I lost a bundle when I bought some stock, but somehow he managed to get rich off it. God damned rich cat—probably made money by selling short."

"And what did you have planned for Mr. Harrington?" Sodini tried hard not to sound too anxious.

Vulkjevich looked coy, and Sodini feared he was at the end of sharing information. But to his surprise, Vulkjevich declared that their plan was foolproof—and totally legal. "We planned to besmirch," he enunciated the word slowly for emphasis, and Sodini was just impressed he knew it at all, "his reputation by giving him false information about companies he was pursuing. Then when he invested and they failed, he would look bad and he would lose money. Pretty smart, huh?"

"But how would you give him false information? And why would someone like him believe it?"

Vulkjevich looked very dejected. "Well, we hadn't figured that part out. I had managed to get a recommendation to do some work for him from that CFO at Jillian's company. When they didn't hire me, I pretended that was O.K. and recommended my friend claiming he was more of a fit for the project, but about then my friend got called home to wherever he lived, so we decided we would get back in touch when he returned. That was a couple months ago, and I haven't heard from him since. But I want you to know that anything we would have done would have been perfectly legal."

"I'm glad to hear that. By the way, what was your friend's name?"

Now Vulkjevich was at the end of sharing. "I'm not going to tell you. He didn't do anything, so you don't need to know who he is. I've said enough for you to know that I had nothing to do with that girl's death."

Sodini considered saying something then decided against it. "Thanks. You've been very helpful and I'm glad to know there are people like you looking out for us. I'll be right back."

Sodini went in search of his partner. He doubted that Vulkjevich was the brains behind the actual crime, but he possibly had the key to the puzzle. Sodini wanted Sherwood to take over the interview to get the name of Vulkjevich's friend or any additional information about him that would enable them to track him down. Although Vulkjevich was hardly smart enough to carry out this crime, this friend sounded more likely. He seemed to be using Vulkjevich to get close to Harrington, somehow, by using Jillian Hillcrest's company maybe. They needed to dig deeply into Vulkjevich's past to see if they could uncover the person responsible. He tracked down Sherwood in the coffee room where he was reading some documents. He looked up when Sodini entered. "Some analyst reports on Hillcrest's company. Just thought I'd get some insight into it. What's up?"

Sodini tried not to appear too excited. "I'm pretty sure that Vulkjevich knows the guy we're looking for. He definitely has a few screws loose and was stalking Jillian—followed her home. She apparently did not find him particularly smart and treated him with less than respect. Imagine that?! Also, he has a deep dislike of the drug-making industry and was out to get the company—and Dan Harrington. Somehow in his mind they are all connected. He definitely was trying to mess with Jillian, and he definitely suspected the affair between the CEO and CFO. But most important he confided with someone else about Harrington and the two of them planned to show up Harrington by feeding him false information on which to make some investments. Apparently this other guy disappeared about then, and Vulkjevich either doesn't know his name, or won't tell. It might be time for you to see what you can get out of him by informing him about Jillian's accident. I still wouldn't tell him about Harrington, because we might be able to use him to get to his friend, if they don't know that we know about Harrington's death. Bottom line: Although I'm pretty sure he isn't smart enough to have planned all this, he may know the person who did."

"Unbelievable. I'm on my way."

The two inspectors rushed to the room where Bill Vulkjevich sat convinced that he was the most righteous financial guy and proud of it. He was determined to bring down the biopharmaceutical industry that had denied his mother the drugs she needed to recover from colon cancer. He grew up in a household watching her die and knew if she had had the right drugs, she would have lived. Ironic that the very industry that could have saved her had denied her. And 30 years later, Bill Vulkjevich faced the death of his father last year with the same animosity toward the drug industry. His father, too, died of cancer—prostate cancer. And Bill was certain the drug industry had also failed him, even though the doctors reassured him they had provided everything there was to fight the disease.

When the two inspectors entered the room, Vulkjevich was sure they would tell him what a good job he had done—since everything was legal. He was not prepared for the animosity they displayed, nor the accusations that followed. He was surprised about Jillian's accident, and, of course denied vehemently he knew about it or had anything to do with it. He also denied having paid $100 to get someone to check out her apartment—although not quite so vehemently as he denied the other events. He screamed that he would never physically harm anyone. He only wanted to get back at the companies that had refused to give Mom and Dad the drugs they needed to stay alive. When he finally broke down, the inspectors stopped their interrogation. They decided to keep him there long enough to arrange for surveillance and wire tapping in case his friend contacted him again, because he still refused to provide that name.

Sherwood left his partner in charge of getting Vulkjevich to sign a statement. He decided it was time to talk some more with Jillian. She seemed to be at the center of all this and might be able to add some information. So, he headed for the hospital. He had a lot to tell her and hoped she was able to listen and that it would all trigger something in her mind.

51

Chad and Vivien were sitting by Jillian's bed when Inspector Sherwood entered the room. Jillian seemed to be sleeping. Chad greeted the inspector and introduced him to Jillian's mother. They decided to talk outside the room so as not to wake Jillian, although Sherwood said he really needed to speak with her eventually.

"I've been gathering a lot of information, and need to ask her a few questions."

He noticed the rather plump security guard sitting nearby. "Are you here to guard Miss Hillcrest? Where were you when I arrived?"

The guard looked at him warily. "Yes, but there's been someone with her since I got here so I just went to get something to eat."

Sherwood started to say something, but Chad pulled him aside. "Cynthia Anderson—she's Jillian's neighbor who used to be a cop—is calling in some favors and getting someone else to stand by—an ex-police officer. Someone called asking for Jillian a while ago, and the nurse refused to tell him anything. I assume they'll follow up on that call, but just in case, I thought you should know. Cynthia went back to her flat and is going to see what she can dig up regarding what's been happening at Jillian's apartment building—just in case there's any connection."

Sherwood was a little uneasy about amateur sleuthing, but he was less concerned than usual because he knew the police were watching Jillian's apartment building for several reasons. Further, he had checked up on Cynthia Anderson and was reassured she would know what to do if she uncovered something useful. "Let me know who she sends so that I can get his name on the list. I'm sorry, but I really need to talk with Miss Hillcrest. Maybe one of you could awaken her?" He looked hopeful.

Vivien smiled. "I'll do it. She's been sleeping for a couple hours, and I think it's time for her to take her meds and to eat something. So it won't be too much of an interruption." She went into the room and quietly spoke to her daughter, who awakened startled.

"Oh, hi, Mom. What's up? Where am I … oh, that's right. Oh, hi, Inspector Sherwood. What's up? Catch any killers recently?" Jillian spoke softly—to preserve energy, they assumed.

"Hi, Miss Hillcrest. Good to see you."

"O.K. I've let you call me Miss Hillcrest long enough. You know me well enough now to call me Jillian."

Vivien and Chad both smiled at her attempts to ease the inspector's obvious stiffness. He seemed pleased she was alert. "Well, in that case, you can call me Loren. I'm sorry to disturb you, but I've been talking to a lot of people and need to ask you some more questions. I'll be as brief as I can; I understand that it's time for you to have some dinner."

"Oh, yeah, food. That's not exactly at the top of my list right now. Actually, now that I think about it, I am hungry."

Again, Chad and Vivien smiled. They both knew Jillian liked to eat, and were relieved that she was hungry.

"Do you know a guy named Bill Vulkjevich?"

"Oh, yes. My god, is he involved in this? If he is, I really underestimated him—I can't believe he would be bright enough to do anything like this and, as annoying as he is, I can't believe he would kill Lisa."

"Agreed. We don't think that he actually committed either the" murders or the embezzlement, but we do believe that he knows who did. And he has been deliberately trying to annoy you, in particular, and cause problems for the company with the false data that he sent to you and to the reporter."

"What's he got against me? I'm a nice guy!!!"

Sherwood smiled. "Indeed you are. But, apparently you must have been somewhat condescending to him, because he followed you home in order to get your address so that he could send you that data to mull over during a weekend. And he hates all drug companies because he believes that they deliberately kept life-saving drugs out of the hands of his dying parents. More relevant to the crimes at hand, he conspired with a friend or acquaintance that he apparently met at a conference to damage the reputation of Dan Harrington, whom he dislikes because he is sure that the guy got rich by making money off the drugs denied to his parents. So, anyway, what I need to know is anything you can tell me about him and whether you know of any relationship between him and Harrington?"

Jillian continued to look skeptical. "Well, I never thought he was a good analyst. Brynn hired him. He worked on a partnered product. Frankly, his first analyses were shallow and had little merit. Then this week he had some decent insights that made me think I had underestimated him."

Jillian needed to rest before continuing. Sherwood waited without interrupting. "However, I was very angry with him for sending me data and misleading me to believe we had a problem. By the way, I was dealing with him that same night I met with Lisa. And Dan Harrington was also calling me at the same time regarding what turned out to be that list of companies. Strange how everything was happening at once."

"Yes. You're doing very well. Can you remember anything else?"

"Not at the moment. But I'm amazed I could think about all that. I can call you if I remember anything else. By the way, did you ever figure out where it was your bogus assistant told me to meet you?"

Sherwood wasn't sure she was ready to hear the results of that inquiry, but knew she was resilient. "Yes. The directions led to an abandoned and isolated diner about three miles beyond where you had your accident. We're investigating the owners to see if there is any connection between them and you or Dan Harrington or Lisa Baumgartner."

Jillian's one eye was grimacing. "I wonder why someone wanted to meet me there? Oh, ouch. Right now I'd really like to see the nurse about some morphine, or whatever they're giving me so I float in that neverland of painlessness. My leg—actually I think it's my whole body— is beginning to throb."

About then, the nurse walked in and asked everyone to leave so she could give Jillian an injection of the sought-after pain drug. Chad fully understood the implication of the meeting location, and gave the inspector a worried look. He decided to take the opportunity to go to the car to retrieve Vivien's bag; she was determined to stay at the hospital all night.

Inspector Sherwood turned to Jillian's mother. "Have you been in touch with your daughter recently? How much did she tell you?"

"Inspector Sherwood, do you suspect that my daughter was lured out to that abandoned diner in order to kill her?"

"I can't deny that the thought crossed my mind. It is possible that the deer and accident saved her life. You can be sure that we're taking precautions now."

Vivien reflected worriedly on that conclusion. Then she turned her attention to answering the inspector's question. "My daughter typically tries to protect me from learning about anything that might endanger her health, her reputation, or her life in general. She chooses to contact me when good things happen. So you can assume I know very little about what's been happening."

"Well, I guess it might help you to know that her ex-husband has been helping her a lot."

"Thank you, Inspector. Good to know. I plan to stay here myself tonight, even if I have to sit in that chair all night."

A nondescript, 50-ish woman dressed in a blue-plaid flannel shirt and jeans approached them. "Are you Inspector Sherwood by any chance?"

"Yes. Who are you?"

"Hi. Cynthia Anderson asked me to help out tonight. I just retired from the force, and, well, I have some time. And Cynthia was my mentor and she asked for help. "

"Great. Let's go introduce you to the nurse on duty and get your name and identification entered. Also, this is the patient's mother. She plans to spend the night as well. I'll see if we can get some beds moved in."

"Good to meet you, ma'am. No bed for me, sir. I'll be awake the entire night. I just need to know where to get coffee."

The two of them went off to the nurse's station leaving Vivien to wonder how her daughter had ever become a primary target in a plot that involved millions of dollars and the murder of two people. This wasn't supposed to happen in her world. She was more accustomed to fighting for budgets and publicity to win over voters and administrators. Nonetheless she had always been resourceful and had found unique and effective solutions to problems frequently enough to have multiple successes. Her daughter had learned the same sense of resourcefulness, and Vivien liked to think it had helped her survive the wreck and her overnight firsthand sojourn with nature. Further, she was sure Inspector Sherwood had learned to trust Jillian's judgment and insights.

However, Vivien knew in addition to her critical thinking capabilities, Jillian also felt the loss of her friend deeply. Further, if she knew this Dan Harrington at all, she would also be sensing his loss. Death had always disturbed her. At the moment, she was euphoric because she had survived a near-death experience. But Vivien was not certain where her daughter would next travel emotionally. She hoped she would not crash until after they caught her would-be killer. She suspected her analytical skills would be helpful in the process, but she knew they could be compromised by her emotions unless they were somehow channeled. Perhaps Vivien could help the process.

The nurse came out of Jillian's room and told Vivien she could go back in if she wished. She warned that Jillian might be a little out of it, but that she was fine. They would be bringing her dinner within the hour, if she wanted to help her eat.

Inspector Sherwood and Cynthia's police friend joined her and they all re-entered. Sherwood seemed eager to leave. He spoke to Vivien. "They said that you can sleep on the other bed in the room tonight. Evelyn here will be staying outside the room. You may not see her, but she'll be here. The hospital's regular security guard will also make frequent visits. He'll introduce himself when he relieves the guy outside. However, call me if anything happens that concerns you. Here is my card with all my contact information. I have to go now. I'm sure that she's going to be all right."

"Thanks, Inspector."

Chad returned with Vivien's bag. "Are you leaving, Inspector? Do you have an extra card for us in case we want to call you?"

"Yes, here's one for you. I just gave one to Mrs. Hillcrest. She can fill you in about Evelyn. She can stay in the room tonight. I didn't know what your plans were, but let me know if you need me to help with any arrangements for you. "

Chad nodded and headed into Jillian's room, not sure himself what his plans were for the night. Jillian was sleeping, and Vivien was arranging the nightstand so the phone was close by. Jillian had already complained that she missed her own cell phone, but the police still had all of her items. Besides, they reminded her, it wasn't charged.

Chad returned to his vigil with Vivien. She informed him about Cynthia's friend, Evelyn, and also that a hospital security guard would be circulating occasionally by the room after introducing himself. She planned to stay in Jillian's room all night. She confided she was concerned that Jillian's euphoria might come crashing down and believed it would be helpful if she were there just in case.

Chad agreed. Jillian would want to keep up a front with him, which was not what she needed right now. She was more likely to show her true emotions with her mother. He would stay for a while, and then go to Jillian's flat for the rest of the night. He owed Cynthia an update and also wanted to join her to investigate Jillian's building and also keep her flat under observation in case someone might try something thinking that Jillian was still there. Good. He'd made a plan. Fortunately, he didn't need to be at work the next day, so he could call in sick, which was easier than explaining that he was taking the day off to stay with his hospitalized ex-wife.

odini disconnected from Harrington's secretary, who did indeed have some new information. Apparently Harrington's assistant— this Lloyd Jenkins—had won a trip to Mexico somehow. There were certain restrictions associated with it that included its secrecy, but the secretary said that Lloyd had been very excited since he could spend some time at his sister's place for part of the time. His business card had been drawn from a depository at a company's booth at some sort of tradeshow. However, for some competitive secretive reasons, he was not allowed to divulge the company name or where he was going. And she thought that there was some kind of focus group associated with it, which might be the reason that they had not been able to reach him. However, she was very surprised that they had still not been able to get in touch with him by e-mail, at least, and that he had not called his sister. Unfortunately, that was all the information that he had shared, although she would look through his desk more thoroughly the next morning—she had done a quick search on Friday—to see if she had missed anything that might give them a clue where he traveled after his visit to his sister's house.

Sodini immediately contacted his friends in Mexico and asked them if they could investigate further. He sent them another photo of Jenkins and requested that they do whatever they could to expedite the search. He explained that he was concerned that Mr. Jenkins could be in danger or that he could be a murder suspect himself. So they would be relieved to find him alive, and they would be anxious to question him regarding Mr. Harrington, his boss. Sodini asked them not to inform Jenkins of Harrington's death—rather just detain him regarding an embezzlement case, and they would fill him in when he returned to the U.S. They were to contact him or his partner Inspector Loren Sherwood if they had any problems.

Then Sodini had another idea. He printed the photo of Lloyd Jenkins and carried it to the room where Bill Vulkjevich sat rigidly with his lips clenched tightly shut and his eyes closed to mere slits. Sodini threw the photo down in front of him and watched for recognition. Vulkjevich simply glanced at the photo and pinched his lips more tightly together, but Sodini saw no signs of recognition. Vulkjevich did not know Jenkins.

"Thanks. That's very helpful."

Vulkjevich just glared at Sodini, determined not to be tricked again. Sodini grabbed the photo and left the suspect to nurse his grievances. He was refusing to sign any kind of statement.

Sodini needed some time to think. He was convinced that at a minimum, Vulkjevich's friend was the embezzler. He was also convinced Vulkjevich did not know Lloyd Jenkins. Therefore, Jenkins was most likely removed from the office so the new financial advisor would have easier access to Harrington's funds. Since the funds were actually transferred after Harrington's death, it was likely that Harrington had discovered the plot before the thief had a chance to gain the assets. So it was unlikely Jenkins had participated. However, if Jenkins could be found, he could probably help to identify the embezzler. This is why Sodini had expedited the search for the assistant.

But how was Lisa Baumgartner involved? And, for that matter, how and why was Jillian Hillcrest involved? Was Lisa killed because of something she knew? Or because she could somehow help to identify the embezzler because of her connection to Jillian Hillcrest? Others were checking the relevance of the list of companies both Lisa Baumgartner and the CFO had been examining. What if the embezzler had become close to Harrington by providing analyses of various aspects of the industry but needed some additional insight into the list of companies to impress Harrington and had hired Baumgartner to supply that information? Then somehow or for some reasons Lisa learned that the list was for Harrington—maybe she even mentioned she knew Jillian Hillcrest, who worked at one of the companies on the list. Given the timing, the embezzler might have gotten nervous she would talk with Jillian and let her know she had been speaking with him—which could lead to Jillian contacting Harrington. If that was his sole motivation, Sodini really wanted to catch this guy.

His reflections were interrupted by a call from an officer who had just finished speaking with Archie Linstrom, the Harmonia executive who had had a meeting with Harrington shortly before he was murdered. The officer reported Harrington had only discussed his assistant to say that he was on vacation. He did not mention a financial advisor. They focused almost entirely on the company that Harrington wanted Linstrom to consider. Other than a stiff neck from his bicycle wreck, he seemed quite fine. The officer said that Linstrom was co-operative and helpful, and said to contact him if they needed anything else.

Just as Sodini was disconnecting from the call about Linstrom, he received another call notifying him the police had installed the surveillance equipment and were ready for Vulkjevich's release. He would be monitored carefully, and if he contacted anyone by phone, in person, or by e-mail, they would know.

Sodini was pleased. Things were proceeding in the right direction. They were on the road to solving this crime.

53 ⋈⋈⋈

C had knocked softly on Cynthia Anderson's door careful not to disturb her fragrant wreath. She opened the door almost immediately although she was on the phone. She motioned for Chad to enter her flat, which was filled with orchids and plants. He noticed that the table was still set for last night's dinner with a lace tablecloth and fine china and crystal. He was wooed by the aromas of cooked garlic and smoldering butter. The black leather sofa and two easy-boy type chairs filled one end of the large room, and faced a reasonably large flat-screen television. Cynthia had filled her loft with plants and orchids rather than use it as an office as Jillian had. Chad briefly wondered how much time she spent caring for the orchids—he didn't know much about them but decided he might consider adding some to his Alameda home. They definitely created a pleasing ambience.

Cynthia disconnected and picked up a plate of something that smelled tempting. "Would you like some of last night's dinner? It's leg of lamb and some Pommes Anna. I finished cooking everything—figured I might as well. Ahhh—I can see that you would like some—your eyes are bigger than I've ever seen them." She smiled her whole-face smile (including her eyes) and went to the kitchen and prepared a plate for him, as he murmured that he wasn't aware of how hungry he really was. She poured them both some wine and they sat down in the living room and enjoyed a few minutes of food and wine, not discussing Jillian or anything.

When she had finished eating, Cynthia grabbed a notepad and turned to Chad to give him the information she had been gathering. "I've been in touch with some friends who have talked with some other friends who put me in touch with the officer in charge of the investigation of this building. Yes, there is an investigation into this building, and our fine concierge here—Charlie. Apparently he has been running or at least participating in some kind of electronics robbery ring. I'm a little embarrassed I didn't catch on—given that I'm an ex-cop. They focus on stealing computers or mobile phones or Kindles or ipads—whatever they can get—and then re-sell them. He even has a virtual company with a webpage where people can order stuff.

"However, they think he was careful not to steal anything from this building specifically. They suspect he used this building as a drop-off place. That is, whenever someone stole anything, they would bring it to him, and he would store it in the back room someplace and then transport it to wherever they actually kept the stuff."

Cynthia looked through her notes. "They're not sure why he broke into Jillian's place or even if he did; that would have been counter to his normal activity. They are working with apartment owners and managers throughout San Francisco to catch whoever they can, and they have arrested Charlie. They think that it is a big burglary ring and it may even be active as far south as San Jose. Charlie, by the way, appears to have ceased activities following the police visits when I caught Pete's brother in our hallway. I don't think the two are connected. So we still don't know who bribed Pete's brother to check out Jillian's floor."

Chad had an idea. "I wonder if Pete knows anything more than he's saying? Jillian really likes him and is sure he is honest, and his actions seem to confirm that. However, he might know something he doesn't know that he knows . . . or something. He was here when I arrived. Why don't we go talk to him right now?"

The two of them headed down to the area where Pete usually waited during his car parking duties. He was not there, so they asked the new concierge if he had seen him. "Oh, yes, he's just parking a car. I'll let him know you want to talk with him. I think he would appreciate an update on Miss Hillcrest. He was very concerned about her." And he called to let Pete know Mrs. Anderson and a friend wanted to talk to him about Jillian.

A few minutes later Pete came into the lobby and joined Cynthia and Chad. He asked immediately how Jillian was doing and whether there was anything she needed. Cynthia updated him on Jillian's progress, and he seemed genuinely relieved. Then she launched into their real purpose. "Chad and I are trying to solve the mystery of who asked your brother to check out Jillian's flat. As you can imagine, given that someone lured her out yesterday, and that almost killed her, it becomes a little more important."

Pete looked genuinely surprised. "Wait. Someone lured her somewhere? I thought she was in a car wreck."

"Yes, she was in an auto accident. But the reason she was in that area was because someone called her representing the police. We're not sure why they did that, but it certainly endangered her life. So we are looking into anything that might be remotely related. What do you know about Charlie and that day your brother was here?"

Pete shook his head. "Well, not much. I told the police everything I knew. Mickey was waiting for me outside here—we were going to buy him a baseball glove. We had both saved up for it, and he was very excited. However, he knew he would not be able to afford the one he really wanted, so when this guy drove up and offered him a hundred bucks to simply go check out an apartment, he figured it would be an easy way to get it. The guy simply wanted him to check out the hallway, and let him know how many apartments there were next to Jillian's—also, exactly which floor was Jillian's, and how close was it to the elevator—stuff like that. The guy told Mickey he was buying her a big gift and just needed to know how easy it would be to get it into her flat."

Pete stopped to consider what to say next. "So, yeah, I'm pretty sure Mickey knew that story was fake, but he really wanted a new baseball glove. His team did well last year and is expected to do well this year; and he plays third base and has a great hitting record."

Cynthia persevered. "I'm sure. Now again, what about Charlie? The police said you came to them directly, that you didn't go through Charlie. Why was that?"

Pete hesitated again and then decided he owed them whatever information he had. "Well, Charlie doesn't exactly have the best reputation. He's worked here for several years, and 'things' just seem to happen. I've seen him talking to a guy I know spent some time in jail for breaking and entering. Also, there were other people who would go into the lobby and give him packages. So I just wasn't sure whether to trust him. He knows Mickey, but he didn't speak up for him that day he got caught in the building. Anyway, I wondered whether Charlie was the one who told this guy to talk to Mickey. I just don't trust the guy, you know?"

"Did you ever see Charlie do anything illegal or disruptive or whatever?"

"No, not really. I just saw other guys handing him stuff in the lobby. He seemed to do his job all right. And he was good to me. That's why I never said anything about him. Maybe I should have. Especially if he had anything to do with Jillian's accident."

Chad decided to join the conversation. "We don't know that, but it would be really helpful if you think of anything else to let us know. Maybe you could ask your brother to remember really hard about the guy who approached him. Like, did he have a beard? Or what kind of music was he listening to? Or was the car old or new—I believe he said that it was white—anything else might help determine who it was. Also, did your brother ever say how he was supposed to meet the guy to give him the information? Was the guy going to be waiting for him in the car? Maybe he told the police, but I don't recall. And, again, thanks for your help. I'll let Jillian know. She'll appreciate it."

They left him looking somewhat dejected, but they were sure he would be grilling his brother that night. Chad was not particularly satisfied that they had learned anything. "We already knew that Charlie was a crook, but now we know Pete knew, too. I wonder who else might have known? If he was selling basically hot electronics stuff, maybe one of his customers was somehow connected to all of this? Did you check with your friends to see if they had questioned Charlie about Jillian and whether he was the one who broke into her flat?"

Cynthia was already on the phone again. "I would think that would be one of their first questions, but I'll double-check." She was busy posing questions to her friend via phone as they headed back to her flat. She finished just as she opened the door. "They are going to check into it more thoroughly. Apparently there was some discussion about Jillian, but not about the day Pete's brother was here. So they will see if possibly Charlie had something to do with it, or if someone else—like one of his customers—asked him for the information. Seems unlikely it would be Charlie since he already knows all that information, like where her apartment is located, and the surrounding area. However, he is being very co-operative right now in the hopes of getting special treatment in the case pending against him and his partners."

"You're right. But wasn't the kid supposed to see if the way was clear, like the hall was empty? Maybe someone wanted to get into Jillian's flat. We know that it wasn't in Charlie's best interest to call attention to this building since he was using it as a way to pass through his so-called merchandise. Maybe it was not related to this incident at all."

Chad stopped to reflect. "But one other question I've had from the beginning is how did that guy get Jillian's phone number who called her to come to Buck's? Her office number is listed as a contact at work, but not her mobile number—which is also her home phone. Granted, she gives it out fairly freely, but only to business acquaintances and friends. So I've got to assume whoever had her mobile phone knew her personally, or knew someone who knows her personally. That concerns me."

"I'm sure it concerns Inspector Sherwood, as well. He mentioned it to me in the hallway at the hospital, which is why they are pleased to have a retired policewoman on duty at her room."

All of a sudden, Chad was exhausted. The wine had had its impact. Looking at Cynthia Anderson, he realized that she, too, was showing signs of having been up all night. He thanked her again for the great lamb dinner, gladly took the replenished glass of red wine she offered, and returned to Jillian's apartment, using a key supplied by the new concierge to get in. Tomorrow was another day, and he hoped it would a happy one.

54 🧬

nspector Sherwood left the hospital knowing he had to get some sleep. He had been up for at least 36 hours. He checked in with Sodini and listened as his partner explained his theory about Harrington's assistant after speaking with the secretary; that it was possible the assistant had received a free trip to get him out of the way. Also, he was pleased to hear Sodini had checked the photo with Vulkjevich, and he agreed with Sodini's conclusion that most likely the assistant might become a victim, not the suspect. He let Sodini know what Jillian had said, and then told him to contact him if he needed, but his plan was to get some sleep. Sodini would pick up Sherwood at his flat to take him to Harrington's the next morning. Maybe in the meantime either the Mexican police or Harrington's secretary would find some additional information about Lloyd Jenkins.

Unfortunately, Sherwood had been pushing himself for too long, and the adrenaline continued to keep him awake even after his shower. He lay in bed fully understanding the meaning of the expression of "wheels turning" in his head. He needed to stop thinking about this case. Although he seldom watched T.V., he decided to look for something that might help him stop thinking about Jillian, her friend, Harrington, and $8 million. So he turned on his television and looked for anything that might brake the "wheels." Something must have worked. He woke up in his chair a few hours later, and headed off to bed, neglecting to set his alarm.

55

Jillian slept fitfully for a few hours, awakening for some unknown reason. She tried to move and then remembered she had been in a wreck because some lunatic had decided she needed to be silenced. She had indeed appreciated the situation, and even though neither Inspector Sherwood nor Chad nor anyone had told her, she was sure that the murderer would most likely have killed her just like he did Lisa—if the deer had not diverted her.

She wondered if anyone had contacted Lisa's mom. She would ask her mother to call her tomorrow to let her know what was happening. Regardless, she was still hoping to get to Lisa's memorial service, somehow, now more than ever. What could Lisa have possibly known that would cause someone to run her over until all life had been crushed out of her? And Dan Harrington? Of all the millionaires to kill, why him? And what did Jillian know that caused the killer to be nervous that she should continue to live?

She tried to relate Bill Vulkjevich to all of this. He just wasn't a likely suspect, but she tried to remember anything he might have said over the past few weeks, both before and after her trip to Geneva. She recalled he talked about some conference he had attended, where he apparently was a speaker, which at the time seemed unlikely to Jillian. However, he had gone on about it for quite a while during a conference call and Jillian had had to cut him short. He talked about meeting quite a few people who were excellent and would be helpful if they needed to hire someone. Maybe that's where he met this friend who Inspector Sherwood mentioned? She decided to call Sherwood in the morning to let him know. She even remembered the name of the conference, and would suggest that they would have a list of attendees. Maybe that would help.

Then she pushed the button she now had to regulate her pain management—and drifted into the land of floating bliss.

56 ⋈⟨⫴⟩⋈⟨⫴⟩⋈

Lloyd Jenkins was indeed enjoying his time in Acapulco at one of the most luxurious hotels he had ever visited. The food was better than gourmet, and it was plentiful. The shows were first class with well-known headliners and, if he were a drinker, he could have whatever he wanted.

However, Lloyd was becoming impatient; the trip was supposed to be connected to some kind of focus group to help determine best practices for a company investigating new ways to reach and serve investors. He had faithfully followed the restrictions to not contact anyone while in Mexico—the sponsor was concerned about competitors learning about this new approach. Given that there so far had been no focus group, Lloyd wondered what had happened. No one had approached him about attending any meetings. When he checked with the hotel concierge, they poured over their itineraries but saw nothing that was likely. However, they let Lloyd know his bills were paid for another week, and they hoped he was enjoying himself.

Lloyd was not concerned too much about work. He had fully informed his boss, Dan Harrington, about the trip and told him the name of the hotel and how to get in touch with him if needed. Dan had told him to have a great time and not to worry about work. He could handle things until Lloyd got back. The past few months had been particularly busy ones, and Lloyd had worked on weekends and at night. So Harrington was pleased that he got the opportunity to relax.

No one had tried to reach Lloyd through the hotel so he assumed everything was fine. Nonetheless, he was growing restless. He wasn't accustomed to days without purpose and his work ethic had been heightened by an upbringing in a frugal family. His parents had left a small amount of money when they were killed in a car crash. His sister had worked her way through college by then, and was earning a small salary as a middle-school teacher, which enabled her to offer her younger brother a sofa in her small apartment and enough food for the growing teenager. He similarly worked his way through college and discovered he had a talent for numbers and the ability to envision new products and to forecast their value.

He had met Dan at a school function intended to connect students with mentors. In addition to connecting intellectually, the two really liked each other. When Dan started his fund, one of the first people he called was Lloyd.

So on the second consecutive Monday morning, Lloyd was not sitting at his desk getting ready for another day of checking out potential experts for Dan to interview or conferences to attend or companies to investigate. And he had to admit, he was a little bored. He decided to check one more time with the concierge about a potential meeting, and then he was going to forego the rules and check his e-mail—assuming the hotel had a computer for guest use. Again the concierge regrettably could not identify any likely meetings and, yes of course, the business center on the third floor had computers.

So Lloyd sauntered up to the third floor to check his e-mail for the first time in a week—with no idea his life was about to drastically change.

57

Sodini was on his way to pick up Sherwood so that they could check out Dan Harrington's apartment when he got the call that Harrington's receptionist had notified them she had spoken with Lloyd Jenkins. First, she apologized for having blurted out the fact of Harrington's death and the embezzlement, which was unfortunate, but understandable. As they suspected, Jenkins had been lured to Mexico under what appeared to be false pretenses. Unfortunately he had received all communication regarding the trip online, and had not met the person or persons responsible for arranging the trip. He had already made arrangements to return to the office, and would be available to do whatever he could to help, arriving by tomorrow at the latest. Apparently he was close to Harrington and was very upset, on a personal level, and he and the receptionist cried together over the phone. He knew nothing of a new account opened in Harrington's name and was surprised it existed. He promised he would say nothing to anyone and would speak only to the police about the murder and the attempted embezzlement. He did, however, immediately contact his sister to let her know he was all right.

Sodini immediately called his friend in Mexico to alert him he had located his suspect, so they didn't divert his return to California. He thanked him profusely and offered reciprocation should he ever need his help. He also promised him a Scotch the next time he was in San Francisco.

They had now most likely eliminated one more suspect. In the meantime, Vulkjevich had not tried to contact anyone so that was a dead-end for the moment. However, Sodini was hopeful they might find something in Harrington's flat that would be helpful. Sherwood was not in front of his building as he was supposed to be, so Sodini tried to reach him on his mobile. He was rewarded with a muffled "What!" and surmised that he had awakened his partner. "Are you ready to go to Harrington's place? Or should I come back in a few?"

"Shit. Sorry about that. Just give me ten minutes. Maybe you could get some coffee down the street?"

"Will do. By the way, we heard from the assistant. We were right. He won a trip to Mexico and was required not to communicate with anyone. He told Harrington but no one else how to get in touch with him. He's pretty upset. He plans to be back by tomorrow or sooner if possible."

"Anything on Vulkjevich?"

"No, nothing so far. We may have to get a search warrant. But let's see what we find at Harrington's. Meet me out front when you're ready. I'll have coffee and pastry."

About 15 minutes later Sodini pulled up in front of Sherwood's apartment, just as his partner was walking out talking on his phone. Sodini honked. Sherwood waved as he headed for the car. "Jillian Hillcrest just called me about a conference that Vulkjevich attended and raved about. She thought that maybe he might have met his so-called friend there. I'll call it in—maybe they'll share the list of attendees and we might recognize someone's name. It's a long shot, but worth a try."

They pulled up in front of Harrington's place, and Sherwood went in to arrange entry to the flat while Sodini found a parking place. The concierge remembered Inspector Sherwood and readily provided a passkey, asking him to sign for it and reminding him to be sure to return it when they were finished. Sodini joined him as they headed for the elevator and Harrington's flat. They decided to focus on the office/den/library; that was where most papers seemed to be located. Sherwood checked the desk itself while Sodini surveyed the rest of the room including the bookcase.

They had been searching for less than an hour when they were startled to hear a key turning in the lock of the front door. Sodini shrugged and both inspectors prepared for what they assumed would be a cleaning person. They were surprised when a well-dressed, distinguished-looking man probably in his late 50s in a three-piece suit carrying a brief case stepped into the room.

Sherwood waited until the intruder had closed the door. "Who are you? What are you doing here?"

The man looked shocked. In fact, he almost looked like he was going to have a heart attack. "Who are you?" He almost screamed at them as he was backing toward the door.

Both men pulled out their badges. "I'm Inspector Loren Sherwood of the San Francisco Police Department. This is my partner, Inspector Joe Sodini. You're not going anywhere until you explain why you're here."

The man seemed to quickly gather himself. "I'm here returning the keys and computer Dan left in my car. He didn't answer his phone so I thought I'd just drop them off. So if you don't mind I'll just leave them here and be on my way." That explained how the intruder got past the concierge—he had Harrington's keys.

Sodini and Sherwood looked at each other and smiled. "I don't think so. We'll need a little more information. Like, who are you?"

"I'm Dan's financial advisor. He'll vouch for me. Just ask him. My name is John Bowersox."

Sodini and Sherwood circled the flustered John Bowersox with the full knowledge that they had their suspect. They both were sure that he owned a white car. They knew he was the one who had opened the new account and embezzled the funds. They knew he had killed Dan Harrington and Lisa Baumgartner. Neither doubted it—not even a little bit.

What was not believable was that he had walked right into their hands.

Sherwood spoke first. "Why don't we all go down to our office and talk about it some more?"

"Wait a minute. I can assure you I have nothing to hide."

"Good. Then you won't mind if we check out your computer?"

"Oh, this isn't mine. I told you. This is Dan's. As I said, he left it and his keys and his wallet in my car. And, here, sure you can check it, if it's all right with him. But I really must be going."

"I don't think so." Sherwood was now between Bowersox and the door. Sodini was on the other side. "You're going with us. Joe, why don't you call for a patrol car?"

The inspectors arranged to transfer their suspect to their office. Neither of them mentioned to Mr. John Bowersox that Dan Harrington was dead. They suggested that he might want to be silent, and he wisely obeyed. While they waited for the car, they were careful to store Harrington's computer, wallet, and keys in the evidence bags Sodini had brought just in case. They did not question the suspect further, waiting for the proper procedure at the station.

Sherwood called Harrington's office and talked with the secretary. "Have you ever met or are you aware of someone named John Bowersox?"

"Yes, that name is familiar, but Lloyd might know for sure. I'll check with him as soon as I talk with him again, and let you know."

When the car and officer arrived, Sherwood accompanied Bowersox, while Sodini decided to remain at Harrington's place to see what else he could find—particularly since they now had a name.

By the time Sherwood arrived at the station, they had discovered quickly that the address on his driver's license was old—he did not live there any more. So Sherwood assumed that they would have to get his address from Bowersox himself. He decided to leave him alone in the room for a while. He wanted to gather more information so he could ask informed, productive questions. This guy was no Vulkjevich. He was smart and careful, although many would question the wisdom of returning to Harrington's flat after he had murdered the guy. Maybe that was one point for the police. By keeping the murder and embezzlement quiet they had lulled Bowersox into believing he had actually gotten away with it. Hopefully Sodini would find something at Harrington's flat that would confirm their suspicions.

Simultaneously, various members of the department were checking out the computer he had brought with him. Also, he had car keys so they were looking for his vehicle while requesting a warrant to search it. So far, he had not asked for an attorney. He probably assumed he was smart enough to outwit the police. Well, maybe he was.

Then, again, maybe not.

C had awakened Monday morning momentarily startled that he was not in his own bed. Then everything came rushing back. He could hardly believe it was past 8:00. He phoned Vivien to find out how Jillian was doing. She answered quickly and cheerfully. "How is she?"

"She's doing fine. She's still in pain, but despite the pain meds, she is fairly alert. Apparently she even remembered something to tell Inspector Sherwood, and she called him to let him know. Ah, you might want to bring her something to eat—you know, something good. I suspect she's not enjoying the food here too much."

"Is she hungry? Well, even if she's not, I'll stop and get her something. I should be there within the hour. First I want to check with Cynthia to see if she's heard anything. She's a really neat lady. I like her a lot."

"It was certainly a relief to have her friend here last night. And she arranged it so quickly and with such little fanfare."

"Yeah. I really like Inspector Sherwood, also. He has been very helpful. I think he'll catch the guy, I really do."

Chad disconnected, took a quick shower, shaved, and dressed in some clothes he had brought in preparation for spending the weekend. The flat was filled with Jillian's presence, but without her it seemed very empty. Chad wasn't sure how he felt. He was angry that someone had tried to kill her, and he wanted to pursue the culprit and protect her from harm. At the same time, his feelings for her had increased, and he was almost as joyful as when he first met her. Regardless, he decided that the best thing to do would be to go see her. He headed for Cynthia Anderson's flat. He knocked on her door, which she again answered immediately. He wondered if she just stood by the door waiting for someone to knock. She greeted him warmly and asked if he had eaten. Chad explained that he was going to get something for Jillian, Vivien and him on the way to the hospital. Did she want to go with him?

She eagerly grabbed her jacket and purse, and the two headed for the elevator. They stopped to speak with the concierge, asking if he could arrange for their car because they didn't see Pete and Chad didn't have his number. The concierge called him, and he appeared within ten minutes in the Porsche. "I sure enjoy driving that machine, if only for a little while. By the way, I spoke with Mickey this morning. He said the guy who talked with him was kind of sloppy, bald, and a fatso. He said the guy's car was littered with junk inside—you know, bottles and wrappers. Also, he isn't so sure any more the car was white, white. Now he thinks maybe it was some kind of dirty white or maybe a tan color. And he was supposed to meet the guy around the corner, but when Mrs. Anderson caught him, he ran without even thinking about talking to the guy again, and he's been a little worried the guy might come back and demand the hundred bucks back, since Mickey didn't give him what he paid for. Don't know if that helps. But I let the cops know the car was not white, because that seemed to make a difference to Jillian."

"Thanks, Pete. That sounds like a description of that Vulkjevich guy who's been a thorn in Jillian's side lately. That's very helpful. If your brother thinks of anything else, please tell us."

"Will do. Tell Jillian I asked about her. We're all pulling for her."

Chad called Inspector Sherwood and left him a message letting him know what he had just learned about the person who had bribed Pete's brother to check out Jillian's flat. He described the person and the kind of car as relayed by Pete from his brother, and suggested the description might fit Vulkjevich as described to him by Jillian. Then Cynthia and he left for the hospital, both looking forward to seeing Jillian.

59 ⋈⋈⋈

Jillian awakened this time relieved it was light outside. It had been a long night; she awoke frequently to the frustration of not being able to move to a comfortable position. When she did drift off to sleep, unfamiliar sounds would awaken her. She was happy now to have the diversions of the hospital daytime rituals. She knew her mother had slept some but assumed she had been watchful during the night. She responded to all of the nurse's questions; and eagerly awaited Chad's arrival. She had heard Vivien mention something about food, and knew Chad would know exactly what she wanted (even if she didn't).

She had not thought any more about Dan Harrington or even Lisa. However, she now recalled she had not spoken with Lisa's mom, and decided to use her mother's phone to send her a message advising her of the accident. She hadn't checked with the doctor yet about whether she would be able to travel by the end of the week, so she at least needed to prepare Madeline for the possibility she might not be able to attend. However, she was going to try her best to be there.

She pecked out her message with her one good hand and hoped it wasn't too brief to cause concern. She let Madeline know she would call her with details either that day or the next. And she hoped Madeline was feeling all right, or at least a little bit better by now. Just as she sent the message, Chad and Cynthia Anderson entered the room. She was indeed delighted to see them, particularly since Chad had brought an awesome breakfast from the Mediterranean restaurant: a goat cheese omelet, potatoes, and a banana nut muffin. He apologized saying he had kept things fairly bland, because he wasn't sure what kind of shape her stomach was in. He had also brought Vivien a similar breakfast, and had stopped at a coffee place and carried in a large 15-cup cardboard coffee "traveler" complete with pouring spout, which he placed on her night stand along with several new ceramic cups (he knew she hated drinking out of plastic).

She really did need to remember why they had gotten divorced. Or maybe not.

The four of them chatted away about how Peet's coffee was or wasn't better than Starbucks (Chad was not part of this conversation since he didn't drink coffee) with Cynthia claiming she knew another brand that was better than either of them. Although Jillian couldn't eat everything Chad had brought, she certainly enjoyed what she did eat. The nurse came in and was happy to help herself to a cup of coffee—she was sure it was better than the hospital coffee. She had come by to give Jillian some antibiotics and other medicine to help prevent infection.

Cynthia had already greeted her friend, Evelyn, whom she thanked energetically and told her they had all slept better because she had been there. The retired officer said no one suspicious had visited the ward, although the nurse had gotten another call enquiring about Jillian, which she had reported. So now Evelyn was headed for home and bed for the day; she said she would be prepared to spend another night there if they needed her.

About that time, Jillian got a call from Inspector Sherwood asking if she knew John Bowersox. She had to think a minute.

"Yes, I remember him. He was the investment advisor I met in Geneva. I invited him to speak on my panel along with Harrington and others. He canceled right after I returned from Europe, claiming he had forgotten a previous commitment. Is he involved? He isn't the one Harrington hired, is he?"

"It looks that way. We caught him in Harrington's flat with his computer and other stuff that ties him directly to Harrington. What else can you tell me about him? Also, did he give you any contact information? And did you give him your contact information? Would he have had your cell number, for example?"

"He seemed quite bright and competent and described himself as a financial advisor for the entrepreneur and investor community. He seemed to know the biotech world. And, yes, I did give him my contact information, and he would have had my cell number."

"What about his contact information?"

"I have his contact information entered into my phone, which I believe the police still have. We can retrieve the information—if you charge my phone. As I recall, it's a phone number and e-mail address. You know, it's hard to believe that he would do all this. Did you find out anything else about Bill Vulkjevich?"

"Not really. I need to go. Thanks for the information. I'll keep you updated. Take care."

As Jillian was speaking with Inspector Sherwood, she realized Chad, Cynthia, and her mother were conspiring together in the corner. She tried to move to see them better, but her restricted leg and painful ribs prevented it. Chad noticed her interest first, and suggested she might want to get some sleep. He was planning to go scouting for their lunch. She told him of the inspector's question about Bowersox. Cynthia chimed in saying they had had some luck double-checking with Pete about the identity of the person who had asked his brother to scope out Jillian's flat, and they had relayed it to Inspector Sherwood. About that time, Jillian's eyelids grew very heavy and she sighed and went to sleep.

Cynthia and Vivien decided to stay in the room while Chad went out for more food. He checked in at work and confirmed he wasn't needed. Then he went to the nearest coffee shop and sat in a corner with a cup of special tea latte pondering what to do next. The past week had shown him a new facet of Jillian's personality—one of determination and independence. He had definitely realized he cared deeply for her. As ex-husband and ex-wife, they had become very close in the past week. While Jillian was a planner and liked to know what was coming next so she could find the best route there, Chad reminded himself he was willing to go with the flow. So he promised himself to stay alert to any signs from Jillian, and if the opportunity arose to advance their relationship, he would take it. But for now, he wasn't going to push it. Having made that decision, he started out in search of lunch.

60 ⌇⌇⌇

Inspector Sherwood reflected on Jillian's information about Bowersox approaching her in Geneva and his subsequent withdrawal from the panel appearance at the conference in San Jose. He shared this with the group investigating John Bowersox. Sodini had decided they should check out Vulkjevich's reaction to Bowersox, but they opted to wait until they knew a little more about him. Vulkjevich would have had Jillian's cell number as part of his work relationship with her, so it was still possible that he was the one who had made the phone call luring her to her near-death accident. However, Bowersox also had Jillian's contact information, since she had given it to him in Geneva. This information from Jillian might get them to that next step of connecting the two.

Also, the message from Jillian's ex-husband that the teenager at her apartment building had corrected his original story to change the color of the car to light brown rather than white and that the guy was short and bald—well, that coincided with Vulkjevich and his car.

Inspector Sherwood relayed this information to the group managing the detail at Jillian's apartment building. They had definitely uncovered an organized ring of burglars. However, their investigation concluded that Vulkjevich was not involved with the burglaries.

Charlie, the concierge, had been co-operating. But he still claimed he had nothing to do with the guy who paid Pete's brother to investigate Jillian's flat. In fact, to the contrary—that event actually caused the thieves' downfall because it drew attention from the police. Inspector Sherwood learned from his fellow officers who were interrogating Charlie that the thieves had used Jillian's flat while she was in Geneva. They had stored some of the electronics contraband there, because the back room was full. Jillian returned earlier than originally scheduled and called Charlie from the airport that evening—to be sure to catch Pete before he went home—to arrange her car the next morning, as she was not expected for several days. Before she arrived, Charlie quickly moved the items that were still in her flat up to her loft, hoping she would not go up there before they could remove it the next day. That's how the lights got left on—the thieves entered her flat after she left for work and removed the items. Mrs. Anderson almost caught them the first day, so they needed to return to retrieve the remaining items. Charlie had to leave the door unlocked so they could get in whenever Mrs. Anderson was out.

But Charlie had no knowledge of Pete's brother, Mickey. He had not hired anyone to check on Jillian. Inspector Sherwood called Chad to let him know this recent information, and to find out if he had learned anything else. At this point, Inspector Sherwood was reasonably sure that the guy who hired Mickey was probably Vulkjevich just trying to stir up trouble.

Sodini called Sherwood to let him know he had found some information about Bowersox among Harrington's folders in his desk. He was packing up what he had so far, and bringing it to the station. One of the folders was labeled "Bowersox" and had the same list of companies the Harmonia CFO, Brynn, had reviewed and that the police had found in Lisa's luggage. In addition, there were several pages filled with a description and analysis of each. Sodini was hoping fingerprints would help connect Lisa to Bowersox and Harrington. That would be a useful piece of evidence.

Sherwood asked Sodini to check for Bowersox's car. One of the officers was bringing the keys to him. According to the DMV, it was a brand new white Mercedes-Benz C300W, so Sherwood was sure that Bowersox would have parked it carefully. They were in the process of getting a search warrant for the car, so he asked Sodini to wait until they had it before opening the vehicle.

In the meantime, the Assistant District Attorney—the ADA—was sure they had enough evidence to hold Bowersox. The broker who had opened the new account for Harrington and received the transfer of the $8 million had identified Bowersox's photo out of a dozen photos (that included one of Harrington himself).

So Sherwood entered the room purposefully where Bowersox waited stoically. After reading him his rights, he informed him that he was being held, and that he might want to consult with an attorney. "You are being held on suspicion of identity theft, grand theft of personal property, burglary and forgery of documents."

The distinguished-looking Bowersox looked incredulous. "I find that very hard to believe. I've done no such thing. I was simply returning the things that Dan had left in my car."

Inspector Sherwood interrupted him. "I suggest you wait for your attorney before you say anything. Do you have one?"

For the first time since they had had brought him to the station, Bowersox looked unsure of himself. "I'm not sure. I'll need to call someone."

In the meantime, Sodini and the officer who had brought him the Mercedes keys located the car. Sodini looked it over carefully for any signs of damage but did not see any dents. They waited patiently for authorization to enter the car, and when the call came, quickly entered it and found items and folders that obviously belonged to Harrington—as well as Harrington's passport and credit/debit cards and a briefcase with Harrington's identification on it. They also found another laptop computer that had no identity tag. Sodini let Sherwood know and suggested they have the car towed to the impound lot. He also said they should check it for recent repairs, possible bloodstains, fingerprints, and DNA evidence.

While they were sure they had a solid embezzlement case against Bowersox, they still needed to gather more evidence to charge him with murder. So after they had turned Bowersox over for incarceration, the two inspectors and the ADA met to discuss what was needed and what the next steps should be. They still wanted to interview Lloyd Jenkins to find out what he knew—if anything—about John Bowersox. Given that Jenkins would be familiar with Harrington's financial procedures and passwords, he would be useful in determining how Bowersox had succeeded in transferring the funds. They would speak with him in the morning after his return from Mexico.

They also pulled in Vulkjevich. Since Bowersox was in custody, they didn't need to monitor Vulkjevich any longer, although he was at least guilty of stalking Jillian and sending false information to *The Wall Street Journal*. More important, he might be able to connect Bowersox to Jillian and/or Lisa Baumgartner.

The two inspectors entered the room where Vulkjevich sat waiting, obviously fuming that he was there again.

"You can't do this. I am a citizen with rights. I'll have your asses up in front of a judge so fast, it will make your head spin!"

Sherwood let him vent a little, then responded with restrained but obvious anger. "Listen, you. We've arrested your friend, John Bowersox." He threw a photograph of the suspect on the table in front of Vulkjevich. "You may be surprised to know—or maybe not—that he embezzled eight million dollars from Dan Harrington, murdered him and Jillian Hillcrest's friend, and tried to murder Miss Hillcrest. You have a choice here. You can cooperate with us, or we can add your name to his as an embezzler and murderer."

Vulkjevich looked dumbfounded. He picked up the photo and studied it intently.

Sherwood continued. "So is this the person you met at the conference and shared plans to do harm to Mr. Harrington?'

Vulkjevich was eager to clarify his role. "Yes, this is him. But I only wanted to besmirch Harrington's name. I never intended to murder him—or anyone. I just want to get the drug industry. They are sons of bitches. But not by killing people. Did you say that he actually tried to kill Jillian? Oh, no. Not Jillian. She's O.K."

"Did you follow her home in order to find out where she lived so that you could send a package of false information to her?"

He looked sheepish. "Yes, and I just wanted to know where she lived. I actually like her. She's only the way she is because she has to be. That's her job." Sodini concluded that Vulkjevich was infatuated with Jillian.

Sherwood continued his questioning. "Did you give information to Bowersox about Harrington?"

"Yes, I gave him all the information I had. Like I told you, we planned to feed him false information so he'd make bad investments. But we never discussed stealing from him. And we sure as hell didn't talk about killing him."

"What else?"

"Well, he helped me prepare the analysis of the Harmonia partnered product that has so impressed Jillian."

"Wasn't that meeting just last week? I thought you told us that you hadn't been in contact with him for months?"

"And that's the truth. He actually did the analysis while we were at the conference to show me how good he was. I never saw him since the conference. He never returned any of my e-mail or phone inquiries. Also, he gave me a different name, including a fake business card. I couldn't track him down." Sodini could understand how someone of Vulkjevich's intellect and skills would have difficulty tracking down the illusive Bowersox.

When they completed their interview, they left him in the room while they pursued some other leads. They also initiated a search on the name that Bowersox had given to Vulkjevich.

In addition to following up with Vulkjevich, they would go back to many of the same places they had originally circulated Lisa's photo and now circulate Bowersox's photo. They also planned to check around the same areas to see if anyone had noticed the Mercedes. And they would be contacting auto dealers to discover if anyone had repaired this Mercedes in the past few days.

It occurred to Inspector Sherwood that the Mercedes could have been out of commission while Bowersox got it repaired, which meant he might have rented a car in the meantime. They would uncover that when they checked his credit card records, which was underway. They would also examine the suspect's bank deposits and/or safe deposit boxes or any other accounts for suspicious activity.

The two inspectors still couldn't believe the guy had actually walked in on them at Harrington's flat. Although they had set the trap for him by keeping Harrington's death and the embezzlement quiet, they hadn't been prepared for the suspect to walk right into their arms. They were very pleased with themselves and said so, while the veteran ADA just rolled his eyes and did his best not to remind them that most criminals are pretty stupid. And, he added, could they please make sure they gathered the right evidence that proved Bowersox was the murderer as well as the embezzler?

Sodini and Sherwood looked at each other then, and decided that it was time to check in with Jillian and her family. She had almost died, most likely because she was helping them track down a murderer. She deserved to know they had caught the guy. So they called it a day and headed for the hospital—stopping en route for a bottle of Champagne.

61

"I don't believe it. I know him. I just can't believe that someone I know would kill two people, embezzle millions, and then try to kill me. It's like a plot from a Law and Order episode." Jillian was reacting to the information relayed to her by Inspector Sherwood, while Sodini was busy opening the champagne. Chad, Cynthia, and Vivien looked anxiously at Jillian, prepared to summon the nurse.

But Jillian was not showing too much reaction to the news, other than relief. "Oh, my. I am pleased that you caught him. And thank you for bringing the champagne so that I could share your victory. And you must be Inspector Sherwood's partner. I don't believe we've met."

Sherwood looked apologetic. "That's right. You two haven't met. This is the world-renowned homicide investigator and my partner, Inspector Joe Sodini. If the bad guys knew about him, there wouldn't be any murders."

Sodini jumped in, sensing that the goal was to cheer up the patient. "At your service, Madame. And very pleased to meet you. I suspect you can't drink very much of this given your meds, but perhaps just a sip would enable you to join in the celebration."

Jillian liked him immediately; he passed plastic cups of champagne to everyone in the room. It went well with the crab and sour dough bread Chad had picked up for lunch. Jillian was sure the hospital staff would make them leave, but instead the nurses, security guard, and several doctors joined them. It was a fun party, if only Lisa and Dan had been there to enjoy it.

As she thought about Lisa and Dan, Jillian began to be depressed. She was happy that they had caught the murderer, but it left her with no reason to drive herself to help.

Her body hurt; her leg continued to throb; she couldn't move. One of her best friends had been killed. A really good guy who was trying to make a difference had been killed. And she had almost been killed. She saw Chad and her mother both watching her while the others were chatting loudly. She smiled weakly, but the tears were starting to come.

At that moment, Chad pulled out his gym bag and removed—Jillian gasped—her bra—the one that had held her leg together just two nights ago. "Here's to Jillian Hillcrest, the survivalist!" She laughed, along with everyone in the room.

"Of course, you saved it, didn't you?" She smiled despite her mood, and welcomed Chad's efforts to cheer her up. Her mind shifted back to analytical.

"Inspector Sherwood, I still don't understand why Lisa was killed."

"We'll need to establish a motive in order to prosecute Bowersox for that murder, but we are well on our way to finding evidence. We're sure that we can connect him to Harrington's murder. Believe me, I am very determined to uncover the evidence connecting him to Lisa's death. We have his car and we have him. And he will not be getting out of jail any time soon. The Superior Court judge has ordered him held without bail. He said he would not even consider it again until the hearing he scheduled three months from now when the issue of bail would be revisited. In addition to the original charges of identify theft and embezzlement, he's being held on suspicion of two murders, one of which includes a special-circumstance allegation of murder for financial gain, which gives prosecutors the option of seeking the death penalty."

The last thing Jillian remembered before drifting off to sleep was her determination that something good had to come out of all this.

62

C had, Cynthia, and her mother visited Jillian daily in the hospital, until Thursday when the doctor discharged her. Jillian had grown stronger, and the throbbing pain had lessened, although it was still there if she moved too much. She was pleased her mother and Cynthia seemed to be getting to know each other. They were always talking briskly when they entered her room, and seemed to be sharing stories and experiences with one another. Jillian hoped their friendship would grow; neither of them seemed to have many close friends.

A steady stream of Jillian's friends stopped by once it became known at Harmonia that visitors were welcome. In addition, her old boss from her previous firm brought several of her friends from there. The room was full of flowers, balloons, candy, and fruit arrangements. Fortunately, the numerous visitors helped to eat the food.

In the meantime, Brynn, Tim, and his wife traveled to New York for the financial conference to meet and greet current and potential investors interested in Harmonia Therapeutics. Tim's presentation was well received by investors, who were aware of it due to a press release Jillian had issued two weeks earlier alerting the investment community to the date and time. The company's stock held its higher price and a new analyst initiated coverage on the company, joining the 12 other analysts whose banks followed Harmonia making recommendations to their institutional investor clients. Although Jillian wasn't there to contribute, Brynn and Tim in their roles as CFO and CEO met with all of the investors who requested meetings. As far as Jillian could determine, Tim's wife, Stephanie, was still not aware of the relationship between her husband and Brynn. Stephanie enjoyed visiting the Guggenheim and the Metropolitan museums during the day and accompanied her husband and Brynn to restaurants and Broadway plays in the evening.

Jillian and Chad were currently very happy together. Whether that meant they would re-marry or not, only time could tell. They both knew they needed to process the two murders and Jillian's near-death before making any commitments. Jillian continued to rely gratefully on Chad's presence to help her through both the emotional and physical healing process. In the meantime, Chad gleefully spent time with Jillian, and looked forward to sharing more with her.

Inspector Sherwood visited Jillian on Thursday at the hospital just before Chad came to take her home.

"We learned much during the last few days, but whether murder was part of the original plan to steal millions from Dan Harrington is still not clear."

Jillian still did not understand the need for killing Lisa. "Given that she was on her way home to Philadelphia and wouldn't even have been around to identify Bowersox—didn't that mitigate any reason to kill her?"

"Bowersox was probably concerned Lisa would speak with you, and you would in turn speak with Harrington. He knew Harrington was thoroughly investigating your company and figured the two of you would be in touch frequently. He could not risk that attention when he was secretly in the process of transferring the eight million dollars worth of stock."

Jillian was starting to understand Bowersox's motive. "That's also probably the reason he withdrew from my panel at the San Jose conference. I bet he deliberately approached me originally to learn what he could about Harrington, and was happy to accept the invitation to be on the panel because it gave him additional access to Harrington. However, as he grew closer to the actual event, he realized his presence might mark him as a possible suspect."

Sherwood continued the speculation. "It was most likely Vulkjevich's rant against Harrington at a dinner between the two collaborators at the now-identified conference that made him a likely target for Bowersox. According to Lloyd Jenkins, Harrington's assistant, Bowersox approached Harrington about two weeks before the Geneva conference. We discovered that this was about a month following the conference Bowersox and Vulkjevich attended."

Sherwood continued. "As a financial advisor, Bowersox pitched to Harrington unique and penetrating analyses of potential high-growth companies. He had solid references—Jenkins had checked them himself. He also had a 20-year history as a CPA working at a financial auditing firm—not one of the Big Firms, but a respectable, mid-sized firm. Since his early retirement, he had worked as a consultant for a variety of companies."

Jillian speculated. "So it was probably easy to convince Harrington that he knew what he was doing?"

Sherwood agreed. "There was nothing in Bowersox's background to suggest that he would become an embezzler much less a murderer. He hadn't tortured animals as a child. He wasn't known as a bully. He didn't shoplift. He wasn't in a gang. He didn't do drugs. He came from a two-parent family. His father was a plumber and his mother was a teacher. He has a brother and a sister who are both professionals without any kind of record—his sister is a corporate attorney and his brother is an anesthesiologist."

"Did he need the money? I mean, why did he do this? Isn't it unusual?"

"Yes, especially since he had money in his bank accounts close to a hundred thousand dollars, and he owned some property left to him by his parents valued at close to a million. We can only surmise that he worked with the wealthy and wanted to join them."

"Pure greed." Jillian grew morose considering that her friend and Harrington died purely to fulfill the aspirations of a greedy man.

Sherwood nodded and noticed Jillian's mood. He looked at Chad for guidance; he signaled him with a curt nod to continue. "Jenkins recreated the path he believed Bowersox took to gain access to the eight million. First, he gained Harrington's trust and respect by conducting some analyses—fairly basic stuff, but he did it with insight. Then, Harrington asked him for additional analysis of the list of companies we had found in Lisa's luggage. Of course, we now know this was the same list Harrington gave to you asking for Brynn's input. Bowersox needed to gain quick information and analysis about them to impress Harrington—and he also needed it fast because he had already arranged for Jenkins to be out of town during that week. We still haven't figured out where he first met Lisa, but we're sure she provided the extra intelligence needed to convince Harrington to trust him."

Jillian's mind was working again. "Is it possible that Vulkjevich gave him Lisa's name? They both worked for the same contractor."

"Vulkjevich denies knowing Lisa. But it's possible that Bowersox represented himself as a potential client under a different name to BIS, and asked for someone to do an analysis. We're checking with BIS, but as you'll recall they aren't too organized, so we haven't been able to track down that information yet. We're thinking that their billing records will be the place to go."

Sherwood stopped to consider what was next. "So when Jenkins was scheduled to go on vacation, Harrington probably asked Bowersox to step in to help with some additional analyses. He worked out of Harrington's flat perhaps claiming it was closer to his home and would be more convenient. That minimized the number of people who saw him. However, when he met with Lisa she maybe mentioned she knew you at Harmonia, one of the companies on his list, and that triggered his concern. He knew Harrington was investigating Harmonia carefully. He couldn't risk Lisa identifying him as the person for whom she provided analysis, because that would tie him to Harrington too early."

Sherwood's phone rang, and he quickly responded with a "Yes, go ahead." Then he returned to filling them in. "Bowersox was ready to leave the country as soon as he got the money. When we searched his safe deposit box, we found his passport, Social Security card, and a document with codes for bank account transfers. We assume his plan was to cash out the funds and move to somewhere like the Cayman Islands. But because Harrington's body was discovered sooner than he had anticipated, Bowersox was unable to complete the transaction."

Chad arrived with the nurse to take Jillian home. She was happy to be leaving the hospital and also concerned about how she would manage in her flat, although her mother, Chad, and Cynthia were all planning to care for her. However, Lisa's death especially was still haunting her.

"Can you please promise me you'll continue to do everything you can to make him pay for what he did to Lisa and Dan?"

"I promise. We'll continue to lead the search for the evidence to confirm or disprove our suppositions. We know we have the killer, but we also understood the need to gather the appropriate evidence to assure that he is convicted."

Despite her determination not to cry, Jillian's eyes filled with tears. The nurse pushed her wheelchair, and the two men followed them and left the hospital room—Chad dedicated to caring for Jillian, and Sherwood committed to finding the evidence to convict the killer who had such an impact on Jillian's life.

63

Jillian sat in a wheelchair in a suburb of Philadelphia at the children's museum her dear friend Lisa had enjoyed so much as a child and generously supported as an adult. The room was filled with displays to encourage exploration—a volcano with baking soda and vinegar to create mock eruptions; a bucket on a spinning rod to illustrate centrifugal force. On one side of the museum were photographs of farms, towns, and soldiers in the eighteenth century next to the daguerreotypes from which they were printed. There were tunnels for kids to crawl through that led to an outside vegetable and flower garden. A huge map covered one wall with buttons and switches for kids to explore distances and track down locations. When Jillian wheeled herself to see it up close, she noticed that Lisa Baumgartner had donated the map. She speculated that was the reason the museum had suggested using this particular room.

They had cleared the center of the room and arranged chairs for the people attending Lisa's service. Madeline sat in front with Beverly—not Harry—by her side. Jillian noticed that Harry and Lisa's brother were in the back of the room. Well, at least they were there. Jillian was pleased to see the number of attendees; there were many of Lisa's friends—both straight and gay. Chad sat next to her, having accompanied her cross-country, helping to get her on and off the plane.

Madeline had hired a guitar player for the service, at Beverly's suggestion. Lisa loved classical guitar, something that Jillian hadn't known. Beverly rose and turned to face the group. She had papers in her hand that Jillian assumed were notes for her remarks. However, her hands started to shake, and she sobbed uncontrollably. No one, least of all her, expected this.

Jillian turned to Chad and motioned for him to wheel her to the front, where she reached out to Beverly. "Let me go first." Jillian used her mother's trick of focusing on something that made her angry—Lisa's murderer—to keep from crying. So her tone seemed somewhat angry when she started her remarks.

"I really want Lisa's death to mean something to all of us. You all knew Lisa. She was a person who met life head-on, with enthusiasm and without hesitancy. The last night of her life, she joked about her problems, not the least of which was her fight with cancer and the insurance companies.

"So why was her life taken? Basically a despicable human being decided she stood in his way of financial gain. Her life and that of another person were worth more things to this monster—perhaps a stable of cars, new house, clothes, and vacations. How can that be?"

Jillian hesitated. "I cannot overlook or forget that some of you in this room—her family—turned your back on her for who she was. What I can hope and plead is that you think long and hard about encouraging and appreciating love over hate. Lisa was born a lesbian. I was born heterosexual. All of us were born one or the other, just as we are each born male or female. What we choose is how we live our lives. We can choose to spew hate. Or we can choose to live like Lisa lived and base our life on love and hope. Despite family opposition, Lisa never hated—she may have laughed about you from time to time, but she never hated. She joked, she persevered, she made choices.

This museum is an example of her positive attitude and choices.

"So, please, let's all be sure Lisa's death is as meaningful as her life. Consider who she was and what choices she made to live a happy life—and to encourage others to do the same. Let's help to educate others and open their minds to judge us for the choices we make, not for who we are."

Jillian wanted to say more, but she could not speak—all of the events of the past two weeks and the sense of the loss of her friend finally caught up to her. She had no more tricks to keep her composure. Chad immediately went to her side and held her hand. She managed to choke out, "Please think about Lisa the person—her joy, her sense of humor, her tenacity and fighting spirit. Her belief in herself." Jillian saw through her tears: There were actually some smiles in the group. "Please practice her values, and help others to do the same. Thank you for the privilege of speaking today."

64

J illian and Chad were back in San Francisco seated at one of Jillian's
favorite Italian restaurants. They had been back from Philadelphia
for a few weeks. Chad had basically carried her out of her flat, to the
elevator, and into a waiting cab so the two of them could enjoy a "Date
Night." As she finished her rigatoni with herbed duck Bolognese sauce,
she debated whether to have the warm chocolate cake with the truffle
center and vanilla gelato or the local cheese plate with honey and
crostini. Chad suggested they get both and share. Ahh, why did they
get divorced? she wondered.

The day had started with a call from Brynn, Tim, and one of the
board members thanking her for her contributions to the company
over the past few months. They gave her credit for the success of the
announcement of the data about the company's lupus product. They
let her know she would be receiving a bonus as a result, and she was
being promoted to Vice President of Communications and Investor
Relations. She protested saying her communication efforts were only
a reflection of the actual successes of the company, and that it was
the outstanding data itself along with the management presentations
that were responsible. Nonetheless, she welcomed the recognition and

looked forward to continuing with Harmonia. She shared with them that she had lots of ideas about communications initiatives and was looking forward to implementing them as soon as she could get back to work. Brynn reassured her they were managing the day-to-day issues and she should focus on recovering.

Right after she disconnected from her conversation from Harmonia, her phone alerted her to a call from Inspector Sherwood. After asking how she was doing, he proceeded to tell her the latest news.

"Just wanted to give you an update on the Bowersox case. We have continued to find evidence to support our theories about Bowersox, particularly with regard to Lisa's murder. Our computer experts have established that the extra laptop we found in Bowersox's car was Lisa's. The ADA believes that information alone will go a long way toward convicting him of her murder."

Jillian received this information somewhat half-heartedly. She was close to accepting Lisa's death, and was not sure if she wanted to be reminded about it.

Sherwood continued with his update. "In the meantime, Bowersox has hired an attorney who's claiming the bruises the Medical Examiner stated to be the result of Harrington's strangulation were really from his bicycle accident. I believe that we have convincing evidence to the contrary, and I'm not too worried about this tactic. Anyway, I just wanted to keep you updated as promised, and I'll continue to do so."

Jillian finally responded. "Thank you so much for keeping me informed. I trust that you'll do your best."

"You're welcome. I understand that you survived your trip to Philadelphia. Here's wishing you a full recovery."

Jillian had been pushing her emotions to the back of her mind over the past few weeks. Sherwood's call forced her to think about what had happened. Enough time had passed that she needed to synthesize the impact of the events. Certainly she had a new appreciation for life that people her age seldom had. She also enjoyed her family and friends more—especially Chad. She was more inclined to want to connect with them. She believed that she was less inclined to need her career to be happy.

That led to a second conclusion, or rather, a personal resolution—she planned to use whatever time she spent with her family and friends to experience them as much as she could. She wanted to laugh and enjoy life, and she wanted to learn from them.

She looked up from her reverie to see Chad smiling at her. She smiled back, contentedly.

The doctor's instructions prohibited Jillian from putting any weight on her broken leg for another four weeks. Her ribs had grown less painful, but they still alerted her that she had done them harm. She was feeling much better now than during the trip to and from Philadelphia. Once her ribs and broken fingers healed a bit more, she would be able to manipulate crutches, but until then she was somewhat restricted.

Cynthia and her mother were helping at home. Although Jillian's mom was not a particularly good cook, Cynthia was superb. She had taken cooking lessons after she retired through a gourmet cooking store chain, and to Jillian's delight enjoyed the art of making sauces and special desserts. Her mother, on the other hand, was good at grinding coffee beans and putting the English muffins in the toaster. She also excelled at walking to the nearest restaurant or market to bring back salads and Chinese food.

In addition to supplying the brawn to carry Jillian out for "Date Nights," Chad also supplied various dinners from local restaurants for everyone. He would bring them to her flat, don his best black suit, and serve them to Jillian, Cynthia, and Vivien with the flare of the most outrageous waiter they could envision. He would open the wine and ask for Madame to taste it before serving everyone. He supplemented Jillian's china and glassware with some of his own so that each course of his purchased dinners was served on the appropriate plate with a special fork or spoon for each course. And he only brought food that was prepared exquisitely, such as duck a l'orange or roast leg of lamb with rosemary accompanied with roasted vegetables and a variety of potato dishes. And the wine he served was usually one of Jillian's favorite cabernets from Napa, like a Trefethen, or occasionally he would surprise them with a Chilean or Australian wine all served in his own special stemware. Although Vivien and Cynthia would help, he even did most of the dishwashing. He seemed to thrive on these performances, and the more the women responded, the more flamboyant he became.

Chad fully intended to become part of Jillian's life and wanted to demonstrate his affection—and usefulness.

Vivien was not sure what would come next in her daughter's life. However, she recognized Jillian understood her future would involve a series of choices, and she knew the young woman understood how to evaluate the pros and cons of those choices. She prided herself on having taught her daughter this process. Whether Chad would become Jillian's husband again was not clear. That he would remain in her life somehow seemed very likely to Vivien. As she experienced so often, she wistfully had the feeling of deep regret and loneliness that her husband was never able to get to know his daughter. He would have liked her very much.

Cynthia was truly benefitting from getting to know her new friends. Vivien and she had so much in common. They were both widows. They both had careers that involved contributions to the community—Cynthia as a police officer and Vivien as a teacher. They both continued to serve in a variety of volunteer positions. And Cynthia really liked and appreciated both Jillian and Chad. They made her laugh. And she really enjoyed her expanded forays into new eating experiences. She was looking forward to sharing more with this exceptional, life-loving family.

Jillian looked at her ex-husband across the table as they shared the chocolate cake and the local cheeses on their "Date Night." She was very aware of her surroundings—the aromas from the kitchen of roasting garlic and baking bread and the hum of patrons sharing the experience of eating a well-prepared and pleasingly presented dinner. She reached over to touch Chad's hand. He looked surprised but immediately responded and held her hand in his. He saw she was crying and was alarmed. She reassured him with a shake of her head. "No, I'm all right. This has been a great evening. Thank you. I don't know what's ahead of us, but I do know I want you in my life. At least, I for sure want you to continue to feed me." They both smiled and enjoyed the moment, full of contentment and quiet anticipation of what might come next.

JOYCE T. STRAND

If you liked ON MESSAGE, watch for the next Jillian Hillcrest mystery

OPEN MEETINGS

Fulfilling her community relations responsibilities as a PR executive, Jillian encounters an investigative reporter concerned about his home town police department.

OPEN MEETINGS

CHAPTER 1

"You absolutely cannot print anything I told you. They'll kill me."

Jillian Hillcrest looked up from the lunch menu. She saw a non-descript, thin, brown-hair-in-a-bun, middle-aged woman dressed in jeans and a white V-neck top frantically approaching her lunch companion, a local reporter. Jillian watched as the reporter quickly stood up, uttered a brief "Excuse me" to Jillian, and put his arm around the woman, leading her outside. He appeared to be trying unsuccessfully to calm her along the way. She continued to plead with him that he must never repeat what she had told him.

Jillian was interested in what the woman was saying to the reporter. Somewhere in his late 40s, the tall and slightly stooped Miles Smith was a stringer for a local newspaper and also had a blog focusing on city, county, and state government. He had a history of investigative journalism that impressed and fascinated Jillian. For example, he had uncovered a county assessor's officer who collected for property value assessments that weren't done, and then funneled the money into personal bank accounts. So she was intrigued about whatever it was the frightened woman did not want Miles to print.

As the Vice President of Corporate Communications for Harmonia Therapeutics, a small local biotechnology firm, Jillian was meeting Miles to discuss her company's role in an upcoming statewide conference of city and county officials. Harmonia had made some noteworthy contributions to the community, including the donation of annual scholarships to outstanding high school science students, employee participation at a variety of fundraisers for youth events, and counseling for local businesses by several Harmonia executives. Miles wanted Jillian to attend the conference so she could be part of the panel he was chairing on the relationship between businesses, city and county governments, and the media.

However, at the moment, Jillian was more interested in the distraught woman pleading with Miles. He returned to their table alone after a few minutes, telling her, "I am sorry about the interruption." Miles enunciated every word to its fullest, no matter what he was saying. He gave the impression of being a bit of a nerd, and his lanky frame and receding hairline reinforced that. "I am working on a story about my hometown up in Troutville, and Margaret was helping. She was here on business and saw me come into this restaurant. She seems a little concerned about nothing—tempest in a teapot, as the saying goes. Just a story for my blog. It is not a big deal. Now, where were we?"

Jillian's instincts told her that Miles was minimizing something that was bigger than a teapot; he just wasn't ready to share it. Nonetheless, she sublimated her chronic sense of need-to-know and turned back to the menu to select her favorite—penne Bolognese—while promising herself to have only carrots and tomatoes for dinner.

The two colleagues spent the remainder of lunch discussing her role in the upcoming conference, and although Miles nodded frequently, Jillian sensed that he was distracted. Normally he would provide more details than were necessary to make his point. Today Jillian had to ask him direct questions to engage him.

"Miles, can you tell me exactly what you want from me for your panel?"

The reporter hesitated as he considered the very reason they were having lunch together. "Of course. That's why we're here. Harmonia participates as a company in the community. Why does Harmonia participate in the community? What does Harmonia get by involving its employees and management team with local businesses, the youth, and the citizens?"

Jillian considered this response. "O.K. That's easy. I can offer that information. But why would the attendees of the conference care? Aren't they largely city, county, and state officials and owners of small businesses?"

As he considered his response, Miles bit his lip, looked up at the ceiling, and rubbed his fingers across the white linen tablecloth. "Well, the ultimate goal, of course, is for you to share how Harmonia's activities with the public can be used by city government officials—even police departments—to help them communicate to the people they represent. There have been a lot of news stories recently about corrupt city officials and police officers especially. How do honest representatives of the citizenry overcome that image? Of course, I'm looking for legitimate tools to open the communication channels. I'm not looking for propaganda or slanderous methods of influence."

"Of course." Jillian was beginning to understand how she could contribute. "So, as a panel member, you're asking me to suggest some PR tactics to help honest city governments communicate better with their constituents. Right?"

Miles nodded vigorously. "That is correct. I want you to suggest PR activities from the business world that might help honest and hard-working city officials to get in touch with the people they serve." He looked thoughtful and appeared to be searching for ways to help Jillian better understand her assignment. "I'll look for some articles that will help you comprehend what many honest officials need to overcome. The number of abuses seems to be increasing."

Jillian was really enjoying her pasta but guessed that Miles was not a foodie, since he had barely touched his lunch. Also, he was fidgeting in his seat, and Jillian suspected he wanted to leave. "Listen, I'll get this if you want to leave. I can send you a list of key points and some backup materials about Harmonia and our community programs by the end of the week."

"Thanks, Jillian. That would be very helpful. I'll get you some articles and also arrange to introduce you to the rest of the panel." Miles got up without further comment, grabbed his briefcase, muttered "Good-bye for now," and left the restaurant.

As she finished her coffee, Jillian looked around for her cane, which she needed as a result of a broken leg that had almost healed. Following the murder of a very dear friend a few months earlier, she had been in a car accident. She still had moments of anxiety and regret when she remembered that last dinner with her friend, the night before she had been killed.

As Jillian limped slowly out of the restaurant, she welcomed the warm summer sun and thought about her situation. She was basically content that her life was almost back to normal. However, she was a little uneasy about the words of Miles' friend. She wondered what story the reporter might be working on that would cause the woman to be concerned for her life.

Unfortunately, her reflection was short-lived. As she limped toward her car, her mobile phone rang. Jillian saw that it was her boss calling, so she answered as quickly as possible while juggling her cane and her purse. She soon realized that her day was about to go south when she heard the disappointing news.

ABOUT THE AUTHOR

Joyce Strand, much like her fictional character, Jillian Hillcrest, served as head of corporate communications at several biotech and high-tech companies in Silicon Valley for more than 25 years. Unlike Jillian, however, she did not encounter murder. Rather, she focused on publicizing her companies and their products. Joyce received her Ph.D. from The George Washington University, Washington, D.C. and her B.A. from Dickinson College, Carlisle, PA

For more information, go to her website at www.joycestrand.com
Photo of author by Erin Kate Photography
www.erinkatephoto.com